DAIQUIRI DOCK MURDER

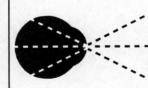

A KEY WEST MYSTERY

DAIQUIRI DOCK MURDER

DOROTHY FRANCIS

THORNDIKE PRESS
A part of Gale, Cengage Learning

Detroit • New York • San Francisco • New Haven, Conn • Waterville, Maine • London

GALE
CENGAGE Learning®

LIBRARY OF CONGRESS CATALOGING-IN-PUBLICATION DATA

Francis, Dorothy Brenner.
    Daiquiri dock murder / by Dorothy Francis.
        pages ; cm. — (Thorndike Press large print mystery) (A Key West mystery)
        ISBN 978-1-4104-4881-1 (hardcover) — ISBN 1-4104-4881-9 (hardcover)
    1. Key West (Fla.)—Fiction. 2. Large type books. I. Title.
    PS3556.R327D35 2012b
    813'.54—dc23   2012008190

Published in 2012 by arrangement with Tekno Books and Ed Gorman.

Printed in the United States of America
1 2 3 4 5 6 7 16 15 14 13 12

For Richard, Ann, and Pat

ACKNOWLEDGMENTS

Roz Greenberg, my editor at Tekno
Tiffany Schofield, my editor at Five Star
Ed Gorman, every writer's friend
Members of the Key West Writers Guild
Dee Stuart, my first reader

ONE

Choking and tasting salt spray, I clawed tendrils of hair from my face and eyes and lowered my head into the stinging wind and rain. Once I stepped onto the swaying catwalk, the world turned into pulsing blackness. Fighting my way forward, I struggled toward the slip where our family docked *The Bail Bond.* I'd promised Mother and Cherie, my sis, to check on the family's cabin cruiser every day while they vacationed in Colorado. Rafa Blue keeps her promises. Once again I lowered my head into the storm. Sometimes lines loosened. Sometimes boats slipped their moorings.

Because Dad, Mother, and Cherie were friends of Brick and Threnody Vexton, our family had rented a slip at their marina the week they opened their business. So far, the Vexton dock masters posted an excellent safety record, but our family never depended entirely on them or any other service people to keep our boat safe. During the past few days, weather announcers had pinpointed a tropical storm brewing in the Gulf. Tonight around midnight the winds escalated to a class one hurricane heading for the Florida Keys. This made my second trip today to Daiquiri Dock Marina to check on our boat. Gritting my teeth, I inhaled the damp sea air and balanced unsteadily against the sway of the catwalk. I took care in walking on the slippery boards underfoot. One misstep could throw me into crashing waves.

I lurched from side to side along the catwalk until at last I reached the row of tethered boats, their bow lines tight and tied to sturdy dock cleats. I read the names on some of the hulls I passed. *Seaduced. Vitamin C. The Sea Witch.* All the boats appeared secure and in place. After tonight's Fantasy Fest parade, a local family threw a party at their private beach home near the marina. Sometimes, unknown to their host, partygoers trespass, board any nearby boat that looks inviting and unoccupied. Dock masters can't guard every place at once. Wise boaters kept an eye on their crafts.

I clutched the brine-crusted line along the side of the walkway, felt it cut into my fingers while my flashlight's icy coldness

10

chilled my other hand. *The Bail Bond*! There! It floated safely in its slip. Relief flooded through me, warming me for a moment. In spite of the storm, I'd kept my promise to Mother and Cherie — and perhaps to Dad, too. He'd always loved *The Bail Bond.*

Turning, I headed back to my car then stopped short. I gasped, stunned by what I glimpsed below me in the choppy water between *The Bail Bond* and the sailboat in the slip beside it.

Impossible! I blinked sea spray from my eyes, squinted, and let go of the security line in order to shield my eyes from the storm. I scrutinized the brine. The wind shrieked at almost gale force now. My imagination had not been playing tricks on me. Someone was swimming in the chop below me. At first I thought the person must be a tourist because the locals know that sharks feed at night. After watching for several moments, I thought I knew the swimmer, and once I saw his uniform, his dark hair, I recognized him for sure.

Diego Casterano! Diego, our family's long-time friend, was struggling in the chop below me. Diego, the subject of my next "You Should Get to Know —" weekly column in *The Key West Citizen.* Brine darkened the pale orange of his Chief Dock Master's uniform and glistened on long strands of dark hair that escaped from his ponytail.

How could this be? Why would Diego swim during a squall, seemingly unmindful of the seas raging around him? The boats beside him bobbed in their slips, tethered, lines taut. I watched for only a moment as his head broke the surface of the incoming tide and almost hit the port side of *The Bail Bond.* For a terrifying moment, I held my breath. His head disappeared, then rose into view again. Maybe he was trying to rescue someone who had fallen from one of the boats or perhaps from the catwalk. I clutched the security line more tightly. Fantasy Fest meant a week of revelry, and anything could happen on parade night. Maybe I could help Diego or at least call for help.

"Diego!" I shouted. "Diego, it's Rafa!" The wind whipped my words into the wet blackness. "Diego!" Squatting at first, and with one hand still clutching the security line overhead for support, I knelt, leaning so close to the water I could taste the salt spray on my tongue and lips. I shouted to him again. If he answered, I couldn't hear his words above the wind and the pounding

12

water. Then in a flash of lightning, I saw a sight that chilled me more than the storm around me.

Strands of Diego's long hair now lay caught and snarled in the anchor line of *The Bail Bond.*

Was he still alive? Was he dead? I knew the stupidity of jumping into the water fully clothed to rescue a drowning person. But was Diego drowning? He wasn't waving to me or shouting for help. I refused to believe he might be dead. He might be alive. CPR might save him. Maybe he was doing the dead man's float, gasping for breath between the times when the waves and the sea covered him.

Cell phone! Find the cell! I slid my right hand down the side of my yellow slicker, feeling for a familiar lump in my jumpsuit pocket. No. No lump. No cell. I remembered leaving it in the glove box of my Prius. Bad decision. My only option now — a dash to the car to call for help.

Diego's head still bobbed in the water, disappearing, then bobbing again. I forgot about dashing. Impossible in this storm. Gripping the catwalk line, I struggled toward my car in the parking lot. No problem finding the Prius. At this time of night and in this storm, it stood alone in front of the marina. Groping in my pocket for my keys, I pressed the open button, missed it, and hit the alarm button instead. In seconds the car horn began an intermittent blaring. I struggled for a moment, trying to quash the noise. But why stop it? Maybe the sound would signal help.

It took all my strength to open the car door and hold it against the gale that threatened to tear it from its hinges before I could slip inside and slam it shut. I welcomed the car's dryness and warmth for a few seconds before I opened the glove box. Scrabbling in its contents, I breathed easier once I found the cell and punched in 911. The dispatcher's voice, tranquil, business-like, helped me calm down long enough to give the necessary information.

"Your name and address please."

"Rafa Blue. The Blue Mermaid Hotel on Whitehead Street. In Old Town."

"Phone number."

I spieled out the number of my penthouse suite.

"Where are you now, ma'am?" she asked.

"The Vexton Marina. Daiquiri Dock." I almost panicked. "Bayside. I don't know the exact address."

The dispatcher's voice calmed me again. "I know the place well, ma'am. You'll have help in a few minutes."

"Catwalk C," I said.

"The officers will find it. You stay right there."

"Yes, ma'am." Where did she think I might go?

I tried to think of friends I might call for more help. Pablo, Diego's son? Pablo lived mostly on the beach. No phone. Brick and Threnody? Yes. I'd keyed their number into my speed dial. Now I punched it and let the cell ring five times. Five rings. No answer. No invitation to leave a message.

Kane Riley? I'd placed my boyfriend's name first on my speed dial. But no. No point in calling Kane. Damn! If he'd spent the night with me as he did many nights, he'd be here right now. Tonight, the Fantasy Fest traffic would be backed up around the Historic Seaport District and the Harbor Walk where Kane docked his shrimp boat. By the time he left *The Buccaneer* and started his work truck, the crisis would have ended. *Stop wasting time, Rafa. Do something. Think!* I debated a moment about leaving the cell or taking it with me, then I tucked it back into the glove box. Better a dry phone here than a wet phone on the catwalk or dropped into the sea.

Leaving the Prius and letting the horn

continue its blaring, I tried to hurry to Diego. The diminishing squall allowed me to jog along the catwalk. What if I couldn't find him again? I peered into the water near *The Bail Bond.* For several moments I didn't see him. Then his head appeared again, a little deeper in the water.

"Diego! Diego! Help's coming!"

Peering into the water, I waited.

Again, I couldn't see him. "I called nine-one-one!" I shouted. "Help's on the way."

After what seemed an eternity, I saw his dark head bobbing closer to the surface again, his hair still tangled in the anchor line. Now he appeared to float. Facedown into the water. I could see his back, his hips. Good sign. No point in exhausting himself trying to swim if he could save his strength by floating for a few moments.

"Diego!" I shouted again during a short lull when the wind dropped.

He didn't respond, but turned his head slightly and looked as if he were trying to raise an arm. Was he trying to motion for me to join him? To help him? I could do that for him, couldn't I? And I could yank his hair free. Or, if he had a dive knife strapped to his leg, I could cut his hair loose from the anchor line.

Seeing someone near might give Diego

the will to hold on until more help arrived. And what about sharks! Sharks fed at night. I couldn't bear the thought of Diego's body, or mine, being ripped to bits by a hammerhead or a yellow. I forced myself to forget that thought. One could never tell about sharks. Even weathered seamen couldn't say for sure what a shark might do.

Skinning from my slicker and the jumpsuit I'd grabbed when I left my bed, I regretted my predilection for sleeping in the altogether. I stood for a moment, shivering until I felt the sting of rain against my bareness. Then I slipped beneath the security line I'd been clutching and splashed into the sea near Diego. I told myself a shark would never notice my small splash among all of Mother Nature's gigantic splashes.

I held my breath, yet I sucked in a mouthful of brine. I tried to stay calm and breathe with greater caution. Tread water. Tread water. Following those silent commands, I kept afloat until I caught a clear view of Diego — until I saw his face. The sea splashed into his open mouth. His eyes looked like white marbles rolled back into his head. I knew then he was dead for sure.

TWO

Footsteps. Stealthy footsteps padding closer, retreating, then padding closer again. Stalking footsteps. I tried to cry out for help, but my tongue clung to the roof of my mouth as if glued there. I couldn't scream. I couldn't speak. With great effort I managed to swallow. Footsteps. Someone walked nearby. Where was I? I turned my head from side to side, trying to shake a memory to a place in my mind where I could think about it. At last, the medicinal smell that permeated the room along with the hardness of the mattress under me told me I lay in a hospital. I peered through slitted eyelids in case someone stood watching me. Crazy idea. Why would anyone be watching? When I saw nobody in the room, I opened my eyes.

I tested my extremities. Feet. Toes. Hands. Fingers. Everything worked. My head felt like someone stood playing "The Anvil Chorus" on a glockenspiel near my brain, but I managed to push myself to a sitting position. Where were my clothes? A hospital gown barely covered me. I felt the lanyard Kane had braided for me around my neck. At least I hadn't lost that.

I reached for a glass of water on a bedside table, sucked great gulps through a straw, and began to think about my situation. I saw no bloodstains. Why the hospital? Did headaches require hospitalization? I couldn't feel any other injuries. Mother. Cherie. Had something happened to them in Colorado? Then snips of memory wafted in and out of my muddled head.

Diego! Dead! Why? How? When? Reporter-like queries floated in my mind, but I found no answers. My head whirled and I felt icy cold when a nurse opened the door and entered the room. Smiling lips. Friendly blue eyes. I imagined MISS EFFICIENCY typed on her badge.

"And how are we feeling this morning?" she chirped.

I didn't know how she felt, but I felt rotten. Before I could reply I heard Kane's voice in the hallway outside my room.

"Rafa Blue," he said. "Rafa Blue. That's her name. I know she's in there. I need to talk to her. I have to talk to her! Tell her Kane's here."

"You have a friend named Kane?" Miss Efficiency asked me, smiling.

"My boyfriend. May he come in? Please?" I tried to scoot from the bed, but she shook her head at me and stepped closer, pushing gently against my shoulders as she eased me farther back onto the mattress and against the wafer-thin pillow.

"No company yet, Rafa. I need to take your vitals and make out a chart for you. Then the doctor will want to see you. How are you feeling?"

"Fine. I want to go home, please. Kane will drive me. I'm sure he's come to get me. Our friend, Diego Casterano, died last night. A terrible accident. I need to talk to Kane."

The nurse smiled but said nothing more to me while she placed the blood pressure cuff around my upper arm and began squeezing the bulb. I squelched my questions while she recorded figures on a chart, checked my temp with a gadget she stuck into my ear, and then took my pulse.

Grim scenes from last night replayed through my mind. What had happened to Diego? He'd grown up in Cuba with the sea for a backyard. He knew how to handle himself around water. Why had he been swimming during last night's storm? I squeezed my eyes shut, trying to blot out the image of his dark hair tangled in the anchor line — and his eyes. I knew I'd never forget those unseeing eyes. And how had his hair become caught in that anchor line? Had there been a problem with someone's boat? A problem Diego felt he needed to deal with during a storm?

Someone banged on the door.

"Rafa?" Kane's voice wore hammer and tongs — a hammer eager to pound his way to my bedside, tongs ready to yank me from the hospital. "Rafa Blue? Rafa, are you in there?"

"Yes." I drew a breath to say more, but the nurse hushed me and strode to the door.

"Sir, I have orders that Miss Blue is to speak to nobody until the doctor sees her — and after that, the police. If you can't sit and wait quietly, I'll call Security to escort you from the building."

"Yes, your highness." Kane's voice dripped sarcasm, but if the nurse noticed, she ignored it. I heard a chair scrape against tile and guessed Kane conformed to her orders. Miss Efficiency left the room, closing the door behind her. I half expected, half hoped, Kane would come barging in, ignoring her orders. But he didn't.

I knew I'd have to talk with a doctor

21

before I could leave the hospital, but the police? Why the police? I hadn't considered talking to them. As a TV viewer addicted to crime shows, I should have guessed the local authorities would want to question me. But surely Diego's death had been an accident. I refused to visualize the police hanging crime scene tape on a marina catwalk. An unexplained death usually called for crime scene tape until the police understood the cause of the death, until the medical examiner finished making his call, until photographers took all the pictures they needed. I couldn't imagine Diego's death as anything but accidental. Yet who knows what might have happened during or after the Fantasy Fest parade? Unless a person was in a celebratory mood, home offered the best place to hang out during the annual Halloween celebration.

A rap on the door announced the doctor's visit. I took another sip of water and hoped I'd be able to answer his questions quickly and to his satisfaction. He ducked his head when he entered the room — a mannerism many tall people acquire to avoid bumps on the skull.

"I'm Dr. Mathis." His voice, soft and low, projected a soothing quality that helped put me at ease. "Rafa Blue, right?"

22

"Right."

Neither of us spoke again until he finished perusing my chart the nurse left for him.

"Blood pressure normal. No temperature. Breathing normal." He laid the chart aside and smiled. "Are you experiencing any pain?"

"No," I lied, hoping he couldn't see my head throbbing, hoping he wouldn't ask me to rate my pain on a scale of one to ten. "I feel fine and I'd like to go home, please."

His smile broadened. "Under the circumstances, the nurse will bring some insurance papers for you to sign so you won't have to stop at the main desk. Once the papers have been approved, you'll be almost free to go."

Almost? I squelched the word from my vocabulary. "Thank you, doctor." Under the circumstances? What did that mean? What circumstances? I began to slide from the bed before he left the room, closing the door behind himself. I took cautious steps toward a tiny closet, then stopped. Where were my clothes? Instinctively I pulled the hospital gown closer around my rear end. Who had found me nude at the marina? How could I leave this hospital with no clothes? Jumpsuit? Slicker? Where were they? Before I could push the call button to summon the nurse, she entered the room.

"Will you please read and sign these forms? We'll need your insurance numbers, too."

My heart sank. More delay. "My insurance cards are in my billfold, and I left my billfold in my jumpsuit. I've no idea where it is now. At the bottom of the sea, maybe."

Kane stepped into the room unannounced. "I have her billfold. I have fresh clothes for her." At first the nurse seemed startled, perhaps by his height, his shaggy blond hair, his black tank top and jeans. She took a step back as if expecting an attack, and Kane, seizing on her hesitation, hurried toward me. We exchanged a long kiss before Miss Efficiency intervened.

"I unlocked your suite for Threnody. Figured she'd be better at deciding what you needed than I would. She packed this stuff for me to bring to you." Before the nurse escorted him from the room, Kane thrust a plastic bag toward me. I sighed in relief when I saw fresh clothes and my billfold, a makeup kit, and a hairbrush.

I perched on the edge of the bed to sign the papers, provide the insurance numbers. When the nurse retreated, I applied a bit of lip gloss. After tugging the hairbrush through my shoulder-length hair, I considered having it styled again in a pixie cut.

But now was no time to be worrying about hair. I'd barely finished pulling on my jeans and tee when the nurse tapped on the door again.

"Chief Ramsey and Detective Lyon are waiting to talk with you, Miss Blue. An informal questioning, they say. May I show them in?"

Informal? Hah! But at least she had asked my permission before she admitted them. I knew police officers geared their questions in ways they hoped would help them catch criminals. They could say anything they pleased, ask any questions they pleased. When spouting questions, they never swore on a Bible to speak the whole truth and nothing but the truth. I pulled myself to my full five feet, eleven inches. Sometimes my height gave me an advantage — perhaps even with police, if the charge in question amounted to no more than some minor offense. I stood beside the bed and waited.

Short, fat, and bald, Chief Ramsey reminded me of the Pillsbury Doughboy. Detective Lyon met my eyes on a level, and his mane of tawny-colored hair might have belonged to the king of beasts. I'd met both men last year when burglars hit The Blue Mermaid three times in one week. Surely these officers remembered me. But if they

25

did, they didn't let on.

"Your name please?" Chief Ramsey asked.

"Rafa Blue." I hoped they'd recognize my name as author of *Rafa's Repartee*, the biographical column I wrote for the *Citizen*. In addition to calling favorable attention to some of Key West's talented underdogs, I wanted to make a name for myself as a writer. But no. These officers didn't remember me. At least not today. If Chief Ramsey recognized my name, he didn't let on.

"Address?"

"The Blue Mermaid Hotel on Whitehead. Penthouse Suite Number Three."

"Your family lives there, too?"

"Yes."

"Are they in residence at this time?"

"No."

"Where are they?"

"My mother and sister are vacationing in Colorado."

"Do you have an address and phone number where they can be reached?"

"The Hand Hotel, Fairplay, Colorado. I don't have their phone number with me. It's on a pad in my suite at The Blue Mermaid."

"Do you plan to make the hotel your permanent residence?"

"Yes."

"For how long?"

"How long is permanent?" What did this man expect to find out from me?

"I've heard a rumor that you're planning a new venture. Are you willing to share that with me?"

"No." It is okay to say no to the police, isn't it?

"Your new venture, ma'am? A novel, perhaps?"

"No comment." So he *did* recognize my name as a writer. Since graduating from Vassar, I'd had a burning desire to write a novel. I planned to use my newspaper experiences as the basis for a book. In fact, I'd already made an outline for a novel. I hoped to begin on chapter one soon, but I couldn't see that as an important bit of knowledge necessary to the police.

I wondered who tipped Ramsey off about my planning a new venture. I couldn't remember talking about it to anyone except Kane, or maybe Threnody, one of my few close friends. Ramsey would probably laugh out loud if he knew Kane had given me a three-hundred-page book with blank pages along with his instructions to fill those pages with a *New York Times* bestseller.

I intended to say no more to Ramsey about my future career plans, and I wished he'd change the subject. Why tell either of these men I was sick of living in my sister's shadow? If my book venture bombed, no one would be the wiser — if I kept my mouth shut about it now. Surely my writing career had no bearing on Diego's death.

I wondered. Had either Ramsey or Lyon ever embarked on a venture that failed?

"Did you know Diego Casterano?" Chief Ramsey asked.

THREE

Ramsey's last question startled me into silence. But I felt more than ready to change the subject.

"Yes, I knew Diego."

"You were friends?"

"Yes, Diego and I were friends."

"How close was your friendship?" Chief Ramsey cleared his throat and looked me in the eye — not easy with his head five or six inches below mine. Detective Lyon stared out the window.

I resented the chief's insinuation. "I knew Diego as a family friend. My mother, my sister, and I — all three of us admired and respected Diego, as did my father when he was alive."

"When the ambulance crew rescued you, your manner of garb indicated that you and Diego may have experienced a relationship closer than that of the rest of your family."

For a moment I said nothing, not wanting

to protest too much or too little. "Diego and I were nothing more than good friends. I admired him because I'm for the under-dogs in society — talented people who have worked hard to be noticed, or perhaps who still have that work ahead of them. A Cuban refugee, Diego came to Key West with empty pockets. He worked up to a position as Chief Dock Master at Brick Vexton's marina. He won the regard of Keys' citizens, who elected him to a position on the board of Monroe County Commissioners. I'm proud to claim Diego as a close family friend. I looked forward to writing about him as the subject of one of my columns in the near future."

I knew I'd said too much, yet I didn't know what I'd withdraw, had I been given the chance.

"That was the total extent of your relation-ship? A family friend? An interesting subject for your newspaper column?"

"Right. I'm a history buff, and Diego's story reaches beyond his life and into Cuban history. His son, Pablo, sometimes plays drums or string bass in the combo that performs in the Frangipani Room at The Blue Mermaid. Our family always enjoyed having Diego drop around after work to watch the action, to enjoy a sandwich and a drink, and to listen to the music."

"When did you last see Diego alive?"

"I thought he was alive last night when I saw him in the water at the Daiquiri Dock Marina. Then I realized, realized he was — dead. You're calling it an accident, right?"

Ramsey avoided my question. "Didn't you think it strange for anyone to be swimming at that time of night?"

"Yes, of course I did. I thought at first he might be trying to help someone who'd fallen from the catwalk while checking on the security of a boat. People do strange things during Fantasy Fest. Sometimes trespassers board and vandalize boats. But I saw no sign of that last night. I realized Diego was in trouble. I saw his hair snarled and tangled in the anchor line of *The Bail Bond.*"

"When was the last time you saw Diego alive before last night?"

I hesitated, wishing I didn't have to answer, wanting to be sure of myself and my next words. The person who last saw a deceased person alive is usually of special interest to the authorities — especially if the victim's death wasn't accidental.

"I saw him at the Frangipani Room the night before the Fantasy Fest parade. That would have been on Friday night. He joined

Mother, Cherie, the Vextons, and me in listening to the combo and watching the people dance."

"How long did he stay?"

"The Frangi closes at midnight. As I remember it, Diego stayed a while after closing to have a drink on the house. The Frangipani Room is roofless — an open-air setting with torches flaring along its outer rim. Friday night Diego helped Brick Vexton extinguish the torches. According to Dad's will, the Frangi is my responsibility, but Mother always likes to oversee the closing of this special dance floor, to be sure it's ready for the next night's opening." I refused to tell him that Mother disliked Dad's leaving me in charge of the Frangi — or anything else. But the court was on Dad's side. Lawyers refused to let Mother change Dad's will.

"Thank you, Miss Blue," Chief Ramsey said. "You are free to leave the hospital now."

"Thank you, sir."

"You are free to go anywhere you please on the island, but if you decide to leave Key West, please get in touch with me or someone in my office first."

"Are you investigating Diego's death as an accident?"

"No. His hair might have been caught in the anchor line accidentally, but the concrete block weighted to his feet rules out an accidental death. Don't you agree?"

"Oh." Surprise left me speechless. I tried to erase the mental image of a concrete block weighting Diego's feet.

"At this point in the police investigation, I'm ordering you to avoid discussing this case with reporters or with strangers."

"Yes, sir." He hadn't said I required his permission to leave the island, but that's what his order about letting him know my plans meant. "Sir, am I a suspect? I called nine-one-one because I needed help. Are you going to hang me without a trial or jury?"

"Nobody plans to hang you, Miss Blue, but everyone close to Diego Casterano may be a person of interest to the police." Chief Ramsey left, making no further comment.

The minute I stepped from the hospital room into the hallway, Kane strode to my side. I knew he must have been listening and I wondered how much of that Q&A session he heard. He linked his arm through mine, pulling me close. After a long kiss, he took my hand and urged me toward the hospital door. Was my shakiness a result of the kiss or was it a delayed reaction to last night's trauma, a delayed reaction to Diego's death?

"Are you okay?" he asked when we stepped into the overcast day and headed toward his truck parked in a visitor's slot.

"I'm okay. But where's my car? Still at the dock? And how did I end up in the hospital? Who brought me here? The last thing I remember, I was choking, trying to tread water — in the sea — with Diego. I don't remember my feet touching a concrete block." I shuddered and eased closer to Kane. "And I realized Diego was dead. Who . . ."

"Officers from Emergency nine-one-one rescued you — pulled both you and Diego from the sea. You were barely conscious, exhausted, and unable to say anything that made sense. They brought you here by ambulance. Took Diego's body to the morgue. I heard the news on the radio and drove to the police station immediately. Since you'd given me a spare key to the Prius, Chief Ramsey trusted me to pick up your car and park it near my boat at the Harbor Walk. You can relax about that. Your car's safe."

"Thank you, Kane!" I squeezed his hand. "How can I ever thank you?"

Kane grinned at me and raised an eyebrow. "I can think of several exceptionally pleasant ways. Want to hear some of them?"

"Not if they require more from me than flowers, candy, or a good book."

"I was afraid of that. But we'll talk about it later, okay?"

I changed the subject quickly. Kane wanted our relationship to progress to a deeper level, but I balked, unready for that change. At least not ready yet. I still needed to face my past, live with what I'd done, my mistakes. Live with my fear of being corrupt. Although I'd always looked forward to love, marriage, and a family, I wasn't sure I'd ever be ready for any of those things. And if I changed my mind, I didn't want Kane to think I came to him in gratitude instead of love. I wasn't ready for Kane to know the details of my past. He was a fairly new resident in Key West, and by the time he moved here a few years ago, the gossip about me had died down — almost.

"Kane to Rafa. Kane to Rafa Blue. Please return to planet Earth and tell me what you're thinking."

"I'm working through the shock of hearing the police calling Diego's death a homicide."

Kane stared into space for a few moments before he spoke. "According to this morning's *Citizen,* the cops first thought he died accidentally, but when, in addition to finding his hair tangled in an anchor line, they found his feet and ankles bound with duct tape and roped to a concrete block, reality changed their thinking. Accident? No way!"

"But why? Diego had enemies? Who?"

"You heard Chief Ramsey's take on it. Back at the hospital, I couldn't help overhearing him say that at this time, any close friend of Diego's is a person of interest. Guess you're not the only one. Be glad of that."

"Has anyone called Mother and Cherie? This news will hit them hard — ruin their vacation. Glad they were off-island when it happened."

"Brick said he called them, but the hotel manager told him they were on a week's pack trip in the Rockies and couldn't be reached for a few days. Guess cell phones don't pick up signals in some parts of the high country."

Kane opened the door to the pickup and helped me inside before he grabbed the newspaper from the dashboard and dropped it into my lap.

"Read all about it. They've managed to keep your name out of it — at least for now."

"Not much to read," I said after Kane

36

pulled himself into the driver's seat. I ran my finger down the couple of inches of type the news editor allotted to the story. "A man dead, an important man in this community, and he rates only two inches of type."

"I'm sure there'll be more later, but for now, just the facts, ma'am." Kane snorted. "They always keep the bad news short and on the back pages. Mustn't alarm the tourists. Mustn't let them know blood has been spilled here in paradise. Where to, Rafa? Your hotel? Vexton mansion? I promised Threnody we'd stop by for a few minutes and bring her up to speed on what's going on. Think you feel up to that now?"

"I guess so. I'd rather not talk to anyone, but I wouldn't have had any clothes at the hospital if it hadn't been for Threnody — and you. So, let's stop at the Vextons', I guess. I feel disoriented. Wonder what happened to my wet jumpsuit."

"The police might have it. Guess someone wrapped you in a blanket for the ride to the hospital. Maybe the police consider the clothes you were or weren't wearing evidence." Kane keyed the truck to life, backed from the parking lot, and drove from the Stock Island hospital toward Key West. When he snapped on the radio, the weather announcer still spouted news about the hurricane stalled off the coast of Cuba. It might turn. It might dissipate. Whatever. Key Westers try to take these hurricane threats in stride, and they succeed most of the time. We locals secure our property as best we can and leave the island only when authorities order evacuation. I can remember a few times when both lanes of Highway One were open only to traffic moving toward Homestead and Miami. This morning we saw little sign of last night's storm other than a few downed palm branches and green coconuts.

Kane slammed on the brakes when the van ahead of us bearing Wisconsin plates jerked to a stop and pulled toward the shoulder of the highway. Two kids jumped from it almost into our path.

"Dumb kids," Kane growled. "Don't they know they could get killed doing that?"

"Dumb parents, Kane. Tourists. It's not the kids. Visitors don't understand how dangerous the traffic on this highway is."

The kids snatched up two coconuts, dashed back to their van, and jumped in. "I suppose they're gloating over having found a couple of free souvenirs to take home." Kane shook his head and left more space between us and the van once we drove on.

A salt-scented tradewind blowing through

the truck windows cooled my cheeks, and the roar of a jet drowned out traffic sounds as it zoomed in for a landing at the air station. The clouds began to lift, and before we reached Old Town, Kane took a roundabout tour along South Roosevelt and Smather's Beach.

Dressed in orange vests and denim pants, inmates from the road prison on Big Pine Key worked at clearing Fantasy Fest trash from the sand and the shoreline. They filled black plastic bags, then, still moving in slow motion, they flung the contents into city dumpsters, making way for the tractor that would rake and smooth the sand into readiness for today's tourists.

Winding back east a few blocks, we turned on Palm Avenue and crossed the bridge spanning Garrison Bight. Before we reached Grinnell Street, I thought for a few moments that a car was following us — a rusty Ford.

"Kane?" I nodded toward the rear window. "We've got a tail."

"Don't think so." The driver of the car tailgating us seized a chance to pass, waving a hearty greeting to Kane. "Ben Bahama. Used to anchor his boat near mine at the shrimp dock before big business crowded us out."

"You and many others, Kane. But that's in the past. Glad you know Ben Bahama. I hate being followed by a stranger."

"Relax. Why would anyone be tailing us?"

"Why, indeed! Someone must have followed Diego yesterday."

Kane turned into The Little Whitehouse gated driveway where a security guard on duty looked us over and then, recognizing me, waved us on through. Along this secluded street, old Conch mansions built decades ago ruled like royalty. Kane slowed at a sign saying THE VEXTONS. I loved living at a posh hotel a few blocks from here and took it for granted as my lot in life — most of the time. But in spite of our upscale neighborhood, the Vexton home gave me the creeps. I squelched a shiver as we drove into the deep shade of two towering banyans. A strangler fig that climbed the trunk of the larger tree threatened its existence.

Brick and Threnody's three-story home could have appeared in an antique, sepia-toned photo as an example of a Spanish Colonial design. Built of age-darkened limestone and native coral rock, it had weathered through the years, huddling under a wide roof supported by iron-flanged pillars on either end of the veranda. A ship's bell, its dull brass unpolished, dangled from

40

a weathered post at the foot of cracked concrete steps.

For a few moments I forced myself to enjoy the breeze that fluttered the banyan leaves until Kane stopped the truck.

Almost immediately we saw Dolly Jass, who called to us from where she stood pulling magazines from the yellow recycling box set near the street. My mood lightened. Only the hard of heart could look at Dolly without smiling. But Kane refused to smile.

FOUR

"Rafa!" Dolly called, walking toward us. "Are you okay? I heard the news. What a terrible scene you've been through. I feel so sorry for Diego. He and I were just getting to know each other well."

"I'm fine, Dolly. Just dropped in to talk with Threnody, to thank her for sending me clothes at the hospital."

"Sorry, but she's out for the morning. I'll tell her you stopped by."

As usual Dolly's silvery hair swirled around the shoulders of her long-sleeved blouse with its elaborate neck bow. I seldom saw her in anything but a poet's blouse and black satin pants, skin-tight across the hips then flaring at the ankles.

"Some work outfit." Kane chuckled as Dolly approached the truck, trying to keep a grip on her armload of magazines. "She's probably hiding a severe case of tattoo regret under those long sleeves. People do that. Women. Even guys who're tired of the macho scene."

"At heart Dolly's a poet, not a cleaning lady. I can't help admiring anyone who works two jobs and still finds time to write poetry."

"Lots of service people having moved to the warmth of paradise work two jobs, maybe three — especially if they've formed the unfortunate habit of eating. Lucky for her Brick gave her a job and the maid's room at his mansion. Good thing he vouched for her work and her honesty with your mother and Cherie."

"A plus for Dolly, and also an extra plus thing for our hotel. We need her help."

"I'll admit she's an asset as kitchen help at the Frangi. Thanks to Brick, she's lucky to have two good jobs." Kane grinned. "Hey! You suppose Brick and Dolly have something going?"

"Kane! Women have a rep for being the gossips of the world, not men."

"Well, even though Dolly's an old lady . . ."

"Hold it right there, buddy." I grinned at him. "I'm guessing Dolly's ten years away from collecting Social Security."

"Humph. No matter her age, she flirts with anything wearing pants, and all the locals know Brick has an eye for the ladies. Threnody better watch her back."

"What's going on with the magazines, Dolly?" I called to her as she reached the truck and two magazines slipped from her grip, flopping to the ground.

"Need a hand?" Kane called, opening his door, offering to help her.

Dolly smiled at me before she batted her eyelashes at Kane. "I can manage okay, but thanks, Kane." She laid the magazines on the ground, tugged a piece of paper from her pants pocket, and tucked it into the pocket on my shirt.

"Threnody asked me to get rid of the mags, but when Brick saw them in the recycle box, he slipped me an extra five and asked me to bring them back inside and stack them in his den." Then she lowered her voice as if someone might be listening. "He's a packrat, you know, a sweet guy, but a packrat. Has a problem letting go of stuff, magazines, old clothes . . . anything. But it's nothing to me. He pays me to do what I'm told." She grinned. "May write a poem about a packrat someday."

With a quick wave, Dolly picked up the magazines, turned, and headed toward the mansion while Kane followed the circular driveway back to the street and pointed us toward the hotel. I guessed Dolly had tucked a poem into my pocket, but I didn't read it right then. No point in giving Kane a chance to laugh at her.

Compared to the Vexton mansion, The Blue Mermaid looked like King Neptune's palace — five stories tall, a lattice-and-vine-covered portico, and hundreds of overhead windows that caught the sunlight and reflected back silvery blue images. Out front, a bigger-than-life sculpture of a mermaid guarded the entryway. Kane followed the bricked driveway that led to our family's private entrance at the back of the hotel. Mother always hated having his battered work truck out front where potential patrons could see it and perhaps decide to book rooms elsewhere. We went inside and took the service elevator to the penthouse.

"I locked the door to your suite this morning after Threnody packed your clothes for you."

The elevator door closed behind us, and we stepped into the hallway where Wyland, famous marine life artist of the day, had painted sea-creature murals on the inner walls — whales, manta rays, and mermaids relaxing in a bed of sea fans and conch shells.

"Glad you locked the place, Kane.

Wouldn't dream of going out and leaving my suite open. Got my key ring?"

Kane pulled my keys from his pocket and unlocked the door for me. I stepped inside my suite, then hesitated.

"What's the matter?"

"Nothing." I walked on, unwilling for Kane to see my nervousness. I refused to admit to fear. A searching look around told me that nobody had been inside the suite except Kane and me — and Threnody. But if someone had murdered Diego, I might be next on the killer's list. To hide my uneasiness, I strode to the refrigerator and pulled out a carafe of iced tea.

"How about a drink, Kane? I'm dying of thirst, and that hospital water tasted like pure formaldehyde."

"You swig down lots of formaldehyde?" Kane stepped close and blew his warm breath into my ear. I laughed, kissed him lightly on the cheek, then eased to the cupboard to get glasses.

"No formaldehyde when there's something better at hand." I poured us tumblers of tea and added some ice cubes before I remembered the special treat Kane made for us yesterday noon.

"Kane! Your crème brulee! We have two ramekins left from yesterday. Shall we eat them now?"

"Glad you remembered!"

Kane carried the ramekins and I carried the tea to the snack bar. Before we sat down to enjoy the treat, Kane kicked off his shoes, walked across the living room to open the sliding doors that opened onto a half-balcony overlooking the hotel pool. Mother and Cherie's suites opened onto full balconies and I tried not to resent that, although, in my mind, it stood as another example of my underdog status in the family. I followed Kane onto the balcony, gazing into the distance where our view included Key West harbor, and beyond that, the Gulf of Mexico.

Kane draped his arm around my shoulder and sighed. "Don't know how you ever get any writing done with a view like this tempting you to relax and enjoy."

"When I'm tempted to goof off too long, my conscience hears my computer and steel files calling from my office." I nodded toward the next room. "The *Citizen* does give me deadlines, you know. Right now, I have a couple of columns written ahead of schedule."

"Good thing. It'll give you some extra time to deal with the police investigation. And I'm guessing there'll be one starting in the very near future — like today."

We returned to the snack bar to enjoy the crème brulee.

"Kane, there's nothing nicer than a man who likes to cook. This custard is delicious — sweet, creamy, and crunchy on top. Excellent. Feel free to use my kitchen any time you choose."

"And your bed?"

I grinned at him. "We'll see about that."

Kane finished his custard and walked toward a hallway wall for a close look at an award I received last year.

"FIRST PRIZE. GRAND SLAM. What's that all about, Rafa? Never noticed it before. Didn't know you played bridge."

"No bridge. That's an award from Florida Keys Sportsmen, Incorporated. Thought I told you about winning it in their contest last summer. I caught a bonefish, a permit, and a tarpon all on the same day. I don't usually display my fishing trophies, but that one's special."

"Wow! I'm impressed. Really, I am. When I go fishing, I can cast a plug or a fly for hours without catching anything. Nada. Congratulations!"

"Thanks, Kane. Glad you noticed the award."

Turning, Kane stepped closer to the

balcony and peered at the ocean. "I can see three sailboats and a catamaran close by. No shrimp boats, of course, now that they've been eased out. And in the distance two freighters are taking their chances with the would-be hurricane."

"I love this suite, Kane. Even though it means putting up with Mother and Cherie's company now and then, they don't drop in unless I invite them. Good thing we have separate quarters." I stood. "Care for something else to eat? A cookie? Some junk food?"

"Another time, thanks." Kane slipped back into his shoes, picked up his tea, and finished it in one gulp. "Let's get out of here, Rafa."

"You must feel as uneasy as I do."

"I can't help thinking about Diego."

"Me, either." I pulled my hand from his, rinsed our tea glasses and ramekins, set them in the dishwasher. "Ever since we left the hospital I've felt someone watching us, following us. Spying on us. It's going to take a while for me to get over the shock of finding Diego — dead, of learning that the police consider me a person of interest — a suspect." I walked around the room, closing the windows and the sliding balcony door.

"Why are you doing that? Your suite will

feel like a potter's kiln when you get back."

"No matter. I'll turn on the AC if I'm too warm. Even though I'm up high, I dislike leaving the suite with the windows open. Last night I dashed away in a big hurry to check on *The Bail Bond* — didn't take time to close them." Now, after I'd secured the windows, I lowered the mini blinds across them, and then followed Kane to the door. As we started to leave, the phone rang.

"Hello," I used a clipped voice, hoping to tell the caller I was in a hurry.

No response.

"Rafa Blue speaking. Hello."

I stood holding a dead line. Irritated, I dropped the phone back into its cradle, followed Kane into the hallway, and flipped the dead bolt in place before we walked to the elevator.

"Guess someone had the wrong number," I said. I kept my voice light, unwilling for Kane to guess I considered the call something more sinister than a wrong number.

"Where to?" Kane asked when we reached his truck. "Want to see if Threnody's returned home?"

"Later, please. Guess I'm unwilling to face people — and their questions, even Threnody's. Let's go somewhere outdoors, yet someplace where we'll have privacy, someplace where you can tell me what you've heard about Diego's death. What's the street talk? What's the gossip?"

"How about going to my boat? The Harbor Walk can be a private place — of sorts — once you reach the last catwalk at the end of the long row of catwalks. We can board *The Buccaneer.* We'll be alone there — except for a few hundred tourists and a few dozen boat owners who dock their boats in those upscale slips. Wish I'd been here in the days when hundreds of shrimp boats filled this harbor. Bought my boat from a guy named Ace. He sold out when the commissioners made him open his boat to tourists one day a week. Now they're trying to make me open *The Buccaneer* to day trippers wanting to go out fishing on weekends. Makes me downright mad the way the commissioners managed to close the working shrimp boat captains out of their working waters."

"But you'll have to admit the city has turned the area into a beautiful place."

"Right, it has, but I'm not going to let those guys force me out. And that's what they're trying to do by insisting I take out day trippers. That's worse than opening it to tourists once a week as a historical monument of sorts."

"I'm ready to think of other things. Let's go to your boat now and enjoy the sea. It'll be good to see my car again, too. Hope cops haven't ordered it towed away from some no-parking zone."

"No tow-away danger. Spoke to some friends. I left it in a legit parking slot. Pays to have friends in the right places. Thought you might rather have the car near the Harbor Walk instead of at the hotel — in case the police come searching for it — or you."

"That's a possibility?"

"Could be. You never know. It pays to be on guard."

Kane drove slowly along the bumps and narrowness of Elizabeth Street to the area once claimed by shrimpers for their shrimp docks. "I haven't worked here all that long, but the old-timers say that before Henry Singleton died and his heirs sold the Key West Bight to the city, they could walk from Elizabeth Street to Grinell on the decks of the hundreds of shrimp boats anchored in the bight. But no more."

"Things change, Kane. Face it. The bight's now Key West's Historic Seaport District. I can empathize with the commercial shrimpers forced to move on and find new waters to work, and I'm glad Ace talked the city into letting him stay. I never knew him, but I'm glad he sold you his boat."

"It's a strange feeling to be the only shrimp boat captain in the area. Believe me. I feel isolated and snubbed by the other boat captains. Sure, I still make my living shrimping, but I had to agree to open *The Buccaneer* to tourists and school groups on Wednesdays as a historic attraction just as Ace did. And now they're talking day trips. No way. The Wednesday groups shoot my Wednesdays all to hell. First I have to clean the boat up to get ready for guests, then I have to clean up again after they leave. And the after-guests-leave cleanup is the worst."

"Hey, there's my Prius." I stopped Kane's rant when I saw my car. Although Kane could remember little of the "old days," he hated seeing government swallow the freedom of the common worker. He parked his truck in a palm-shaded space reserved especially for him, and we walked back to my car. Opening the driver's door, I slid under the wheel, turned to inspect the rear seats, opened the glove box.

"Everything's as I left it, Kane." I smiled at him. "Thanks for taking care of it for me."

"That's the sexiest thing you do, Rafa."

"What are you talking about? I didn't do a thing."

"Not a thing except smile at me. Your smile is one of my favorite things. It's like the sun roof in a car — lights up the whole area, especially my heart."

"Thank you for being so sweet. It's nice to know something about me pleases you."

"Your smile's not the only thing. Want to hear more?"

Now I felt self-conscious every time I smiled, but I smiled at him again. "Not now, okay? I might get the big head. Let's go on to your boat. I'll try to forget all the glitz and glamour around it. It's still just my favorite shrimp boat."

"Glad to know that."

"As a child the shrimp docks fascinated me. The unique smell, of course, but after a few deep breaths, I got used to that. Gulls swooped and dived. Watchbird pelicans perched, statue silent as they guarded dock pilings and waited for handouts. White boats trimmed in black dotted the sea, their riggings pointing skyward like dark swords. We lost an interesting scene when the shrimp fleet left Key West."

"You're good at painting word pictures."

Today, *The Buccaneer* lay moored beside the last of the sleek sailboats. I could imagine their captains looking down their noses at a smelly shrimp boat. Kane's boat floated many yards from the seawall and Kane strode toward it. I followed him onto the swaying catwalk, grabbing the security line on my right for support.

When we reached *The Buccaneer,* Kane boarded in one quicksilver movement, then turned to give me a hand while I stepped over the gunwale onto the gray deck. I've never been a sailor at heart, and the roll of the boat even while secured in its slip made me feel unsettled and vulnerable. Shadows of running clouds plunging us from shade to light and back to shade again left me off balance and I looked at the horizon hoping for stability as I moved about.

Kane had raised the iron outriggers until they formed a black V against the sky. The pink chafing gear designed to protect the trawl nets from wear as they dragged against the sea bottom looked like two blobs of rouge applied to wrinkled faces. I wished I knew more about the boat, but Kane always said it was a working boat, not a pleasure craft. He'd only invited me aboard for a tour one Wednesday last year — a very brief tour.

"Want to sit in the wheelhouse?" He nodded toward the cabin.

I wanted to see more of the boat, but today was no time to expect another guided tour.

"How about sitting aft where we can catch a few rays and see the action around us. We can keep our voices low."

"Suits me."

I helped Kane pull two canvas chairs onto the deck, positioning them so we'd have an almost unobstructed view of the Gulf. The sea always makes me feel miniscule and unimportant, but it never seems to affect Kane that way. He stood for a moment looking at the horizon, completely at ease as captain of *The Buccaneer.* I thought and hoped he'd want to talk about Diego, but he surprised me.

FIVE

"Rafa, I'm mad as hell at the commissioners for passing legislation that forced hardworking shrimpers from what they had claimed for years as their working waters."

"There's nothing anyone can do about it now. The *Citizen*'s printed news of that controversy for months, no, for years. Politics. But it turned out to be good news for you. You have a great boat slip right here at the harbor walk, and I guess there's no shortage of shrimp waiting for your nets."

"The *Citizen* may have dropped the subject of working waters as they relate to Key West shrimpers, but I checked recently, and *no* shrimp docks remain on Stock Island either. Not only that, but the artisans on Shrimp Road worry that they'll be forced from that area, too. Painters, woodworkers, craftsmen — their quaint shops are on the last available land near working water space in the lower keys. When the landowners decide to sell, those businesses are doomed."

"I read the commissioners' thinking on the subject. Politics! They try to make the changes sound as if they're benefiting Stock Island, but I doubt it. It's all politics. The only good thing about proposed laws is that changes take a long time to happen in Monroe County."

"But eventually they do happen." Kane pounded a fist into his palm. "They happen exactly as the majority of commissioners plan for them to happen."

"You mean the Gang of Three? Diego was one of the commissioners." I hoped mentioning Diego's name would remind Kane of last night and get him off the topic of politics.

"Don't know about any Gang of Three, Rafa. Don't know the insider scoop on things going on at the courthouse, but folks who ignore stuff that happened years ago might need to wake up — me included. History has a way of repeating itself."

"Like making the free-loading live-aboards along Houseboat Row move their boats to paying slips at Garrison Bight?" I asked.

"Right. If we don't remember things that happened in the past, we condemn ourselves to repeat similar things. I read that somewhere, but it's true." Kane brought us sodas from a cooler in the wheelhouse. "Old-timers tell me the live-aboards fought moving for over thirty years, but a few years ago, the change took place."

"I think Diego lived on Houseboat Row when he first came to Key West." My trying to get the conversation back to Diego failed.

"Diego told me that he left Houseboat Row willingly," Kane said, "but some of the captains left their anchorages kicking and screaming, when new laws forced them out."

I sipped my drink, enjoying the tingle on my tongue. "Everyone has to face change."

"And Houseboat Row no longer exists. It's a thing of the past. Personally, that area didn't bother me. I was one of many who thought it offered a picturesque attraction for tourists visiting the island for the first time."

"Opinions differ." I said. "And those who preferred *E coli*–free water won out."

"So maybe Houseboat Row posed a health hazard. Nobody doubts that those boaters sometimes dumped their waste directly into the sea. But that wasn't the case with boat captains at the shrimp docks."

"You squeaky-clean guys kept your boats shining with spit and polish?" I took a deep breath and grinned at him. "Can't imagine what caused the smells in that area."

"A little shrimp fragrance never hurt anyone, Rafa. We shrimpers dumped waste in the sanitary stations the city provided for that purpose. The only reason the city fathers wanted to get rid of the shrimp docks with their 'working waters' ordinances was so they could attract wealthy yachters from Miami — even from Europe or Australia. In today's world, the bottom line's always money, and yacht captains have more of the long green than shrimp boat captains."

"I didn't know you felt so strongly about the politics of it, Kane. I knew you put up a strong fight to keep *The Buccaneer* docked in Key West, but . . ."

"You bet I felt strongly about it. Still feel strongly about it. I've seen pictures of that upscale yacht basin in Marathon. Old-timers tell me it used to be an area where shrimpers kept their boats and sold their catch to locals and tourists who stopped to chat with their favorite captain and buy shrimp fresh from the sea."

"You're right about that. Dad sometimes took a five-gallon bucket and paid old Captain Anders to fill it with fresh shrimp that Mother served to guests that night. Even Cherie had to help when we shelled and deveined those whoppers."

"Then politics took its toll. Commissioners forced those captains to leave. And that's what happened here a few years ago. Ace told me all about it before he sold me his boat. Diego talked and voted for clearing out the shrimpers. As a commissioner, he led a group of followers. He led, and his opinions and his vote counted with the other commissioners — counted big-time. It's one area of thinking where Diego and I disagreed."

For a few moments Kane and I sat in the deck chairs sipping sodas and enjoying an unrestricted view of the bay. Although the vastness of the sea made me feel smaller than a grain of sand, sometimes it gave me a sense of all's-right-with-the-world. But not today. Kane's effort to divert my attention failed. I couldn't forget Diego's body floating in the black water at the marina. Nor could I forget that in Chief Ramsey's eye, I was a person of interest.

The impact of Diego's death, the finality of all death, left a sadness in my heart that I couldn't eradicate. Kane broke into my morbid thoughts, but he still didn't mention Diego. I tried to turn my ears off to his chatter. Impossible.

"Sometimes I wonder how old *The Buc-*

caneer is, Rafa. Old-timers say boats can remain seaworthy for years if their owners follow the rules in maintaining them. Got a buddy who claims he celebrated his cabin cruiser's hundredth birthday last year."

I wondered why Kane avoided talking about last night's murder. Did he think avoiding the subject would spare my feelings — or his own? Surely he must know Diego was uppermost in my mind this morning.

"How old do you think *The Buccaneer* is?" I forced myself to go along with Kane's trend of thought. Time enough later to think about Diego — maybe the rest of my life. A life behind bars? I forced myself to bury that thought. Surely the chief would find other people of interest.

"I've told you I bought *The Buccaneer* from a guy named Ace Bradford about five years ago. He moved back to Iowa. Said he missed early-onset flu season and December's ice and snow storms."

"Maybe he was kidding."

"Yeah. I guessed he missed his girlfriend who he said waited for him in Des Moines. Ace told me he bought this boat from a guy named Red Chipper."

"You ever met him?" I asked.

"Red still lives in the Key West area, I

think. He used to drop around now and then to talk a bit. I changed the boat's name to *The Buccaneer*. Don't think Red minded. More than likely he renamed it when he bought it."

"Wonder where he got the boat. I mean, did he buy it from a boatyard new, or maybe buy it secondhand from a friend?" I took a deep drink of soda and let it trickle down my throat, still hoping to work our conversation around to Diego and last night.

"Said he bought it from Captain Snipe Gross and that Snipe bought it from a captain name of Bucky Varnum. That dates it back to nineteen-eighty."

"Almost thirty years ago. How'd you pinpoint that date?"

"That's the year the Mariel Boatlift began — and ended. Lasted about six months. Bucky made big bucks off the boatlift — the Cubans. At that time, Castro let everyone leave Cuba who wanted to leave — and plenty of people wanted out of there, wanted to come to America. Diego was one of them. He came here on that boatlift — along with about a hundred twenty-five other people."

Good. Now the conversation was touching on Diego. "Do you know what kind of a job Diego held in Cuba?"

63

"Worked with his family in the cane fields, I think. Guess they owned a big spread in the countryside somewhere near Havana. He never talked much about it. My guess is that they didn't want him to leave."

For a moment I thought I'd succeeded in directing our talk back to Diego. Wrong.

"Castro opened his prisons and gave free and legal passage to any criminal who could find space aboard a boat. Plenty of hardened criminals sailed to the Keys — the closest land to Mariel Bay."

"Kane! Are you hinting that Diego had been a criminal in Cuba? Is that what you believe? I suppose that might be true, but . . ."

Kane ignored my question, which made me even more curious about Diego's family and his past. Someone had murdered him. Could it have been someone from his Cuban past? Now I listened with more interest.

"Rafa, we're both too young to remember this, but I've always liked history, and I've read about the boatlift. Never talked much to Diego about it. For a while, President Carter didn't realize Castro had opened Cuba's jail cells. He welcomed the immigrants, and Florida offered the closest shore. I knew an old guy who hung around the Raw Bar. He told anyone who'd listen to him about his flight from a stinking Cuban jail."

"He rated criminal status in Cuba, but he became a free man in Key West?"

"Right. You got the picture."

"That must have been scary for the locals."

"This guy didn't impress me as a dangerous person, but he told the Cuban authorities he was a druggie. Castro's officials wanted the druggies out of Cuba. They put them on any boat handy that headed away from Mariel Harbor."

"Kane! Are you sure that's true? After all, the guy admitted to being a druggie."

"Who am I to doubt? Nobody, no country, wants to claim a hop-head. Anyway, that guy said he came over for free. Said he stood waiting on an almost-collapsed dock in Mariel Bay and then followed the guy ahead of him onto the boat. He had no big plans for his life in Cuba. Didn't even think about a goal for living free in America."

"Sounds like a great fellow. Surely Diego wasn't anything like that. Diego seemed like a guy who knew where he was going." Again I tried to direct the conversation back to Diego and keep it there. Again, I failed.

"Castro and Carter changed shrimp fishing in the Keys — for a while."

"Kane, do you think someone from Diego's distant past could have murdered him last night?"

"It's something to think about. May not be a bad thing to point out to Chief Ramsey."

"I'm certainly willing to think about it. Tell me more. I'm guessing shrimp boats became water taxis — something like the gondolas in Venice only a lot less glamorous."

"Right. Shrimp boats and any other crafts that would float became taxis. But boat captains didn't haul Cubans here for free. Old-timers on the island say Bucky Varnum grew rich overnight on the backs of Cubans. They resented him charging those who had money for passage, but leaving the poor behind. He made trip after trip to Mariel Bay and solicited passengers to Key West. Socked them two grand each."

"Where did Cubans find that kind of money?"

Kane shrugged. "Life savings, I suppose. Maybe relatives helped them, perhaps on promises of future aid from them once they found jobs in America. Maybe the Cuban government paid to get the druggies out. Anyway, thousands of Cubans found the money for passage to America."

"And Diego must have been one of them. How many Cubans could Captain Varnum carry at one time?"

"Take a guess. Look around. This boat isn't very big, but I'm guessing he could get fifty or more aboard if they didn't demand too much comfort. Probably lots of them had to stand up the whole trip. Maybe some of them rode below deck in the hull. I'm sure the boat left Mariel Bay overloaded."

"You know how long it took a boat to travel from Cuba to Key West?"

"It'd have depended on the weather, the condition of the boat — on lots of things, including the captain's ability to handle a craft loaded overcapacity in all kinds of weather. Diego lost his wife at sea when a sudden squall caught them. Of course they were unprepared for such danger. Diego's wife drowned. Only with luck on his side was he able to save Pablo, little more than a baby at the time."

I looked around the boat, trying to avoid imagining Diego losing his wife, trying not to imagine fifty people jammed aboard, all the time knowing shark-infested waters lay only a few feet below their toes.

"Didn't they have laws in those days about overloading the boats?"

"I suppose the Coast Guard tried to maintain laws, but with so many boats at sea, officials faced an impossible job. They couldn't monitor all of that vast number of boats and enforce safety regulations. But after a few trips, Captain Varnum must have become a wealthy man."

"I wonder what happened to him — where he hangs out today."

"Nobody seems to know — or care. The boatlift ended when President Carter realized Castro was sending murderers, thieves, and mentally deranged people as his gift to America. It's a time lots of people like to forget. Probably several of today's Key West citizens along with Diego arrived here on that boat lift."

Murderers. Thieves. I refused to think of Diego as anything but a good guy and an honest citizen. "And many of today's Cubans may have tried to enter Florida illegally, trusting the wet-foot-dry-foot law to help them — if they're lucky enough to reach dry land."

"Yeah," Kane opened a package of chips and offered me some.

I enjoyed their salty crispiness, but I wanted to forget the long-ago boatlift and focus again on the here and now. "Kane, many of my columns touch on people and history, but let's forget the past for a while. I'll label Bucky Varnum a crook and a cheat, but I want to hear what you know about last night and Diego."

"People forget history at their peril, Rafa. Didn't mean to bore you."

Six

"You weren't boring me. You never bore me. The history of your shrimp boat fascinates me — especially since Diego was a part of it. But for Pete's sake, please tell me what you've heard about Diego's death. What's the street talk?"

"Haven't had much time to listen to street talk. Been busy getting your car and finding legal parking for it. Getting you out of the hospital."

I smiled. "Sorry to have been such a bother."

"No bother at all. Consider me at your beck and call — especially when you smile."

"Come on, Kane. Give! Quit teasing and stop stalling. You must have heard some rumors."

"Okay. But they're just rumors. Some people are asking where Pablo's hanging out."

"Hmmm. Diego's son."

"Right. His son has frequently been heard arguing with Diego — over money. Pablo wanted more. Claimed he owed college debts and that Diego should help pay them. Pablo is Diego's next of kin. And several people overheard him demanding money from good old dad."

"I don't know Pablo well — just from meeting him when he plays drums with the combo at the Frangi. Although I've heard he's little more than a beach bum, giving tarot card readings under a palm tree during the sunset celebration at Mallory Dock, I can't imagine him as a killer. What else have you heard?"

"That there's bad blood between Diego and Brick Vexton as well as hard feelings between Diego and Jessie, Brick's son."

"So for a busy guy, you've heard quite a few rumors. Glad Mother and Cherie were off-island when the murder took place. Someone might have tried to work them into the gossip, too."

"Gossip's all it is. Keep that in mind. And don't forget to include me among the suspects."

"You?"

"Sure. I told you Diego and I disagreed big-time. He was one of the commissioners who voted for closing Key West's working waters. He wanted the shrimp boats out of Key West Bight." Kane waved an arm, gesturing at the yachts and sailboats around us. "Diego voted for turning our former shrimp docks over to moneyed interests. He backed the developers who lined their pockets at the expense of the shrimpers, honest fishermen who struggled to eke out a living and who had no place else to go."

"County officials held an election, Kane. I remember that. The majority of voters agreed with Diego and the rest of the commissioners or the new laws would never have passed."

"Perhaps. But before the vote took place, I'm the one who blasted lengthy letters to the *Citizen* on the subject. My name's out there as an avid protestor. At the time, most of the other shrimpers used good sense and kept quiet. Or at least they kept their names out of print."

I didn't know what to say next. I'd seen Kane's letters to the editor, but arguments concerning island politics don't hold my attention for long. In this vast ocean, I figured the shrimp boat fleet would have no trouble finding another place to dock their boats. I knew Diego had odd-jobbed around Key West for years until Brick opened his marina and gave him steady employment. Diego

72

had a way with people. Everyone liked him. Brick backed Diego in his bid for a job as county commissioner, and when voters elected Diego, he thanked Brick by continuing to work as his chief dock master. They were friends as well as business partners.

"Guess I asked to hear your take on the local gossip, didn't I? I never imagined political differences could fall so close to home." I tried to relax and enjoy the chips and soda, but our conversation about Diego's murder and county politics had ruined the beauty of the sea scene for me.

"Yeah, you asked all right. And I told you. At least those are this morning's gossip tidbits along with my take on local politics."

"Kane, I can't imagine you or any other shrimper murdering Diego over the closing of Key West's working waters. Surely any gossip about you will blow over and be forgotten once the police start investigating other angles."

"I hope so. Police investigations draw little print, but the cops are tenacious when they think they're on to a clue that points to a culprit. Many people may be sucked into the aftermath of Diego's murder. He cut a wide swath in this community."

Kane's words chilled me. I'd heard enough — for now, at least. When I leaned over to drop my soda bottle into the trash can, the paper Dolly had stuck in my shirt pocket crackled. I pulled it out, again more than ready to change the subject, to think of something other than Diego's murder and possible suspects.

"Look Kane!" I waved the paper in his direction. "Dolly's given me a poem."

"Big deal. Has she pinpointed the killer in iambic pentameter?"

"An original poem from the poet who wrote it *is* a big deal, Kane. Please don't make a joke of it. Dolly considers herself a poet, a poet awaiting her big moment in print."

"Big deal!"

"I think it's a big deal, and in the near future I may choose Dolly as the subject of one of my columns. People need to know more about her, to be aware of her goals and her struggle. I enjoy using my column to help the underdog — talented people awaiting recognition. Look, this poem's about a cat."

"No surprise there." Kane stared into the distance.

"Dolly loves cats. I see her feeding a black stray at the hotel almost every morning."

"Surprised she didn't make you pay a dime for the poem."

I grinned. Dolly might or might not become known as the Poet Laureate of Key West, but she is known for leaving copies of her poems beside the cash registers in many Key West stores. A small sign beside the poems asks patrons to take a poem and deposit a dime in the Poet's Jar nearby, the proceeds going to poet Dolly Jass.

"I've bought several of her ten-cent poems, Kane. I consider the gift of a poem from Dolly an important gift, generously given."

"Okay. Okay. Read it and forget it."

"Aloud?"

"If you insist. But it won't influence me to drop any dimes in her Poet's Jar."

I read the poem silently before I shared it with Kane.

"The title is 'Sir Cat and the Spider Plant.' " I smiled. "It's a bit of whimsy."

"A lot like Dolly, right?"

"Perhaps. But it may lift your spirits, shift your thoughts from Diego and murder."

I began reading:

When life gets so boring
That fits aren't worth throwing
I slink to the porch
Where Spider Plant's growing

It thrives in a clay pot

That hangs from a bracket
And one spider baby
Swings low. Watch me whack it.

It flies to its siblings
The whole plant's aquiver
I smack it again and
Green leaves start to sliver.

Ma'am runs to the porch to
Protect Spider's babies
And I'm in big trouble —
No ifs ands or maybes.

Ma'am stamps and she storms. She's
A mover and shaker
But watch! I'll start purring.
That's my great peacemaker.

After I read the poem and received no comment from Kane, I refolded it and started to tuck it back into my pocket. Then I saw three more lines Dolly had added like an afterthought toward the bottom of the page. They were untitled.

Wise cats wait till night
To stalk the land and prowl earth's
Haunted hidden spots.

I read the lines twice and felt hairs rise on

my forearms before I folded the sheet and tucked it into my pocket. I didn't read those last lines to Kane, but I wondered if they carried an esoteric clue concerning Diego's murder, or if she was experimenting, trying her hand at creating haiku. I stood and began pulling my deck chair back into the wheelhouse.

"Want a quick tour of the boat?" Kane asked.

What was going on here! "Sure you've got time?"

"You being sarcastic?"

"No. I didn't mean to sound that way. You've seldom invited me aboard *The Buccaneer,* and I'd love a tour. But I hoped you'd have more to tell me — more rumors about the murder." Kane ignored those last words.

"There's little to see on *The Buccaneer* that you haven't already seen. I haven't made many big changes during the past weeks. You've seen the big three, the main deck, the wheelhouse, the hull down below."

"Where does your crew sleep?"

"In the bunks at the front of the wheelhouse." Kane led me forward. "But first, here's the galley. I did add a new camp stove last summer." He pumped some water into

77

a small sink and pointed to a Coleman stove."

"And now the bunks?"

Kane moved forward in the narrow wheelhouse and pointed to two bunks, a built-in chest of drawers, and two lockers for stowing gear.

"Not much space for personal things," I said, laughing.

"Shrimpers don't bring many personal things aboard." Kane lifted the thin mattress on one bunk and propped it against the bulkhead then stepped aside to give me a better view. "There's a small compartment under each bunk. Go ahead. Open it up if you're curious."

A pine board with a blue rope handle at each end lay fitted into a rectangular indentation. I grabbed the handles and tugged on the board. It didn't budge.

"Let me give you a hand. That board's been there since I bought the boat. The compartment underneath doesn't get much use. Never thought it important to work on the sticky lid." It took two tugs before Kane pulled the board up, revealing a small space that held a catalog of nautical equipment, a couple of salt-water fishing magazines, and a deck of playing cards.

I laughed. "Enough recreational equipment to keep any sailor happy."

"Dampness makes the lid warp, but no matter. Shrimping crews don't have much time for fun and games."

"What do you do for sleep space if you have several crewmen aboard?"

"There's another sleeping compartment that opens into the hull next to the ice bins."

Kane didn't offer a tour of the hull and I didn't ask.

"You ready to go? You can stay here and rest a while longer if you aren't up to talking to people yet."

"I'm ready." I leaned against the wheelhouse doorway. "Guess I hoped to hear more talk about the murder."

"I haven't heard any more talk this morning, but a week or so ago, Brick told me about some problems between him and Diego." Kane gave a short laugh. "Sounded like labor-management stuff. I never thought too much about it at the time."

"What kinds of problems? Surely none that might escalate into murder."

Kane shrugged. "You never know what sort of argument might precipitate a murder. Diego had worked for Brick for years as chief dock master — an important job at any marina and ship's chandlery. After Brick read my letters to the editor and realized

79

Diego and I stood at odds, he told me some of his problems with Diego that had nothing to do with Diego's job as chief dock master."

"They had to do with the working waters dispute?"

"Brick thought their differences more serious than that. The commissioners have a lot of say about the functioning of the ROGO."

"The county's Rate of Growth Ordinance. I've heard Mother scream about that — about the difficulties she met when applying for a permit to build a new work shed or even to add a windbreak onto the hotel's back entryway. Laws forced her to wait for weeks for her name to reach the top of the ROGO list so she could buy a permit to add the dance floor in the Frangi."

"Lots of people think the ROGO sucks. If someone tries to hide doing a little construction on his property without going through the ROGO, a jealous neighbor may report him to authorities. And that usually results in the would-be builder facing a fine."

"Mother mentioned a neighbor who had to buy a permit to build a simple pine box to cover his air conditioner."

"Right." Kane lowered his voice. "Rafa, this information must go no farther. It's between the two of us. Agreed?"

"Agreed."

"Brick wants to add a hotel to his marina and he wants his son, Jessie, to manage it once it's in operation."

"And the commissioners have a problem with that?"

"One commissioner did — Diego. Diego liked the idea of Brick building the hotel, but he wanted Brick to name him manager, not Jessie. That hotel manager job would have meant big bucks to Diego. Brick balked at that idea and so did Threnody. Guess we both know that around Key West, Jessie carries a bad-boy rep. He's a wild card, doing as he pleases, getting whatever he wants whenever he wants it — and his folks want to see him gainfully employed in the family business."

"And what could Diego do about it? Seems to me that a guy's son would be the logical person to manage his dad's hotel if that's the way they both wanted it."

"Right, but Diego's position as a commissioner gave him lots of power, lots of ability to influence the commissioners regulating the ROGO."

"Sounds like a lot of shenanigans could be afoot, right?"

"Key West politics are full of red-neck shenanigans, good-old-boy-behind-the-scenes stuff that most citizens know nothing about. Most people don't give a rat's eyebrow about a ROGO decision unless it's *their* building permit that's being delayed."

"So you're saying that maybe Diego might have been using his influence to keep Brick's name low on the ROGO."

"I'm not saying that, but it could be true. Also, it could be true that Diego might use his influence to move Brick's name forward on the ROGO and get the permit sooner if Brick would agree to hiring Diego to manage the hotel."

"Did Jessie want to manage the hotel?"

"Brick said Jessie wanted anything that meant more money in his pocket."

"Wonder if Jessie would settle for being chief dock master."

Kane snorted. "The Jessie I know avoids hard labor, and dock masters face a lot of that."

"Kane, due to the building permit disagreement, Threnody and Jessie, as well as Brick — all of them could be among the suspects in Diego's death. We're not the only ones."

"I never said that."

"You hinted that, Kane. You know you did."

"And you promised to keep my hints top secret."

"Of course. Depend on it. I keep my promises." I stepped inside the wheelhouse and sat again in a deck chair. "Kane, even if I'm a suspect in this murder, I'd like to do some private investigating into Diego's death."

SEVEN

For several moments Kane stared at the horizon before he growled a response, his voice so low I had to lean forward to hear his words.

"Don't do it, Rafa. Don't even consider it."

Kane seldom gave orders — at least not to me. I hesitated before I met his gaze. "Why not, Kane? I can't see any harm in doing a little investigating on the side. Why shouldn't I?"

"Because at this point you'd be smart to keep out of any investigation. Because you're the one who found Diego's body, and you're a suspect in his murder. Because you're a person of interest. Want to hear more? If you step forward and start your own investigation, you could damage both your present and your future writing career. You'd be smart to hang back for a while and see what happens."

"You may be right." I stood facing him, our eyes almost meeting on a level. "I don't intend to step forward. So far nobody has asked me to do that. And I'm guessing nobody will. But I don't think I can live with myself if I don't make an effort to help find Diego's killer. I'll never forget seeing his head bobbing in the water below that catwalk, never forget feeling that raging sea pounding his body — and mine. Kane, his eyes rolled back into his head like a death mask. Can you imagine that horror?"

Kane's involuntary shudder spoke louder than words. "Let it alone, Rafa. Let Key West's finest do their job without your help."

"Diego was my friend, Kane. My good friend. I wish you'd tell me more about what you've heard about the murder so far. Let me in on what you know — or what people have said to you. I have a strong feeling you're withholding important information from me."

"I've already told you all I know. Remember, I wasn't out and about last night. I skipped the parade. Spent most of the evening aboard my boat tinkering with one of the motors before I heard the police broadcast and drove to the marina and then to the hospital. Not much chance to talk to anyone. And I've already told you what I

85

know about Brick and Diego's differences."

"If Brick wanted to build a hotel, Threnody must have wanted that, too."

"I vote yes on that one. Few wives wouldn't welcome more money in the family till. Threnody's a high-maintenance babe — a social light, as the saying goes. At least that's what I've heard from your sister."

"Kane! I've never thought of Threnody as a babe. High maintenance, yes. Meaning she has to wear the *right* kind of designer clothes, has to drive the *right* kind of car — probably a new car every year, has to get her name in the *Citizen* as a supporter of worthy causes."

"Right. You've got the picture. According to Cherie, Threnody holds an office in the Lower Keys Women's Club. She's on the board that books top-notch entertainers to appear at the Tennessee Williams Theater. Also, she just finished a term on the school board."

"She keeps busy." I shrugged. "Some women enjoy those activities. Her kind of women need lots of financial backing so they can finance charity balls and that kind of thing. I leave that life to Mother and Cherie, but I do like Threnody. She has a kind way of listening to me and cheering me on when I'm discouraged. Writers lead lonely lives."

"Sometimes I think you hide in your penthouse suite, hide and perhaps glory in the solitariness of your writing."

"Nothing wrong with preferring to be alone. I learned that from my grandmother, Kane. She taught me to love fishing as a child. That's a solitary occupation, and I didn't need to learn to love it. My love of fishing came naturally."

"Maybe because practice made you so good at it. I've watched you cast lures almost into a fish's mouth."

"Got to be able to cast to a target, Gram always said. People used to watch us practice fly casting on the lawn at Bay View Park. Gram would drop hibiscus blossoms on the lawn as targets, then we'd back off several yards and practice casting to them. We kept score. Gram usually won. But back to the Vextons — Threnody."

"Yes, Threnody." Kane chuckled. "That woman spends money like water. I'm guessing she'd welcome the income from a hotel at their marina."

"Sometimes it surprises me that she's willing to sing a few numbers with the combo at the Frangi."

"You've heard her sing, Rafa. You know she has a trained voice. I heard her tell

Dolly that when she was in her teens and early twenties she studied voice at Julliard's. In Key West, her church choir is about her only outlet for singing. I can understand her wanting other places to use her talent. I'm guessing she doesn't mind the applause at the Frangi, either."

"If I were to investigate any murder, I'd start by trying to learn who last saw the victim alive."

"In Diego's case that might be a hard fact to learn. Fiesta Fest Parade night was at full swing. Dozens of people might have seen him helping with the floats, helping traffic control, or just mingling with the crowd."

"True, but it's strange that the murder took place at the marina. Who knew he'd be at the dock so late last night?"

"I have no answer, Rafa. None."

I had no answer either, and for a while I said no more. Nor did Kane. Maybe I needed to sort out my own feelings, the true causes for the differences between Kane and me that kept us from growing closer. In my heart, I knew my feelings could be touching deep secrets, fueling buried reasons for my need to investigate Diego's death. I could hardly bring myself to admit my secret life to myself, to admit the mistakes I'd made years ago, let alone to reveal them to Kane who might consider them reason to walk away from me forever. My deepest desire was for a home and a family. That certainly came before hostessing in the Frangi and before a writing career. But that desire was a secret known only to me. I wouldn't let it cause me to break my deathbed promise to Dad.

"Kane, who will replace Diego on the commissioner's board?"

"You're already planning your investigation, right?"

"Wrong. I'm just asking myself some questions that need to be answered. Quite likely the police will be making similar queries. Any idea who will replace Diego on the board?"

"Haven't the slightest. Don't even know who decides stuff like that. Some political bigwig probably appoints a capable person to fill out the board until the next election. Maybe the mayor. Maybe the county administrator. Maybe someone in the state department. I've never been into city, county, or state politics. Until the 'working waters' issue came up, I had no personal reason to be interested. Don't go poking around for clues, Rafa."

"If I do any *poking around,* as you put it,

I'll keep my actions covert. You'll never notice."

"Be real. I've already noticed. You're asking me pointed questions. Are you thinking that being in line to be selected as Diego's replacement on the board might have motivated some guy to bring out the duct tape and rope?"

"Guy? Are council members always men? I don't think so! Murder's an equal opportunity employer. Maybe a woman will replace Diego on the board. But whether the killer's male or female, there's one important thing to consider in this case. The culprit had to be strong enough to lift a body — a body attached to a concrete block. All that grunt work might not have been a woman's sort of thing. I'm guessing the killer was a man."

"Although you say you have no plans to investigate this case, seems to me you're getting deeply into it. Right?"

"Wrong. Well, maybe not totally wrong. I've read that many killers are sociopaths — men without a conscience who like to murder women for the fun and pleasure it brings them. I can't imagine Diego's killer being a fun-and-games guy. I think he knew exactly who he wanted to kill and why. I think he had strong motive for his actions

— probably financial."

"Are you ready to go now, Rafa? Want me to drive you back to the hotel?"

I knew I'd already said enough, perhaps more than enough, about finding Diego's killer. Maybe Kane knew best. Maybe I should stay out of it — except for being a prime suspect. It looked like I couldn't avoid that.

"I'd be glad to have your company, Kane. I'm going to have to talk to people sooner or later. I'll try to start gradually." I glanced at my watch. "Mother has hired the multi-talented Mama Gomez away from that soft drink bar on Caroline Street. She'll now be making sandwiches at the Frangi as well as taking charge of the combo."

"You're not telling me anything new, Rafa. Mama G's a hard taskmaster. Loves her little bit of authority. She have a key to the Frangi?"

"No. But the desk clerk would let her in. Guess I should be getting over there before long. She sometimes wants someone to taste her sandwich fillings and offer an opinion."

Kane sighed. "As I remember it, Mama G only wants opinions if they are favorable. Very favorable. I think she'd like to see her name in lights on The Blue Mermaid marquee as Sandwich Queen of Key West."

"Isn't that the way with most people? We all like praise and applause. Most of the sandwich fillings I've tasted are really good — maybe both delicious as well as different."

"Different. That's for sure. Not many tourists come in asking for a chopped escargot sandwich on rye. Or Cuban pita bread with a conch and capers filling. I think she makes the crazy recipes up herself."

"Who knows? But she loves telling the tourists about smuggling her Tia Louisa's sandwich recipes to America stitched into the hem of her skirt back in nineteen-sixty. And the tourists love hearing about her parents sobbing as they abandoned her to the hush-hush Pan Am flight that brought children from Havana to a Catholic Charities orphanage in Miami to escape the Castro regime."

"Are you stalling, Rafa? If you aren't ready to face going to the hotel yet, we can hide out here a while longer. I can walk to the Raw Bar and bring us back a picnic lunch to eat here in privacy."

"That might be a good idea, but I think it's too late. Our privacy is about to end." I nodded toward the dock. "The blue and whites have found us."

Now I wished I'd told Kane about my past. Better he should hear of my youthful escapades from me than from the police officers — should they choose to refer to my waywardness as a basis for accusing me of murdering Diego.

Kane followed my gaze to a police car parking in a tow-away zone. Cops can do that. It's a decided advantage for them. But I thought detectives used unmarked cars. Kane and I stepped farther into the wheelhouse and out of sight, peeking through cracks in the siding. Detective Lyon left his car and strode onto the catwalk, heading toward *The Buccaneer* as if unmindful of the boards swaying under his feet. But I noticed that he slid one hand along the security rope, ready to clutch it if he lost his balance.

"What do you suppose he wants?" I asked.

Kane had no time to reply. Lyon reached the bow of *The Buccaneer* and stopped.

"Anyone aboard?" he called out.

"Yo!" Kane stepped onto the deck. "How can I help you, detective?"

"Rafa Blue with you?"

Now it was my turn to step forward. "Yes, sir." I waited, determined to make Lyon do the talking. Another thing Gram taught me. Few people can stand silence. They feel an atavistic need to fill it — usually with their own voice. Lyon was no exception this morning.

"Chief Ramsey wants to see you both at the police station."

"Why?" Kane asked.

"Why both of us?" I asked. "He already talked to me this morning at the hospital."

"The chief wants to ask a few more questions. He's inviting several of Diego Casterano's friends and acquaintances to attend an informal meeting at his second-floor office. He says it won't last long."

"Has anyone been arrested?" Kane asked.

Detective Lyon met Kane's direct gaze. "No arrests have been made at this time. If you'd like, I'll be glad to drive you to the station. Or if you'd prefer to provide your own transportation, that would be fine, too. Sometime in the near future the chief would like to have access to Ms. Blue's car. Again, it will only be a routine check because the nine-one-one call came from her car last night."

Kane continued to meet Detective Lyon's gaze, but his words were for me. "What do you want to do, Rafa? Shall we ride with him or shall we provide our own transportation?"

"Let's go in my car. I have nothing to

hide. If the chief wants to inspect the Prius, it will be at hand."

"Fine." Detective Lyon glanced at his wristwatch. "I'll see you in Chief Ramsey's office in about ten minutes."

"Agreed," Kane said. "Depending on traffic, of course."

"Of course." Lyon turned, leaving us.

EIGHT

I asked Kane to drive my car because he knows how to make quick work of reaching the police station. It wasn't that he knew a shortcut or that he goes there often, but he does know how to maneuver the Prius through traffic without hitting mopeds, whose drivers have never driven a moped before or RVs almost wider than our streets. I allow, few people to drive my car, never Mother or Cherie, but I don't worry when Kane's at the wheel.

Horns blared. Brakes screeched. I braced against the dashboard, feeling myself thrown toward the windshield in spite of my seatbelt. We both choked on diesel fumes when the Bone Island Shuttle cut ahead of us and came within inches of ramming the rear end of a slow-moving Conch Train.

I still sat gritting my teeth when Kane sliced a sharp turn into the driveway of the police station. We narrowly missed hitting a fire truck exiting on a nearby strip of concrete with horns blaring and lights flashing. I gasped, not realizing I'd been holding my breath.

"I hate having to answer questions again. Ramsey and Lyon already questioned me this morning."

Kane grinned. "Maybe the chief has a crush on you, Rafa. Not every day a tall redhead drops into his lap — figuratively speaking, of course."

"Be real, Kane."

Kane arrowed my car into a narrow visitor's slot. I sighed, admitting to myself that this questioning might be one in a long string of Q&A sessions Ramsey and Lyon pre-planned for suspects. I remembered Lyon saying others would be with us answering questions this morning. I wondered who.

Leaving the car, we approached the buff-colored building on foot, skirted around the coral rock fountain in front of the doorway, and stepped inside a small entryway. The police stations I see on TV with their green walls and their tobacco-spit brown floors always give me a stay-out-of-here feeling. Key West's station offered a more benign look. White tile floor. White walls. White plastic chairs alongside one wall near the elevator. Everything gleamed in a whiteness that contrasted with the dark smell that descended on us like an evil miasma.

After we entered the building, I stepped outside again long enough to grab a deep breath of fresh air. I held it, refusing to fill my lungs with secondhand cigarette and cigar smoke for as long as I could. Kane strode to the elevator and punched a button and in moments we entered a compartment small enough to cause claustrophobia. After listening to elevator hum until we reached the second floor, we stepped into the hallway. Detective Lyon emerged from a doorway where he'd been waiting and motioned us to join him. With great reluctance, I let myself exhale and breathe again.

Although we had driven here quickly and circumvented several situations that might have delayed us, we were the last to arrive. Everyone stared at us when we entered the room. I hated the "bug under a microscope" feeling. I'm not afraid of snakes, but I always like to see one before it sees me. But why was I comparing these people to bugs and snakes? I knew everyone in the room, and none of them had frightened me before. But today Ramsey and Lyon thought one of these people might have murdered Diego. Which one? I hated the idea of being in the same room with a killer.

The group waited, sitting in a semi-circle of straight-backed folding chairs arranged in front of a battered oak desk. The fragrance of gardenias permeated the room — a pleasant scent that frequently traveled with Threnody. Did she use eau d' cologne to help her pretend the air in Ramsey's office was smoke free? A good idea. At least nobody in the room was smoking.

Brick and Threnody sat side by side. Brick wore one of his many specially tailored silk shirts, khaki Dockers, and beach Crocs. His bald head and his carefully trimmed beard pulled my gaze away from his weathered face and steely blue eyes. I felt sure he prided himself on his penetrating gaze that tends to make the other person look away first. That morning I looked away first.

I returned Threnody's weak smile. Kane's "high-maintenance" description popped into my mind. Her dark hair, styled in a casual do, touched the shoulder of the hand-print caftan that matched her sling-back sandals. Today she projected a Sunday-morning look suitable for a trophy wife a decade or so younger than her husband.

Their son Jessie had practiced his casually elegant look to perfection. I wondered if he'd planned for his black silk shirt and white slacks to contrast with Kane's faded jeans, tank top, and flip-flops. Don't know why Jessie always reminded me of a one-eyed Jack — maybe because his eyes weren't a matched set — one blue, the other brown. Nobody knew why. Sometimes Jessie seemed secretive about it. I thought he used his eyes like magnets — attracting women to him.

To my surprise, Dolly Jass sat near the door in her trademark poet's outfit. How did she fit into this scene? But much more important than these people's costumes were their closed-book expressions.

So far nobody had said a word, and we listened to the breathing of the air conditioner until Chief Ramsey entered the room and stood behind his desk. I'd been so busy noticing the people present that only now did I study the mix of items on the desktop. For a few moments, he looked down at the clutter. Then he lifted his chin and peered at us, his gaze traveling around the room and stopping briefly on each of us as if in silent greeting.

"Ladies, gentlemen." He paused to clear his throat. "I've brought you here this afternoon to show you items pertinent to Diego Casterano's murder, to show you some photos of the death scene, and to ask each of you a few questions. The police found Diego's body, his personal effects, and these other items shortly after midnight last night in the sea beneath a catwalk at Daiquiri Dock Marina."

Opening a manila envelope he'd been holding in his right hand, he withdrew several glossy photos, which he began passing out, three to each of us. The photos carried a chemical scent, perhaps of developing fluid, and they felt slick to the touch. I could hardly bare to look at them. One showed Diego's partially submerged body in the water. Another, Diego's body lying prone on the rain-slicked catwalk. A distance shot that must have been taken from the end of the catwalk showed sailboats, cruisers, runabouts — all moored in their slips. It also showed a sign with the words DAIQUIRI DOCK MARINA in black print against a white background. I shuffled through the pictures quickly then turned them upside down in my lap.

Without speaking, Ramsey waited until everyone finished studying or at least looking briefly at the photos.

"Does anyone care to comment on these pictures?" he asked.

Nobody spoke. What did he expect? Perhaps a denial that the person was Diego? A denial that the photos had been taken at the Vexton Marina?

Ramsey collected the photos — slowly, deliberately — and returned them to the manila envelope that he then laid on his desk. Next he began touching each of the other desk items and naming them. I cringed inwardly, imagining the sensations his fingertips must be conveying to his brain.

"A diver found this concrete block roped to the victim's ankles, which had been bound together with black duct tape." He ran his fingers over the concrete and twined the blue rope around his fingers. I folded my hands in my lap, avoiding the thought of feeling the roughness of the concrete under my own fingers.

Then, leaning a bit forward, Ramsey picked up the tangled clump of duct tape. He said nothing as he dangled it before us. After a few moments he dropped it and we heard a dull thud as it hit a bare spot on his desk. He made no comment, nor did anyone else.

"Have any of you seen any of these items before this morning?"

Nobody spoke. All eyes met the chief's. Brick cleared his throat as if he might say something, but he remained silent. The blue rope caught my attention because it seemed similar to the rope I'd just seen in the bunkhouse on *The Buccaneer.* But so what? Rope is rope, right? I tried to remember that seamen called rope "line." Chief Ramsey hadn't called it anything. He gave the impression that he hadn't noticed it. I knew his seeming lack of notice must be a ruse of some sort. A trap. Did he expect one of us to incriminate him- or herself by accidentally mentioning it? If so, nobody obliged him.

Next, Ramsey picked up a dock master's jumpsuit, gathered at the back with a wide elastic band. He held it in a way that made it impossible to ignore the words DAIQUIRI DOCK MARINA embroidered in dark brown against the melon-colored fabric. Melon as in cantaloupe, not honeydew. Why were such crazy thoughts racing through my mind? When Ramsey turned the front of the uniform toward us, we saw that all of its buttons were missing and that someone had ripped the fabric from neckline to crotch. I tried to squelch my mental picture of Diego in a death struggle with his killer — with someone sitting near me in this room right at this moment. Or maybe not. Again I wondered who would replace Diego on the board of commissioners. Maybe a stranger appeared in the dark of night, killed Diego, hoping to be appointed to replace him as a commissioner. Maybe nobody in this room was guilty of this horrible crime.

"Have any of you seen this uniform before?" Ramsey asked.

We all nodded as Brick spoke up. "Of course I've seen it — or one like it — many times. It was the chief dock master's work uniform at my marina. Diego owned several of them, and I kept a couple of extras in an employee's closet at the chandlery in case I needed to call in a sub."

Ramsey nodded. "I feel sure you've all seen such a similar uniform before. But did anyone see it last night?"

Nobody answered and Ramsey picked up a closed plastic bag, the kind with a bright-colored zipper across the opening. A bit of coarse, dark hair almost filled the small container. A strand of it hung outside the bag, caught in the zipper. I could hardly bear to look. I focused my gaze on the bag, but I let my eyes glaze, forcing myself to avoid looking at Diego's hair by concentrating on other things. My car. My computer. The Blue Mermaid. For a few moments I could avoid facing the hair, but I couldn't avoid Chief Ramsey's intrusive voice.

"This hair came from the victim's head."

Ramsey's voice forced me to look at the bag and think about the hair. It had been tangled in the anchor line of *The Bail Bond.* Perhaps the murderer intended to make the death scene look as if the victim died accidentally. Perhaps. But no. The perpetrator knew someone would find the concrete block soon. He had tangled Diego's hair in the anchor line for shock value.

Next, Ramsey displayed a leather thong holding a medallion that advertised the Vexton Marina. Again nobody spoke. Ramsey laid it on top of the concrete block and picked up a bit of hand-tooled leather. "Anyone seen this before?"

I spoke. "I've seen it many times. I know it belonged to Diego because my father made it for him many years ago as a gift. As a craftsman, Dad enjoyed tooling objects from leather."

Ramsey laid the thong aside. "And this?" Now he stepped in front of his desk and held a diamond stud earring in the palm of his outstretched hand as he passed in front of each of us, offering the stud for our inspection. His pudgy hand matched the rest of his body. At times, the gem shifted its position and almost disappeared in a fleshy crease below Ramsey's index finger. Everyone except Brick examined the diamond from a distance. Brick reached to touch it.

"I can't be sure that earring belonged to Diego," Brick said. "But I know he owned and usually wore a stud similar to this one."

While the chief displayed his exhibits, Lyon scribbled in a small notebook. Now he jammed the notebook into the pocket of his suit coat. Suit coats. I guessed that's the way the chief and his detectives set themselves apart from ordinary citizens. They wore suit coats even on days like today when the temperature threatened to hit the high eighties. I wondered if Lyon had been jotting down our reactions to the desktop exhibits. I'd been making mental notes, but I'd noticed little reaction from anyone.

I wondered how difficult it would be to hold one's expression in a neutral mode while looking at the last effects of a man you'd murdered the night before. Surely a brow would quirk or a jaw clench.

NINE

Ramsey pulled a cardboard box from under his desk, placed Diego's effects in it, and shoved it back under the desk.

I shuddered as I thought about the grisly items in that box. Had I been the one found dead, what evidence would Ramsey have deemed important enough to save in my cardboard box? Forcing myself to pay attention, I shook that grim thought from my mind and tried to concentrate again on matters at hand. The blue line the killer tied to the concrete block stuck in my memory, but why? Maybe because it matched the shade of my favorite turquoise ring. Maybe because I saw a line of similar color on Kane's boat only a few minutes ago. Kane said the compartment lid under the bunkhouse mattress was there when he bought the boat. Several years ago. Did Ramsey think he could drop the blame for Diego's death at Kane's bulkhead? Crazy idea. The chief had no way, no way at all, of knowing about the rustic furnishings in *The Buccaneer*'s bunkhouse.

The chief began talking again. I tucked my thoughts about the blue line to the back of my mind — in a place where I'd remember to pull them out and give them more consideration later.

"Now I want each of you to tell us the last time you saw Diego Casterano alive. Brick Vexton? I'll start with you since you worked closely with the victim."

Brick met the chief's steady gaze. I wondered who would exit from this eyeball-to-eyeball encounter first, Brick or Ramsey.

Brick cleared his throat, never allowing his gaze to waver. "I saw Diego arrive at work yesterday morning around seven o'clock. He checked in at the desk in the chandlery as was his custom every work day."

"You didn't see him at any time later in the day?"

"No. I left Jessie and my usual weekend employees in charge of the dock because I needed to tend to my volunteer duties on the Duval Street parade route."

The chief nodded. And looked away first. Score one for Brick.

"And you, Mrs. Vexton. When did you last

see the victim alive?"

Mentally, I cringed every time Ramsey said Diego's name, but hearing him called "the victim" was even worse. The word grated against my eardrums until my head threatened to start aching again. Threnody thought for several moments before she answered.

"I saw him Friday night at The Blue Mermaid. Yesterday, Saturday, I spent the day at home until parade lineup time. Fiesta Fest officials scheduled me to sing a solo seated on the first float as the parade passed the judges' reviewing stand in front of Sloppy Joe's. I spent part of my day vocalizing, memorizing lyrics, and practicing for that event. Singing outdoors, even with a good mike, takes lots of early-on rehearsing, yet I have to take care not to tire my vocal cords and cause hoarseness. Singing while seated requires more breath control than singing while standing. So, after practicing, I spent more time adding the finishing touches on my Mrs. Neptune costume. I didn't see Diego at any time Saturday."

The chief hadn't interrupted Threnody's prima donna account of her rehearsing. Was I jealous of Threnody and her talent? No. Threnody was a singer. I was a writer. We'd both worked hard for any recognition we'd won.

Ramsey continued, "If you didn't see the victim yesterday, please tell us again about the last time you did see him alive."

"I saw him Friday night, mingling with guests who came to enjoy dancing and refreshments in the Frangipani Room at The Blue Mermaid."

"Did he stay there all evening?"

"I have no way of knowing that," Threnody said. "I was only present a short time before I sang the sign-off number with the combo. After I finished singing, I helped Dolly Jass, who sometimes tends bar or helps out in the kitchen. Rafa Blue is manager and acts as hostess in the Frangipani Room. While Cheri and her mother are away on vacation, Rafa asked Dolly to help out wherever she needed her and she asked Brick to mix drinks and tend the cash register. After Brick closed the bar for the night, he and I drove home."

Chief Ramsey next turned to Jessie Vexton. "When did you last see Diego Casterano alive?"

Jessie looked directly at Ramsey. "I'm not sure, sir."

Even while seated on an uncomfortable chair in a dreary office, Jessie managed a slight shrug that revealed his cocky I'll-do-as-I-please attitude.

"I worked at the cash register at our chandlery most of the day on Saturday. I only saw Diego now and then as he performed his various dock master duties during that time. I closed and locked up before I left sometime around seven o'clock."

The replies to the chief's queries were all of a similar nature until Ramsey's gaze and attention focused on Dolly Jass.

Dolly looked down as she patted the head of a black kitten that peeked over the edge of the straw tote on the floor beside her chair. If Ramsey or Lyon noticed the animal, they never let on. Nor did anyone else. I'd seen Dolly's kitten many times around our hotel and it didn't surprise me to see that she brought it with her.

"Miss Jass, please give your full attention to my questions."

"Of course, sir." Dolly looked directly at Chief Ramsey, but she continued to pat the kitten's head.

I smiled to myself, wondering if the chief resented being upstaged by a kitten.

"Miss Jass, when did you last see the victim alive?"

Dolly looked around the room at each of us before again meeting Chief Ramsey's

111

direct gaze. She crossed her legs. She moved her tote bag to a spot on the floor near her left foot. I sensed her enjoying her moments in the limelight as everyone awaited her reply.

Dolly reached down to give the kitten one more pat before she raised her eyes slowly and looked at Ramsey in the flirty way she reserved for most men. "I saw Diego late afternoon yesterday." Her low, sultry voice might have held the promise of a fun time to come, had she been speaking under different circumstances.

"Saturday, right?"

"Yes, Saturday. Yesterday. The afternoon before the Fiesta Fest parade." Dolly lowered her gaze.

"How late in the afternoon?" Ramsey asked. "Do you remember the exact time?"

"Around five o'clock or perhaps a bit after five."

"Where were you at the time?"

"At Vexton's Marina."

"Do you go there often at that time of the day?"

"No, sir."

"What were you doing there yesterday afternoon?"

"I sat relaxing, sitting at an umbrella table a few yards away from the chandlery office and near the water. I took my time enjoying a cup of tea — hot tea, because a cloud bank covered the sun and an onshore breeze suddenly chilled me."

"Was going to the Vexton Marina for late afternoon tea your usual habit?"

"No. Not at all." She fluttered her eyelashes, first at Brick and then at Ramsey before she continued. "I went to the marina yesterday afternoon to compose a poem — free verse — a poem about the sea. I need to surround myself with the subject I'm writing about in order to start my creative juices flowing. I also chose to go to the marina because I needed to get away from the parade noises and the rambunctious crowd taking over many of the streets in Old Town."

The chief nodded as if he understood, as if he, too, sometimes sought out quiet spots amid turmoil. "And were your creative juices flowing yesterday afternoon at the Vexton Marina?"

Was Ramsey making fun of Dolly's response? Patronizing her? Either way, his question raised hackles in my mind. In most situations, I'm usually for the underdog. This morning Dolly displayed an innocent schoolgirl persona when answering Chief Ramsey's questions. I wanted to help her stand up to this man, but I couldn't. Not today. Not at this time. I kept silent.

"No," Dolly replied. "No creative juices flowed for me yesterday afternoon. Sometimes that's how it goes, and I accept a writer's block as a part of a poet's life. I merely nodded a greeting to Diego as he passed me on his way to welcome an arriving boat captain and help him claim his slip and hook up to an electric outlet. Soon after that I gave up creating a new poem and left the marina, biking to my room at the Vextons' mansion with a blank notebook."

"Rafa Blue."

I jerked to attention, startled to hear my name when I expected the chief to have more questions for Dolly.

"Rafa Blue." Ramsey called my name again, pausing for a moment as he looked directly at me. "When did you last see the victim alive?"

I tried to choose my words carefully. "I believed Diego was alive when I first saw his head bobbing in the water at the marina late last night around midnight."

"What were your first thoughts on seeing him there?"

"At first, it startled me to see anyone in the water. It took me a few moments to recognize Diego in the choppy waves, to be

114

sure it was he. It astonished me to realize he chose to swim after dark. Few people swim at night."

"Did you think he might be in trouble?"

"Not at first. Diego grew up around the sea. My first thought was that he might be trying to help another person who could be in trouble."

"So what did you do?"

"I called to him, shouted to him. The roar of the water and the storm drowned out my words so I called several times."

"Did he respond to your call?"

"No. He did not. By that time I knew something was wrong. He seemed to be floating, and I thought perhaps he was saving his strength by doing the dead-man's float instead of swimming or treading water. I knew he needed help."

"And you called nine-one-one, right?"

"That's correct. I'd left my cell phone in my car parked near the chandlery. It took me several minutes to reach the car and the phone as I fought my way slipping and sliding along the swaying catwalk."

"You never saw Diego any time earlier in the day?"

"No."

"I understand you're living at The Blue Mermaid here in Key West and writing a weekly column for the newspaper."

"Yes, sir." Why he was dwelling on information we'd discussed at the hospital?

"Good luck to you, Rafa Blue."

Good luck? What was that supposed to mean? Good luck? With my writing career? Or good luck in avoiding being considered a murder suspect? I leaned back in my chair, but I couldn't relax.

TEN

"Kane Riley?"

"Yes, sir."

"When did you last see the victim alive?"

"I saw Diego Friday night at the Frangipani Room."

"What were you doing there?"

"I work there sometimes when I'm not out on a shrimp run."

"What are your duties, Mr. Riley?"

"I'm a plainclothes security guard — a bouncer — a peacekeeper, if you will."

"The Frangipani Room's in a rough-tough area of the hotel?"

"No. Hardly ever, but after Mr. Blue died, leaving his wife and daughters in charge of the hotel, they felt it added protection, an air of safety, to have a security person present in the Frangi."

"You were paid for this job?"

"No. Rafa and I've been close friends for some time. It's my pleasure to help out at the Frangi."

"And Diego was there, too, on Friday night?"

"Yes. Diego Casterano sat at the refreshment bar eating a sandwich."

"Did you talk to him that night?"

"No, sir. He arrived shortly before Mama G — she's the combo director and pianist — before she announced her special medley of golden oldie piano selections. That number usually lasts several minutes. It's an ad-lib bit of entertainment she keeps going as long as the audience claps and whistles and demands more."

"Yes," the chief said. "I've seen and heard Mama G perform her specialty on many occasions. Tell me about last Friday night."

"Nothing unusual about it. When Mama G ended her number, she announced a short intermission. I noticed then that Diego was no longer present."

"The two of you didn't speak?"

"No. I didn't see Diego again until after your men removed his body from the water at the marina. Dead."

Chief Ramsey stopped the questioning and stood for a few moments as if deep in thought. Nobody spoke. We sat again listening to the thready breathing of the AC. Nobody actually relaxed, but when the chief

118

spoke again, I sensed everyone pulling to a higher degree of alertness.

"Does anyone know the whereabouts of Pablo Casterano this afternoon?"

Nobody replied.

"And Rafa, can you tell me if Pablo worked at the Frangipani Room last night?"

"No, sir. He did not. Pablo does work with the combo — sometimes. We're glad to have him, and although he's sometimes undependable, he's a good drummer when he's there — an excellent musician."

"And you don't miss him when he doesn't appear for work."

"Of course we miss him, but he owns the trap set. When he doesn't show up, we go to plan B and call on Dolly Jass to sub for him."

"Using Pablo's drums?"

"That's right."

"With Pablo's permission?"

"Don't know anyone ever asked for his permission. The trap set is there. We need a player, so we call Dolly. She's not a trained musician, but she can keep a steady beat."

"And Jessie Vexton plays string bass?"

Kane started to speak, but Jessie interrupted him.

"I play at playing the bass," Jessie said. "I just perform often enough to keep my fingers calloused so they won't blister. Years ago, I strummed guitar with a garage band while attending high school. I know the one, four, five chords well enough to get by on the bass for an evening at the Frangi."

"And you have your own instrument?" Chief Ramsey asked. "That's the one that looks like an oversize violin, right?"

"Right." Jessie didn't smile at the chief's description, but his desultory shrug showed his opinion of it. "Mama G understands about musical instruments and so does Rafa. They let the musicians cover their instruments and keep them on the combo stand between gigs. The Frangi's in an open-air setting, and the maintenance crew keeps a plastic roof and drop-down walls in place during daytime hours. The outdoor dampness wreaks havoc on drum heads, and it's even harder on strings and wood, so we keep our instruments covered after the Frangi closes."

"And you get paid for playing?" Ramsey asked Jessie.

"Yes." The corner of Jessie's mouth curled downward. "A pittance. I play mostly for the fun of playing."

I raised an eyebrow. That was the first time I knew Jessie considered his evening's take a pittance. Mama G and Pablo always

seemed eager enough to collect their pay-
checks. Neither of them had asked for a
raise.

Now Ramsey looked around, gathering all
of us into his gaze. "Can anyone tell me
where Pablo Casterano is at the moment?
Detective Lyon?"

"I was unable to locate Mr. Casterano,
sir. I could find nobody who had seen or
heard from him this morning. All leads led
nowhere."

"Where does he live?"

"My understanding is that he's a homeless person," Lyon said. "Many times he
sleeps on the beach, and many times he appears at Mallory Dock's sunset celebration,
offering tourists tarot card readings."

Ramsey cleared his throat. "I wanted
everyone connected, even remotely connected, with the victim to appear at this
meeting. That certainly includes his son.
Does anyone in this room know anything
concerning the whereabouts of Pablo Casterano?"

"I haven't seen Pablo lately," Jessie replied.
"Sometimes he hangs out with friends
either at Smathers or the state park beach
— the one here on Key West."

"Once he disappeared for almost two
years," Kane said, a frown punctuating his

121

words. "During that time nobody saw him or heard from him. Not even Diego"

"Pablo doesn't surprise us when he doesn't show up for work," I said. "The surprise comes when he does show up."

"Where did he go for two years?" Ramsey asked.

Jessie shrugged. "He wouldn't say. After some of us asked the question once, Pablo made it clear he didn't want to hear it again."

No one else spoke up and Ramsey looked again at Kane. "Mr. Riley, you're a writer, are you not?"

"No, sir. I am not. I make my living here in Key West as a commercial shrimper — and I moonlight at The Blue Mermaid as a security person — no pay."

"But lately I've seen your name on several letters to the editor — in the *Citizen* and sometimes in the *Keynoter.* Isn't that correct?"

"Yes. I've written a few letters, but I certainly don't think a couple of published letters makes me a writer."

"Your letters showed your deep concern for commercial fishermen working in the Key West area."

It wasn't a question and Kane made no response.

"You feel strongly about Monroe County's interest in what the commissioners refer to as our island's working waters?"

"I do."

The steely look in Kane's eyes bespoke his interest in the subject more than his clipped words.

"Perhaps your thoughts and Diego Casterano's thoughts concerning the working waters differed."

"They did, sir. They differed a great deal."

I wanted to signal Kane to hush. Surely he could see that to reveal a conflict of interest with Diego was unwise at this point. Why was Ramsey going out of his way to try to connect Kane to Diego's murder?

Eleven

Ramsey changed tactics and let his gaze touch on all of us again — one at a time. "Since Dolly Jass says she saw the victim alive late yesterday afternoon, I'm led to believe his murder took place sometime between five o'clock and midnight when Rafa Blue made her nine-one-one call for assistance. This's tentative. The medical examiner will announce the official time of death. This might not happen until tomorrow. But until we hear from him, I'm going to assume we have a seven- or eight-hour time frame in which the victim died. Do you agree?"

Nobody responded to his query.

"Does anyone disagree?" Ramsey asked. Again, no response. "Since nobody disagrees with this time frame, I'll ask each of you to tell us where you were and what you were doing from five in the afternoon until midnight last night. Brick Vexton, what do you have to say?"

"Not much, sir. I spent most of the day and the evening helping with the parade and I worked at many places, marking the route, erecting barriers across some of the major street intersections, posting signs — that sort of thing. That work took me nowhere near my marina."

"You have witnesses to corroborate your statement?"

Brick blinked and hesitated. "Of course I saw a few friends and acquaintances now and then. But I doubt that I can find anyone who will vouch for my whereabouts for all of that time, actually most of the day. Threnody and I did meet friends who managed to get seating for four for a late supper at Red Fish, Blue Fish."

"Threnody Vexton. You said you were home practicing your vocal solo and working on your costume. Was there someone at your house who can vouch for your late afternoon and early evening hours? Dolly Jass has quarters at your home, does she not?"

"She does. Dolly lives there. She works for us, but not on Saturdays. That's her day off. Her room has a private entrance and I do not keep track of her comings and goings."

"And you saw nobody else during the day?"

"No, sir. Well, nobody outside the family. Brick stopped by for a sandwich around noon. He stayed only a few minutes. Nobody else called or checked on my whereabouts until I arrived at the parade's starting point. Lots of people saw me on the parade float at that time."

"And after the parade? Where were you then?"

"As Brick told you, he and I joined friends at a restaurant for a late supper. Bernice and Clayton Johnson. I'm sure they'd vouch for us for the few hours we spent together. As I remember it, service was slow due to the huge crowd, but even so we were home shortly after midnight."

"Jessie Vexton, where were you from five o'clock until midnight yesterday?"

"I was on call at the marina during some of that time. Dad gives the employees, including Diego, time off on parade night, so I remain on duty in case a boater arrives late and needs help. Last night was a slow night. Guess everyone was attending the parade. Around seven, I closed the chandlery and went home."

"You didn't mind missing the parade and the festivities on Duval Street and elsewhere on the island?"

"No sir. We've lived here a long time and I've seen lots of Fantasy Fest parades. During my teen years, nude women with their clothes painted directly onto their skin held a certain fascination for me. Even today I sometimes enjoy seeing the drag queens in full regalia looking more beautiful than most of Key West's women. But last night I left the marina and went home."

"Got anyone to vouch for you?"

Jessie shook his head. "At the marina, customers come and go — most of them strangers. Last night, few people stopped by. And nobody called me or came by my home."

"Rafa Blue? I have an account of your nine-one-one call around midnight, but what were your activities earlier in the evening?"

"I attended the parade for a short time, went home around ten o'clock, and stayed in my suite alone until I drove to the Vexton Marina to check on our family's boat."

"Kane Riley?"

"No alibi, sir. I attended the beginning of the parade, but after watching a few floats, a few marchers, I boarded my boat and remained there for the rest of the evening, keeping the lights on and making myself visible. Sometimes vandals hit on unoccupied boats, and I didn't want any bad stuff to happen to *The Buccaneer*. Saw few people around the Harbor Walk that could vouch for my presence."

Chief Ramsey directed his next question to Brick. "Mr. Vexton, what were your feelings toward Diego Casterano?"

For an instant Brick looked startled and a muscle tightened along his left jaw. His reaction didn't surprise me. I'd have tried to avoid such a question, too.

"What sorts of feelings?" Brick asked. "Feelings relating to our business dealings? Feelings relating to our long-time friendship?"

"Any sort of feelings you care to share with me."

Brick hesitated so long, I wondered if he was going to refuse to answer Ramsey's question. But at last he spoke. "Diego and I were long-time friends. Diego had worked for me for many years, and in casual conversations we learned that during our lifetimes we shared many common experiences. I grew up in a Miami orphanage, abandoned at birth by my parents for reasons unknown to me. Diego arrived in Key West during Castro's nineteen-eighty Mariel Boatlift, also abandoned by his family. But he knew why. They hated to see him grab that once-in-a-lifetime chance to legally leave his homeland. The Casteranos raised sugar cane, and Diego played an important part in their operation."

Brick hesitated and I didn't blame him. Police officers can twist words — sometimes to their choosing. And once a person has said a thing, made any sort of a statement, it's almost impossible for him to withdraw it. And I empathized with people who had been abandoned by their families.

However, I couldn't blame my family for their reaction to my childish run-away-from-home act at age thirteen. The streets of Miami were no place for a young girl living on her own, especially a rich kid who took off after stuffing her purse with a couple hundred bucks in cash — a kid who thought she knew everything. Just thinking about it now still made me pull farther into the protective shell I'd built around myself while living in a luxury suite in a luxury hotel. Poor little rich girl. Some time I'd have to tell Kane about my past. But not today — or tomorrow. I could only guess at his reaction, and good or bad, I hated the thought of facing it. When had I fallen in love with him? My story might send him out of my life forever. I couldn't face that, either.

Suddenly Brick's flushed face and harsh words about parents he never knew yanked my attention back to the here and now.

"If you're going to expect me to answer more questions," Brick said, "I'd prefer to have a lawyer present." His right hand clenched into a fish. "Shouldn't you have given all of us here this afternoon a *Miranda* warning?"

Chief Ramsey cleared his throat again, but before he could say more, Brick continued, "Maybe other people in this room today also would like to summon legal protection and advice. I'm ready to call a lawyer. It may be Sunday, but Diego's murder may evolve into a major court case. I'm guessing most lawyers would be interested in representing any of us, regardless of the day."

"Nobody here is under arrest, Mr. Vexton. Authorities don't *Mirandize* everyone during an informal questioning."

"Then we're free to leave the building?" Kane shifted forward in his chair as if about to stand and go immediately.

Detective Lyon dropped his notebook and pen into his coat pocket and stepped back, blocking the doorway.

"I'd like everyone to remain here until I

finish asking a few more questions." Ramsey glared at Kane.

"But anything we say can be held against us, right?" Brick rose and eased a few steps closer to the exit. Threnody and Jessie stood, ready to follow him.

"Are you ordering us to stay here?" Kane asked the question before Ramsey could reply to Brick's question.

"I want to ask more questions," Ramsey said. "You would be wise to remain here for a few more moments and answer them."

"Then we're not really free to leave, are we, sir?" Jessie directed his question to Ramsey, but he looked at Kane as if for confirmation.

"You're all free to leave," Ramsey said, "but although I'm asking you to stay, no way am I forcing any of you to remain here against your will."

"Then if we're free to leave, we're not in your custody," Kane said.

"True," Ramsey replied. "You aren't in police custody."

"You're not giving anyone a *Miranda* warning at the moment because it's against the law to give *Miranda* warnings to people not in your custody. I heard that on TV — *Law and Order* — and I'm leaving. Right now. And I'm asking Rafa Blue to leave with me."

131

I wasn't sure whether I should remain seated or rise and follow Kane from the chief's office. Brick made the decision for me by standing beside his chair, easing toward Ramsey and abruptly changing the subject.

"Before any of us decide to leave or stay, I'd like some information about setting a time and place for Diego's funeral service."

Ramsey stood his ground and Brick took another step forward — a step toward the door where Detective Lyon stood. I wondered if Lyon was playing guard, if he had orders to detain us if we started to leave.

"Mr. Vexton." Chief Ramsey spoke in a stentorian voice that let everyone know who was in charge. "The photographer has finished his work, but the medical examiner has not yet released the victim's body. Officials are still running tests and recording details concerning the homicide."

Brick raised his chin and his voice and took a step closer to Ramsey. "To whom will the body be released when the medical examiner and his people finish their work?"

Ramsey hesitated and Brick pounced on that hesitation.

"Pablo Casterano seems to have gone missing — at least for the moment. Since the victim was one of my most respected employees, I'd like the privilege of claiming his body and arranging for his funeral unless Pablo appears before you and objects. I'm sure Threnody will agree to this."

I spoke up. "Since the victim, er, Diego, was my friend and a close friend of my family, I'd like to volunteer to help Brick and Threnody with the funeral arrangements in any way I can. I know Mother and Cherie both would make that offer were they on-island at this time."

Chief Ramsey shook his head and stepped behind his desk. His action made me wonder if he felt the desk gave him protection from us. Or maybe he felt it reinforced his rightful authority. When he spoke again, his words commanded our full attention.

"When the medical examiner releases the victim's body, his next of kin may claim it."

"And what if his next of kin doesn't do that?" Brick asked.

"Then a friend may claim the body in the absence of family. Under those circumstances, you will be well advised to seek legal guidance."

Everyone started heading for the exit. Detective Lyon opened the door, but moments before anyone stepped into the hallway, Chief Ramsey called out.

"You may go now. I thank you for coming

here this afternoon. Please do not leave the island before making me or someone in my office aware of your plans."

Brick and Threnody headed for the elevator first with Jessie following close behind. Dolly Jass hung back, and Kane motioned for her to go ahead of us. She smiled and batted her eyelashes at Kane as she stepped ahead.

"Let's go someplace for lunch, Rafa," Kane said in a voice that would carry to Chief Ramsey. "Maybe The Square Grouper."

"That's on Cudjoe Key, Kane. Off-island."

"I know." Kane linked his arm through mine, turned to grin at the chief, and gave a casual goodbye salute to Detective Lyon.

TWELVE

When we were out of Chief Ramsey's hearing in the parking lot, I headed for my car, slid behind the wheel, and sighed in exasperation when Kane thumped into the passenger seat.

"Kane, the chief said we're not to leave the island without telling him or someone in his office. Why ask for trouble by driving off-island for lunch? We're already persons of interest. Let's don't give the authorities reason to become more interested."

"Okay. So you're right, but his questions irritated me. Guess he intended them to irritate me, hoped I'd react by blurting something I'd regret."

"But you didn't. Good thinking."

"Guess I wished I hadn't written those letters."

"Dad always advised me to set aside any letter written in anger and to let it cool overnight. Whenever I did that, I almost always destroyed the letter before it reached the post office."

"If I'd known Diego was going to turn up murdered . . ." Kane pounded his knee with his doubled fist. "No. I'm not sorry I wrote those letters. Not sorry at all. I needed to let people know how strongly we shrimpers feel about our working waters. People need to know the inside scoop. They need to pay attention when a commissioner resigns from her job because she feels other committee members, secretly working on the side of land developers, pushed through legislation detrimental to the majority of citizens."

"So you know who you'll vote against at the next election, right?"

"Fat lot of good it'll do now that the legislation has passed. Let's forget it and find a place to eat."

"Nobody should be at my place right now. We can go there. Or we can have the Frangi to ourselves, too — for a while at least. Better yet, let's go to the hotel, order lunch, and eat outdoors beside the pool."

"Fine with me. Maybe we can plan a strategy that will keep us low on the chief's list of suspects."

"Right. But I want to hear more about what you've heard about Diego's murder. And maybe we can catch some news on the

136

radio or TV."

"Not if we're outside by the pool, unless we want to advertise our interest in Diego's murder to the hotel guests."

"You may be right about that. Let's skip the radio." I drove slowly to The Blue Mermaid, careful to obey all traffic rules and to attract no undue attention. Croton bushes lined the paved entryway to the hotel portico where several drivers waited behind their steering wheels for valets to take their cars into the ground level covered parking area. I drove on to the back entry.

Kane spoke up. "This hotel is a good example of the illegal stuff white-collar crooks can sneak into legislation before honest Key West citizens know what's happened to them. A similar thing happened to our working waters."

"I don't get the connection, Kane."

"The guy I bought *The Buccaneer* from told me that years ago, building contractors and the commissioners, supposedly working on behalf of local citizens, agreed that hotels would be limited to a height of four stories. That way, homeowners in the hotel area would still have their view of the sea."

"Guess you've noticed this hotel has five stories." I parked in my usual spot.

"Right! Somewhere in the legal maneuvering, the building contractor slipped in a zinger that made it okay for the covered ground-level parking area *not* to count as the hotel's first floor. But counting the parking area, there are a total of five floors. When citizens growled that the hotel blocked their ocean view, the builder laughed and waved his contract at them. Very sneaky."

"That must have happened years before Dad bought the hotel."

"True. But I'm pointing out that it happened. And the same thing is happening to what remains of our working waters."

"I'm glad Dad had no part in that bit of underhandedness." I cut the motor, noting that Dolly had left her bike propped on its kickstand nearby. Finding a parking place on the island is such a hassle that Dolly refuses to own a car. She bikes everywhere, so far without mishap.

"I'm starving, Kane."

Kane laughed. "It's too late for lunch and too early for dinner. Want to settle for a sandwich beside the pool? We'll call it lunner."

We strolled toward the pool gate before we stopped, realizing our faded jeans and tees would stand out like barnacles on a boat hull in this crowd of sleek-bodied sunbathers in their bikinis and low-rise briefs. "Okay, but maybe we need to change into more appropriate attire."

For a few moments we stood at the pool gate, listening to shouting kids, watching them splash water onto lounges bearing ladies who had no intention of getting wet. We grinned as the women flailed their arms and tried to protect their pricey hairdos. Even from this distance, I inhaled mingled aromas of hairspray and coconut-scented sunscreen.

"On second thought, why don't we go to my suite, order from room service, and eat on my balcony? Food. Privacy. Sunshine. What more could we want?"

"Sounds good to me."

"On third thought, why don't I toss a fresh fruit salad, pour us some iced tea, and order hot garlic toast from room service?"

"Sounds even better. How can I help?"

"You can pour our iced tea and help carry stuff to the balcony, okay?" Before we took the elevator upstairs, I picked a banana, an orange, and some mint leaves from our private garden near the pool. In only a few moments we sat on the balcony munching on the tangy fruit salad and the soothing flavor of the garlic toast. Although we took care not to sit near the balcony railing or make ourselves visible to the revelers in the pool below, we enjoyed hearing them shouting, splashing, and having fun.

When I looked into Kane's eyes, he must have guessed what I was about the say.

"Don't expect any more news about the murder from me, Rafa. I've told you all I know — all I've heard. Diego must have had an enemy we're unaware of."

"Who's his next of kin other than Pablo?"

"You know more about Diego's family than I do."

I shook my head. "I'm guessing any other relatives live in Cuba."

"Think a jealous relative paddled here in the dark of night to off him?"

"Don't know what to think. I wonder. Was he wealthy? Wealthy enough to make his next of kin interested in a quick inheritance?"

"You think Pablo might have murdered him?"

"I've no idea. But it's a thought. Didn't someone say they heard Diego and Pablo arguing about money?"

"I heard them argue several times. The gist of it being that Diego thought Pablo should give up his beach-bumming ways and find a steady job."

"A job in addition to playing here in the

combo?"

"Of course. The combo job's a great way to earn a little extra pay, but it's by no means self-supporting — not on this tourist's paradise of rip-off prices."

"Strange that Pablo chose this week to do a disappearing act. If he expected an inheritance, he must have known he'd have to show up to claim his father's body, arrange a memorial service."

"Maybe he couldn't face that."

"Too grief-stricken. Let's give him the benefit of the doubt. After all, he lost his father. I could still remember the shock and sadness I felt at losing my own father." I shook my head.

"I hate to see you looking so sad, Rafa."

I managed a smile. "In spite of his grief, Pablo must have known he'd be one of the first persons of interest in an investigation. Kane, I don't think Pablo had anything to do with his dad's death. I've wondered now and then why Mother and Cherie were so close to Diego. You know the skinny on that? Guess I was never interested enough to ask, just sorta took his friendship for granted."

"Anything I know is gossip. Old-timers say that after only a short time on the island, Diego fell in love with Key West, settled down here, and planned to stay. He met Brick Vexton when he stopped at his marina trying to buy a boat. For a while he used the runabout for making a living of sorts by doing small chores for people around the waterfront.

"I've heard Brick say Diego soon learned a boat was only a hole in the water where you poured your money. But Diego was a hard worker, and Brick hired him to help out at the marina. Eventually Diego worked up to the position of chief dock master. Guess he met important people at the marina."

"That figures," I agreed. "Diego's outgoing personality and reputation for honesty must have helped get him elected as a councilperson. But he continued to work at the marina. Didn't want to let Brick down."

Kane nodded in agreement. "The news of his death must have hit the Vextons hard. And it will hit your mother and Cherie hard, too. Wonder when they'll get back home."

"Soon, I hope. I rather enjoy working alone at the Frangi, but I'm eager to get back to writing full time. Of course everyone's been a great help to me the past few days. Couldn't have kept the Frangi running so smoothly without help."

"You've done a great job, Rafa. Don't put

yourself down."

No point in telling Kane I was used to putting myself down where Mother and Cheri were concerned. The black sheep of the family. That was me.

"Kane, I need to investigate Diego's murder. I need to do it to help get that killer off the streets."

We'd finished our salad, and when we stood, Kane pulled me into a deep embrace. We exchanged several long kisses before I pulled away reluctantly, and I tried not to let his nearness distract me from what I'd needed to say.

"I have to investigate Diego's murder, Kane. I have to."

"Nobody's asked you to do that."

"And I've thought of another thing."

Kane shook his head and sighed. "I'm almost afraid to ask. But what else have you thought of?"

"Maybe I have an agenda that goes beyond taking a killer off the streets. I can't help thinking I could take careful notes during my investigation and use them later in my writing — in writing a book, perhaps a mystery novel. Having my name on a dust jacket is high on my list of lifetime goals."

"You were planning a column on Diego, right?"

"Right. And maybe I'll still write it after the talk about his death dies down, but one day I'm going to write a novel. It could be a book based on this horrible murder. I'm going to involve myself in primary research, in unearthing facts that nobody else is privy to. My need to write a book may help solve Diego's murder, and every case that's solved takes a criminal off the streets. That's important to me and to everyone who lives here."

"Guess there's nothing I can say to stop you." Kane shook his head in defeat. "But Rafa, please remember this. I insist on fitting into your life somewhere — somewhere important to both of us. And remember that right this minute a killer who might harm either one of us walks free on the streets of this island. Also remember that anyone officially or unofficially trying to nab that guy could be the next person on his hit list."

"I'll remember all those things. I'm well aware of them."

"So where do you intend to start your investigation? I want to help you if I can."

"Thanks, Kane. I appreciate that, and I'll call on you for help anytime I need it."

"That sounds like my exit line." Kane grinned and we left the balcony, carrying our salad dishes to the dishwasher before he headed for the door and the elevator. "I'll walk to *The Buccaneer.* Need to rest a while before I get ready for our night at the Frangi. Okay?"

"You could rest here. Bed's made up."

Kane patted my fanny. "Too many distractions here. I think we both need to rest — really rest."

"Okay, if you insist." Reluctantly, I followed him to the door. We shared another kiss before he stepped onto the elevator. Closing the door to my suite, I was headed for the shower when I thought I heard someone call to me. I turned to see if Kane had forgotten something.

Before I reached the door, I heard my name again.

"Rafa? Rafa Blue?"

The sound came from outside my suite and I hurried to the balcony entrance, listening. Then, hearing nothing more, I stepped onto the balcony and peered over the railing at the revelers in the pool. I saw nobody I recognized. I had started to lean farther over the railing to peer directly below when I heard an ominous creaking and grating. I gasped when I felt the railing sway.

It took me seconds to realize the scream

came from my own throat. Clutching at air, I felt myself falling.

THIRTEEN

I felt a wild fling through space before something jerked me to a stop. Every joint in my body ached. I thought my neck might be broken and I lay there dazed and hurting. I wiggled my fingers first, glad they still worked. And then my toes. They worked, too. No broken neck. That was first aid information Gram had taught me in my childhood, because I was the tomboy of the family, prone to taking falls — especially when I was staying at her home on Big Pine.

"Rafa! Rafa!"

Now I recognized Kane's voice. Very different from the voice I'd heard shouting my name before my fall. Lower. More authoritative. But where was he? I welcomed hearing his voice and knowing he was near, but I had no strength to raise my head and look for him. No strength to answer him.

It took me several moments more to realize that a pile of sheets on the slightly protruding balcony of the hotel's laundry room below my penthouse balcony had broken my fall — maybe saved my life. In moments a Cuban laundry worker ran toward me, shock and fear etched onto her face.

"*Señorita! Señorita* Blue." Perspiration dampened her forehead when she pushed her dark bangs to the side, her hands trembling.

Her name tag identified her as Maria. She babbled at me in Spanish, trying to lift chunks of plaster and iron spikes from where they lay on and around me. Grabbing my hand, she tried to ease me from under the debris.

"*Gracias. Gracias.*" Using my limited Spanish vocabulary, I punctuated the words with what I hoped was a smile. By the time I managed to pull myself to an upright position on the pile of sheets, someone in the hallway began pounding on the laundry room door.

"Rafa! Rafa!" Kane shouted. "Tell that woman to let me in there. Now. Now!" He continued to pound. "Rafa? Rafa?"

Growing even more round-eyed and open-mouthed, Maria ran to the door and admitted Kane into the steamy room. The commercial-size washers and dryers were doing their best to overcome the work of the A/C.

"Rafa! Are you okay? Can you stand?" Kane reached toward me. The touch of his strong hand encouraged me to cooperate with his effort to pull me to my feet. "What happened? What happened? Can you tell me what happened?"

For several moments I said nothing, concentrating on walking and getting out of the laundry room.

"*Gracias,* Maria. *Gracias.*" Kane reached into his pocket, pulled out a bill, and thrust it into her hand.

"*Gracias, Señor.*" She babbled more Spanish, which we could only respond to with smiles as I limped painfully to the elevator.

"What happened, Rafa? Shall I call nine-one-one? A doctor?"

"No nine-one-one, Kane! Don't you dare. I'm over the worst shock of my fall and I'll be fine in a few moments. The nine-one-one guys don't need to hear from me two days in a row."

"Then how about calling your doctor or reporting to the ER? Doctors are on duty there twenty-four/seven."

"I'm feeling better already. Relax, okay?" In spite of my optimistic words, I clung to Kane's arm and he inched toward the elevator, accommodating his pace to mine.

When we arrived at my suite, I followed Kane inside and then eased onto the sofa. He rushed to the refrig, rattled cubes into a glass, and then poured me some tea. Before I could take a drink, he dashed onto the balcony, stopping abruptly when he saw the bent and broken railing.

"How did this happen, Rafa? We were on this balcony only a few minutes ago." He squatted to examine the balcony floor and the few railings that remained intact. "You must have leaned with a lot of force against these spindles to break them. What on earth were you trying to do?"

"I'll admit I was leaning over the railing a lot farther than usual. I thought the call might have come from someone below me, someone out of my sight. But I didn't lean hard enough to break wrought-iron spindles and cause them to crash down."

"The call? What were you doing the moment before the crash?"

"I thought I heard someone calling my name from the pool area. At first I thought it might be you, that you'd forgotten something."

"Not I! Did you see anyone at the pool you recognized?"

Feeling stronger, I set my tea glass on the

coffee table and joined Kane at the edge of the balcony, keeping far back from the damaged railing.

"Take care, Kane. More of the railing may break off. You're very close to the edge. I need to call a maintenance person before there's another accident."

"Rafa?"

"What is it, Kane? You see something special in the rubble?" I hesitated before inching another step closer.

"I'm not so sure your fall was an accident. Think carefully. You saw nobody below that you recognized?"

I stepped back into the safety of my suite, far from the break in the balcony railing. "So many people crowded the pool and surrounding patio that I couldn't focus on each one. The kids were playing volleyball in the shallow water, splashing and yelling and batting at the ball. Most of the adults were relaxing on chase lounges and sipping drinks. I saw nobody I could recognize from up here."

"Before you call Maintenance, I think you should call the police."

"And have them come tromping into my suite? I don't think so. Give me a break, Kane! It's been a long, long day. We've had enough interaction with the police. And we still have the evening to face in the Frangi."

"Humor me, Rafa. You say you want to investigate Diego's death, right?"

"Right. I want to investigate without the help of the police. I want to investigate slowly — at my own pace."

"But right now you need the police to see this latest scene. Let them decide whether or not it was an accident or a scene more carefully planned. You're a person of interest, remember? We're both persons of interest. I think the police will want to know about this so-called accident."

Much as I hated to, I saw Kane's point. If the balcony scene hadn't been an accident, I needed to know the truth of it. If I was a target, I needed to be aware of that fact and be prepared to protect myself — if I could.

"You want to call, Kane? Or should I?"

"You call. The accident happened on your property. I don't want any more police activity in my life if I can prevent it. But I'll stay here to give you moral support while you deal with the officers and their questions."

"Okay. And thanks. I'll call Detective Lyon. If he wants Ramsey in on it, he can decide that."

I made the call, and while we waited for Lyon to arrive, I changed from my ripped jeans and shirt and flung them into the hamper. After donning fresh clothes and tugging a brush through my hair and applying a touch of lip gloss, I felt up to facing whatever came next. I suppose I knew all along that both Lyon and Ramsey would arrive. And they did. They brought a photographer with them. I told them the same story I told Kane. They both took notes. The photographer took at least a jillion pictures before they all started to leave.

"Miss Blue," Chief Ramsey said, peering directly into my eyes. "Do you feel that you're in danger?"

"No, sir. I think this was a freak accident. I'll call a maintenance person and have the rail repaired either today or first thing tomorrow morning."

"Good idea." Ramsey thrust his notebook into his jacket pocket.

"I'm sorry to have bothered you over nothing."

"One never knows when something is nothing or when something is something. No apologies needed. I'm pleased that you called. My officers will give you and The Blue Mermaid some extra attention for the next few days."

"Thank you, sir. I appreciate your interest." I felt guilty at that lie. I wanted no special interest from the police.

FOURTEEN

After the police left, I sat on the couch for a few minutes, resting and trying to avoid wondering if my fall had been an accident or if someone had planned it and I had stepped into a trap.

"Want a ride to your boat?" I asked Kane at last. "I've some errands to do and *The Buccaneer*'s right on my way."

"I could walk to the dock, but if you feel up to driving, I might as well ride. Mama G can get into the Frangi if she decides to bring tonight's sandwich things over, can't she?"

"Yes. Mother gave her a key. And if Dolly arrives while I'm gone, she has a key, too. Anyway, I won't be away long."

I closed and locked the glass sliding door between my living room and the balcony and we took the elevator to my car. After I let Kane out at his boat, he didn't question me about where I planned to go from there.

Thank goodness. I wasn't really sure of the answer myself. I still felt shaky and queasy from my fall. I watched until Kane stepped over the gunwale, waved him a farewell, and headed for Duval Street before I turned toward the police station.

For a few moments after parking in a visitor's slot, I sat behind the wheel, planning my strategy. If I were to investigate Diego's murder, one of the first things I needed was a piece of the blue cord the police found binding his feet. I needed that for starters. Other needs could come later.

I opened the car door, startled to see Chief Ramsey exiting the station. We saw each other at the same time and he walked toward me. If my presence surprised him, he didn't show it.

"Miss Blue, are you returning to talk with me? Perhaps you've thought of something else that might be of interest to the police?"

"Sir, I have a favor to ask."

"Then let's go inside where we can talk in private."

And that's what we did. Once the chief unlocked his office door, we entered, and I saw the box of evidence still under his desk.

"Sit down, please. I hope you've recovered from your fall."

"Thank you, sir. This won't take long. I've

come to ask you for a small piece of the blue line you found at the death scene."

"A strange request, I must say." Ramsey seated himself behind his desk. He said nothing more, and I guessed he was using one of my favorite tactics when interviewing a subject for a column. Silence. Let the other person break it. Ramsey asked no questions, so I made no response. Sometimes keeping silent is much more difficult than speaking. It's a hard thing to do. During awkward moments of quiet, a nervous person tends to speak. I wasn't that nervous, and when I didn't oblige the chief by breaking the silence, he waited for several moments before he spoke.

"What are your plans for the line, Miss Blue? I find your request a strange one."

"Chief, I'd like to play at least a small part in finding Diego's killer. He was a friend who had done me many favors in the past, a friend I'd intended to feature in my weekly column. Someone got that blue line from somewhere, true?"

"Of course."

"I'd like to learn where it came from. Almost every marina and tackle shop carries many varieties of nautical line. I'd like to make a covert check on shops carrying that blue variety."

"What makes you think it's special, Miss Blue?"

Nonplussed, I hesitated for a moment. I couldn't tell him I saw line similar to it on Kane's boat this morning.

"I think it's special because, well, for one reason, because of its color. I've not been around a lot of nautical line, but I've helped Mother and Gram with their boats and boating supplies from time to time. I've never seen that shade of blue rope before. If you'll lend me a snippet of it, I can save you and your men some time and lots of leg-work."

"In what way?"

"By visiting the local chandleries and looking at the various kinds of line they carry. Just an interested buyer, that's all I'd be. And wherever I find similar line, I'll let you know the name of that store. Knowing where the line came from would surely be a starting point in finding who bought it, when they bought it, why they bought it. Don't you agree?"

"Yes, I consider that a good starting point, but although the department's shorthanded, I don't want an ordinary citizen working on this case. That could cause too many prob-lems."

"Sir, I'd keep our agreement a secret. A

policeman approaching shop owners and asking about the line would alert the owners that something was up. But I'd just be an ordinary citizen searching for craft material to make a wall hanging."

Chief Ramsey twisted in his chair. I won't go so far as to say he squirmed, but he came close to squirming before he spoke again.

"All right, Miss Blue. I'll let you check out a segment of the line as long as you're willing to sign a release that indicates this evidence is in your possession."

"And when I return the evidence, you'll return the release with your signature?"

"That is correct."

"Agreed. May I take the line with me now?"

With only a nod of consent, Ramsey pulled a printed form from his desk drawer, filled in some blanks on it, and shoved it toward me along with a ballpoint. I signed the form and he placed it in a folder, securing the folder in the gray steel file behind his desk. He then pulled the evidence box from beneath his desk, snipped off a piece of line about six inches long, tucked it into a manila envelope, and sealed it before releasing it into my possession.

"Thank you, sir. I'll get back to you about this after I've had time to visit some nautical shops and ask a few questions."

"I'll expect to hear from you soon. After twenty-four hours a trail grows cold. Time is of an essence."

His tone and a nod dismissed me, and when I left his office, he stood puttering with the contents of the evidence box. Once in my car, I drove to Chitting Marina first because it was close by. Would Ramsey follow me? Some careful glances in my rearview mirror showed no evidence of that.

At Chitting's, I parked in the graveled customer's area. After I pulled the snippet of line from the manila envelope and tucked it into the pocket of my slacks, I left my car. I crossed a planked dock where incoming waves splashed against an array of boats tethered in their slips. A pelican perched on a pine piling hunched forward as if starting to fly, then changed its mind and resettled on the piling. I entered the chandlery and headed for the business desk. In the distance someone worked with a jackhammer.

The smell of hotdogs turning on a small grill beside the cash register blotted out the stench of gasoline and diesel fuel. My mouth watered even though Kane and I had eaten only a short time ago. In moments the sound of the jackhammer ceased.

"May I help you?" A young man approached, smiling.

"Perhaps." I pulled the line from my pocket. "I'd like to buy several yards of line similar to this."

The man examined the line and pointed to the wall across the room. There, a large display of caddies held coiled line that grew in size from very thin to almost thick as one's wrist.

"We have many types of line. Perhaps you can find something in our display that you can use."

I followed him to the display. "I'm looking for something in blue. I'm planning to make a wall hanging for the great room in my home. I really need sea blue."

The clerk shook his head as he glanced at the snippet of line I brought in and then at the wall display. "Sorry I can't help you, ma'am. We don't seem to carry any in your shade of blue. Maybe another chandlery or tackle shop will have some different colors. Or perhaps you'd like to look in our catalog and find something you'd care to order."

"Thank you, but no. I wanted to get to work on my project tomorrow, if at all possible." I turned and walked to my car. I checked out three more chandleries and a bait boat without any luck. At the next store along the street — George's Tackle Shop —

an old man shuffled forward to greet me. The scent of cigar smoke clung to his gray jumpsuit that matched his beard and his gray eyes. He peered at me from under bushy white eyebrows, eyebrows that made me think of Andy Rooney.

"How may I help you, ma'am?"

Again, I pulled out my sample of blue line and made the request I had memorized by now.

"Let me get a closer look at this." Taking the line, he carried it to a cluttered desk where he pulled on a string attached to a huge bulb that brightened the whole area. After turning the line this way and that and then picking at its frayed end for a few moments, he chuckled. "Where'd you get this line, miss? None of my business, but I'm curious."

I preferred being called miss rather than ma'am, and I smiled at him, wondering how old he was — eighty, ninety, maybe even older than that.

"Oh, it's just an old piece of line I found tucked away in a friend's boathouse. Can you match it for me?"

"Afraid not, miss. I've been selling nautical supplies for a lot of years." He examined the rope again before looking at me. "This kind of line was a bestseller — in its day.

But according to my memory, no company has produced this type of line in this blue shade for twenty-five, thirty years. This sample may be older than you are."

"Oh, my. I wanted to get to work on my wall hanging today, if possible."

"Had you considered making the hanging in neutral shades? I have lots of neutrals in many different sizes."

"Thank you, sir, but I've set my heart on blue."

"Sorry to break your heart over a piece of line." He laughed. "Been a long time since I broke anyone's heart."

"Thank you, George." I risked using the name of the shop, and I guessed right.

"Been a long time since a young miss has called me George, too. You stop by again. Anytime."

"You've been a big help to me, even though you can't supply the line I need."

Leaving the shop, I felt George's gaze following me as I ambled to my car and sat thinking. I tucked the line into the manila envelope and shoved it into my shoulder bag. So this line wasn't of a kind that anyone might find readily available in today's Key West shops.

That bit of information tempted me to report what I'd learned so far to Chief

Ramsey immediately. Then I thought better of it. If this line matched the bunk box handles I'd seen on Kane's boat . . . I didn't want to do anything that might direct suspicion to Kane. But I had no way of comparing the two pieces of line without Kane knowing what I'd discovered. And if I returned the sample to Ramsey too soon, he might wonder why I hadn't worked harder at finding a match.

The sun was dropping low, so I decided to return to the hotel, freshen up, and change into an outfit more suitable for appearing in the Frangi tonight. A long skirt? A sequined tee? Maybe some glamorous barefoot sandals? When I opened the elevator door at the penthouse floor, Dolly came running toward me from the Frangi.

"Rafa! You've recovered from your fall?"

"Sure. No big problem." It surprised me to realize some truth in the little white lie. I'd been so caught up in searching for blue line, I'd almost forgotten my bruises and sore muscles. "What's up?"

FIFTEEN

I thought Dolly might ask more about Diego's murder, but no.

"Brick asked me to change the bulb in his desk lamp. He wants to start using the new energy-saving bulbs in all lamps in their mansion."

"Good idea. I ordered our maintenance crew to use compact fluorescent bulbs in our hotel lamps some time ago. How can I help you now?"

"I have the new bulbs, and I've removed the old one from Brick's desk lamp. Problem is I can't get the new bulb to fit. If you're feeling up to it, maybe you can take a look and figure out what I'm doing wrong. Could you go with me to the mansion now? Of course, if you're not feeling up to it . . ."

"I'm okay, Dolly. Don't treat me like an invalid." I glanced at my watch. "But we'll need to hurry."

We took the elevator down, slipped into

my car, and drove to the mansion. I parked to one side of the strangler fig threatening the banyan tree and followed Dolly inside. I'd expected to see ecru and brown décor that blended with the outside of the mansion, but no. The living room lay awash in light flowing through the jalousie windows and an overhead skylight onto off-white walls. Jewel-toned cushions on a white wicker couch and matching chairs added spark to the room. The multicolored terrazzo floor spoke of long ago when that type of flooring was popular in both private homes as well as in public buildings. Threnody had spiced the room with bright area carpets.

"How beautiful! Threnody has a great sense of color and design."

"Threnody and Madam Carmelina at the furniture shop on Duval. Threnody fell in love with Madam Carmelina's suggestions, but the madam met her match when she faced Brick." Dolly grinned. "Surprises me that Brick will even get rid of an old light bulb."

I followed Dolly into Brick's study, looked around, and returned her grin. It was like entering a time warp into another day and age. Did I imagine that musty smell, or was it real? Braided throw rugs covered the floor. Two Danish Modern chairs that might have been modern in the 1950s sat near a much-used oak desk. A brown cylinder-shaped shade lay upended beside a lamp made of foot-long lengths of copper tubing set in a brass base.

Picking up the new bulb, I tried to fit it into the lamp. "You're right, Dolly." After several unsuccessful attempts, I shook my head and shrugged. "Guess old lamps sneer at modern bulbs."

"Drat! I thought maybe you could get it to work. I like to please Brick whenever I can."

She tried the bulb again and then I gave it a second try. "Guess Brick will have to make do with old-time bulbs."

"Threnody wants him to redecorate his study, but I don't think that's going to happen anytime soon. Brick wants to leave everything just the way it is. But thanks for trying to help, Rafa. I really try to please Brick. He's very good to me, but this time it's impossible." Dolly glanced at her watch. "I've got to be going. Want to give the balcony at the Frangi one last sweep before you open for business tonight. I'm helping with the sandwiches, too."

Dolly's words made me wonder just how good Brick was to her, but maybe I was letting Kane's comment about them influence me.

"I'm returning to the hotel. Want a lift back?"

"No. I'll ride my bike. I'll need it there in the morning."

Leaving the mansion, I headed home. This long day began to take its toll. My left shoulder still ached from my fall off the balcony, and my knees developed a shaky, I'm-about-to-give-out feeling. I flopped onto my bed for a short rest without taking time to turn the satin spread aside. I didn't wake up until an hour later when my phone rang.

As I jumped, startled at the sound, pain stabbed my shoulder. The phone rang again while I reached for the bottle of pain lozenges I'd used earlier. Drat! Empty bottle. Forget that idea. I answered the phone. Nobody replied.

"Hello? Hello?"

Dead line. I scowled, wondering who awakened me — for nothing. Maybe a wrong number. But in an instant, the phone rang again. I picked it up wondering if I'd get another dead line, and it didn't help my mood or my shoulder to hear Dolly's voice begging me to hurry to the Frangi ASAP.

"Have to run an errand first, Dolly. Be

there soon as I can."

My gum-shoeing, along with the time I'd spent with Dolly trying to change the light bulb, had taken longer than I realized. Twilight falls quickly in the Keys and already the outside light had faded. I grabbed a green ankle-length skirt and matching tee, dressed quickly, and headed for my car. I could have called room service for a pain pill, but sometimes that takes longer than getting one for myself.

I usually love the tourist Conch Trains with their quaint canopies and clanging bells, but this evening I wanted to honk at the driver slowing me down on Duval. I didn't honk, but I did grit my teeth, a habit my dentist deplores.

Inching along toward Fausto's Pharmacy where I knew I could find my special brand of lozenges, I suddenly came alert. Pablo! Pablo strolled along the cracked sidewalk to my right.

"Pablo!" I called to him through my car window. "Pablo!"

His head turned toward me for a moment then in the next instant he began jogging, almost bumping into a woman carrying an armload of packages. He entered a nearby bar. What was going on here? I wanted to go after him, to talk to him, but no parking place. Bumper-to-bumper traffic. Sloppy Joe's. That's where he went. I could call there later. But he'd been running from me. I felt sure of that; he started jogging the minute he saw me.

I found plenty of parking slots at Fausto's, paid for my lozenges, swallowed one with a gulp of the bottled water I always carry in my car. Don't know if it was the pill or the psychology of taking medicine, but after a few moments, my shoulder and knees felt better and I headed home. When I reached the Frangi, most of tonight's workers stood gathered there, and now they hurried to greet me. I knew Dolly and Kane must have informed them of my fall. Had I been an advertising exec, I'd have snapped their picture. What a wonderful ad they'd make for the Frangipani Room.

Brick's maroon silk slacks and a dark hand-print shirt set off his gleaming head and dark beard. He looked like a model from a seaman's catalogue. Threnody, her hair sprinkled with glitter and piled high, matched the ambience of the room. Jessie stood at the bar waiting for the evening to begin. Tonight he wore chinos, a tank top, and sandals — and a golden hibiscus tucked behind his left ear.

Kane, in his black jacket–white pants

bouncer's uniform, hurried toward me. Before I could tell everyone I'd seen Pablo, Dolly also rushed forward, waving a sheet of paper. In the background, Mama G stood on the tiny bandstand, tapping her foot and looking grim and dour. I smiled, but only to myself. We depended on Mama G for many things, and we all humored her — sometimes. Tonight her signature look included her braided crown of black hair held in place with tortoise-shell hairpins and her scarlet caftan and black Birkenstock sandals. She glared at Dolly, unused to being upstaged by her, her cat, or her poems.

"Rafa! Guess what!" Dolly waved the sheet of paper toward me. "Made a quick stop at the mailbox on my way here. And look! I've had a poem accepted. This may be the big time for me."

I corked my own news about seeing Pablo and listened to Dolly.

"Weeks ago I entered a contest. Thought I'd never hear from the judges. My poem's been selected from those of thousands of poets who entered this contest." Dolly paused to grab a breath. "Rafa! It's going to be published! In a *book!* A hardbound book. My poem will be in libraries all over the country. I can hardly believe it — a book! It's true. A book! Read the letter if you don't believe me."

"Book people do not know you sell poems ten cents each." Mama G snorted. "Dime may be more than they be worth."

Again, Dolly fluttered an envelope and a sheet of paper toward me, ignoring Mama G's put-down.

"Only five hundred poems have been selected for *Poet Lover's Paradise.* Only five hundred! It's an honor to have a poem chosen. There'll be a hundred-dollar cash prize for the grand winner, and all five hundred authors have a chance to win one of ten additional cash prizes. Read the letter they've sent me, Rafa. Read it if you don't believe me."

"I believe you, Dolly." I scanned the letter she thrust toward me and I knew almost immediately she'd been caught up in a cruel scam. The letter offered her publication of her poem *after* she'd agreed to buy a copy of the expensive book her poem would appear in. And, of course, extra copies could be purchased for friends and family at a slightly reduced cost. I couldn't bear to break bad news to her at the peak of her excitement.

"I'd like to see your poem. You have a copy, right?"

"Right." The long sleeve of her poet's

172

blouse caught in the pocket of her black satin pants as she tugged a sheet of folded paper out and held it toward me. "It's about a cat."

"We'd never have guessed." Kane rolled his eyes.

"I think it's a cute poem," Threnody said, "I've read it and, Dolly, I hope you win one of the cash prizes. I love poetry and I've always loved cats. I certainly plan to buy a copy of *Poet Lover's Paradise,* and maybe some extras to give to friends."

Kane rolled his eyes again, but if Dolly noticed, she didn't let on.

I took the sheet she offered and read the poem aloud:

CAREER CAT

When Madam's Music Club meets here
I get up with the sun.
The cleaning person comes at eight
I'm ready for some fun.

I paw-print on her fresh-scrubbed floors
And when she screams, I leap
Onto the countertop and sniff
The tea cakes. See her weep?

At last she's gone. I nap and yawn

173

In a velvet easy chair.
So watch your backs, guests dressed in
   black
Or you'll wear my gift of hair.

While Madam's guests perform
   downstairs,
Upstairs, I frisk in furs.
Guests sing. They swing. Their loud
   applause
Masks my contented purrs.

To show that I appreciate
Their meeting at our house,
I stalk and pounce. I bring our guests
A trophy — fat gray mouse.

My Madam faints. Guests hurry off.
I hope they'll come next year.
I've many months to plot new plans
To boost my cat career.

I grinned and handed the poem back to Dolly. "I like it a lot. I agree with the contest judges. It deserves to win a prize, but I'd check into this publishing company before I sent them any money."

"Then you don't really think it's a top-notch poem?"

"Yes, I do," I said. "But there are so many

scam artists these days, you can't be too careful. When someone wants you to send money in order to be eligible to win a prize, watch out. That's the hallmark of a scam."

"It could be a scam, Dolly." Brick gave her shoulder a pat then rested his arm there until Dolly moved away from his touch. "I've read about companies that make most of their profit from selling a book to authors, a book that includes an author's story or poem. Most writers realize how hard it is to get original work from the computer to the published page and then into libraries and bookstores. Scam artists take advantage of that."

"It's called vanity printing," Kane said. "Think about it."

Dolly took three steps toward Kane, sparks shooting from her eyes.

SIXTEEN

"Hey guys," I said, seizing the opportunity to break into the conversation and change the subject, "I just saw Pablo."

"Where?" Kane stepped from Dolly's path. "Was he headed this way?"

Dolly saw this as her cue to retreat to the kitchen. Nobody said anything more about her prize-winning poem.

"I saw him go into Sloppy's. He saw me, and I called to him, but he didn't answer or wave a greeting. I couldn't stop. No place to park. He ticked me off, acting as if he didn't know me. But we can call him now. At Sloppy's."

"His dad dies, and he's hanging out in a bar?" Kane shrugged. "I guess he can grieve in a bar as well as anyplace."

"You going to call him, Rafa?" Jessie asked.

"Maybe we should back off — leave him alone," Brick said. "Give him a chance to

176

approach us in his own way. He could show up here tonight before we open. Let's grant him some space."

"*Hola!*" Mama G shouted before we could answer Brick. She'd been on the bandstand a few minutes ago, but now she approached us from the kitchen with a tray bearing a bowl of sandwich filling.

"Time to think about business. Frangipani Room business. Time to forget about wannabe poets and don't-wannabe drummers. Mama G needs your say-so on my sandwich fixings. My *Tia* Luisa in Havana created the recipes back home in our country, but Mama G bring them from Cuba to Key West many years ago."

"We've heard your story before," Kane said. "Lotsa times."

"I'm sure your sandwiches will be fine, Mama G," I said. "All our patrons always rave about them. And sometimes ask for your recipes."

"Secret recipes," Mama G insisted. "No give to strangers. Come now. Taste recipes I prepare for tonight."

"They'll be fine, Mama G," I said.

"How you be sure without tasting?" Mama G offered crackers, the filling, and a small spreader. "Conch salad with ripe olives. Try.

177

Taste. Then say fine — if you think it be fine."

Kane turned and headed toward the bandstand, suddenly concerned about the well-being of Pablo's drum set. Threnody stepped forward and spread some sandwich filling on a saltine.

"Wonderful, Mama G," she said. "It's a unique taste. I'm sure our guests here this evening will love it and ask for more."

Brick tried the spread and nodded in agreement with his wife. When Dolly returned from the kitchen to taste the mixture, Mama G held the bowl out of her reach and scowled.

"Don't need your opinion," Mama G said. "You just stick to writing your poems."

"And I didn't need your put-down of my poem, which professional editors accepted for publication," Dolly said.

"Ladies!" I interrupted. "It's almost time to open the Frangi to our patrons. Mama G, I'm sure everyone will love your sandwich fillings. Why don't you blow your conch shell now to announce we're ready and waiting for guests?"

"*Si,*" Mama G said, distracted from her argument with Dolly. "The wail of the conch shell, it appeal to the curious. They hear. From all over the hotel, they hear

178

Mama G play the conch. It draw people here. It get our evening off to a grand start."

"Some grand start we'll have without our favorite drummer," Kane grumbled. "Guess we really didn't expect Pablo to show, did we? We've been depending on Dolly too much. Maybe we'd better hire her on a regular basis — show Pablo that he's not indispensable."

"I'll call Dolly from the kitchen," Brick said. "I'll sweet-talk her a bit to get her over the poetry thing."

"I'm guessing she'll be willing and eager to sit in on drums again tonight," Kane said. "She's probably looking forward to it. Dolly loves the limelight — almost as much as Mama G."

"You'll pinch-hit for her in the kitchen?" I asked Brick.

"As usual," Brick said. "Promised your mother."

For once, Mama G didn't grumble or protest. She picked up the conch shell from the top of the piano and began blowing. Her face grew stroke-red from the effort and, although she looked as if a seizure or a heart attack might be eminent, she continued making conch shell music.

When Brick returned from the kitchen and his talk with Dolly, he gave us thumbs-up. Tonight he claimed the chore, or the honor, depending on how you looked at it, of lighting the torches that ringed the balcony outside the dance floor. I loved the sight of the torches sending their flares into the late-evening darkness, the smell of the lighter fluid. The open-air Frangi was one of my favorite places in the hotel.

Guests began exiting the elevator and easing closer to the bar and the dance floor. I stepped forward to greet them, knowing the flaring torches and Mama G's conch shell wailing intrigued them.

"What's going on?" one lady asked. "I've never heard anything like it before."

"Mama G's playing 'Row, Row, Row Your Boat,' " I explained. "She produces her music by blowing across the cut-off end of a conch shell. It's a talent she's developed from childhood."

"I don't recognize the tune," the lady said, after listening a few moments. "Don't recognize it at all."

I couldn't recognize the melody either, but I smiled. Mama G's puffed cheeks threatened to flush from crimson to purple, but she kept on blowing. Soon people gathered at the bar or found seats at the edge of the dance floor, waiting for the combo music and the dancing to begin.

At last Mama G passed the shell to Brick with a dramatic bow. Brick then made a mini-ceremony of polishing the conch with a flowing silk scarf, holding it high in the torchlight before placing it on a silver salver atop the piano. Mama G gave Brick his moment in the sun before she swooped to the raised combo platform. Threnody followed her across the dance floor and stood near the piano. The two of them always opened and closed the evening with Threnody singing a soulful rendition of "Harbor Lights." Tonight she also sang two jazz numbers. I guessed the combo was prolonging the evening's opening, waiting to see if Pablo might arrive.

I couldn't help wondering why Pablo stopped at Sloppy's tonight instead of coming straight to the hotel. And why had he avoided me? Did Ramsey and Lyon know he was back on-island? I hoped none of the tourists here tonight noticed the plainclothes detectives watching our dance floor from the sidelines while they kept the Frangi under surveillance. But I noticed. The officers were strangers to me, but once you've been in the hotel business a while, you can spot a cop at a glance. Jessie noticed, too. He kept looking from the cops to Kane, perhaps hoping Kane would

181

bounce them onto the street. I saw Mama G scowl at Jessie once when she had to wait for him to get the correct arrangement on his music stand.

She started to scowl at Dolly too, pointing to the title of the tune they were about to play. Dolly ignored her, tilting her chin toward the stars and smiling. "I don't use music," she said to Mama G and also to a patron who stopped to compliment her. "I play from my heart and soul."

Mama G let her get by with ignoring her, and I shrugged. *Was a drummer's sheet music all that important?* I wondered. I'd glanced at Pablo's music one night, and it looked like several lines of the same notes printed across the page with little variation. How could anyone read that and turn it into music?

Threnody and Dolly had arranged several dozen open-face sandwiches on hors d'oeuvre trays ahead of time. Brick knew how to serve them with a flourish, so I decided to go to the kitchen and try to call Pablo at Sloppy's. I hadn't expected him to come rushing right to the hotel the minute he saw me, but he could at least have let us know he was back on-island. The telephone hung very close to the door separating the kitchen from the dance floor, so I went to my suite to make my call in privacy.

Would the plainclothes guys follow me? I watched for them, but no. I was alone. Inside my suite, I relaxed on my bed and used my bedside phone. After punching in Sloppy's number, the phone rang ten times before a gruff voice answered.

"Sloppy Joe's Bar. Hemingway's favorite watering hole. Sylvester speaking."

"Will you call Pablo Casterano to the phone, please?"

"You sure he's in here, lady?"

Ma'am? Miss? And now I was "lady." Guess I should have given my name before I asked for Pablo. "This is Rafa Blue calling Pablo from The Blue Mermaid."

"Hold on a minute or ten. I'll give him a shout. Pablo, right?"

"Yes. Pablo Casterano."

From a distance I could hear Sylvester bellowing Pablo's name. He said Castellano, but — close enough. I waited several minutes and was considering hanging up when Sylvester spoke again.

"He ain't here, lady. Not tonight. Why doncha come on down anyway? We could have some fun."

"Another time." *Another century,* I thought.

"Lady? Rafa Blue? Lady, you in the book?"

I replaced the receiver, glad I wasn't in the book — at least not Sylvester's book. I stood for a few moments in my living room, looking through the sliding glass door and trying not to think of my fall from the balcony that afternoon. I peered into the darkness surrounding Key West Harbor before I slid the door open a few inches and felt an onshore wind blow the sea scent of the tradewind to me. I imagined I could taste salt on my lips. And that reminded me of Saturday night, Diego, the Vexton Marina. I slid the door shut, making sure to lock it.

SEVENTEEN

I hurried back to the Frangi, stepping into the entryway in time to see a crowd of patrons parting to allow Pablo to stride to the bandstand. He wore black jeans, black tee, and a palm frond hat that revealed diamond studs gleaming from both earlobes. For a moment he glared at Dolly sitting at his trap set, then he smiled at her and bent to brush a kiss onto her cheek.

"Thank you for holding my place for me, Dolly. I appreciate." Then he turned to the crowd.

"You're in luck, folks. I just got back to Key West, and I'm ready to play for you this evening. Thanks for waiting for me."

For the first time, I noted Brick's reaction to the scene, and I remembered Kane's words about Brick having an eye for the ladies. He stood watching Dolly, and when she left the bandstand, relinquishing the trap set to Pablo, she approached him at the bar. He gave her a playful pat on the fanny. I hoped Threnody hadn't noticed, but I felt sure she had.

Most of the patrons at the Frangi tonight were tourists on vacation who had no insight into the personnel problems plaguing the combo. With Pablo at the traps, the rest of the evening passed smoothly. Once Threnody finished singing her farewell rendition of "Harbor Lights," the crowd, including the plainclothes cops, gradually disbursed, heading for the elevator or perhaps for another hotel, another bar.

When only the few of us involved with operating the Frangi remained in the room, Brick made no move to extinguish the torches — his chore while Mother and Cherie were away. Kane broke the tension that gripped everyone.

"Welcome back, Pablo." Kane extended a hand in greeting, which Pablo ignored. "Long time, no see."

Pablo's gaze bored into Dolly. "Who gave you permission to use my trap set?"

"I didn't know anyone needed permission," Brick said before Dolly could reply. "The combo needed a drummer. The drums were in place. Dolly volunteered. So how cool is that?"

"Pablo, welcome back." I stepped between

the two of them, soft-voiced and smiling. "We're glad to have you on-island, and we all want to offer our condolences on the loss of your father."

"Thank you. I appreciate that." Pablo spoke in a calm voice that helped ease our tension.

"We know your father's death must be a terrible shock to you," Threnody said. "It's left all of us devastated."

"A shock at first," Pablo agreed, then he slapped a deck of tarot cards onto one of the glass-topped tables that ringed the bandstand. "But I saw the forewarning right there in the cards. Dad belittled my tarot predictions, but if he'd listened to me during the past year or two, he might have avoided his killer."

"And I suppose you intend to tell the police who that killer is." Jessie held his head in a way that caused one of the patio torches to reflect flashes of amber light onto his brown eye while it hid his blue eye in deep shadow.

Pablo glared at him. "You might be surprised at the info I intend to tell the police."

When Pablo turned and headed down the hallway toward the elevator, I followed him until we were out of earshot of the others. I managed to pass him, step in front of him.

He stopped and looked me in the eye, and I spoke before he could push the elevator button.

"Pablo! We need to talk."

"What about? Maybe you'd be happy if I sold my trap set to Dolly or Jessie. Or maybe you'd like to buy it for the hotel and find a replacement for me in the combo."

"We aren't trying to replace you, Pablo. No way. But be fair. You disappeared and we had no idea whether you planned to return. Even Diego didn't know your whereabouts. When you failed to show up for gigs, we needed to find a drummer. We asked Jessie — sometimes, but if he played drums, that left us without a string bass."

"Hmmm."

While Pablo trailed along behind me, I unlocked the door to my suite and invited him inside, trying to hide my nervousness. My fear? Perhaps. I glanced toward my balcony, wondering if Pablo could have been the person calling to me from below before the railing gave way. I offered him a stool at my snack bar and sat down next to him.

"Pablo. Here at the hotel we're all your friends. Be reasonable. Treat us like friends. Be on time for the combo gigs and you'll be welcome. We need you and we want you."

"Got an attitude. Guess I should apologize. And maybe I will — some fine day in the future."

"I'd like to talk to you for a few minutes. Could I bring you a sandwich from the Frangi? I'm sure there a few leftovers."

Pablo shook his head. "You don't have to bribe me with food to get me to stay. We do need to talk. In spite of the tarot forewarning, I'm still in shock over losing Dad. Heard about it on a TV newscast. Rafa, I don't even know where Dad's body is or where to go to claim it."

"I know you're hurting. I wasn't trying to bribe you with a sandwich. Mama G didn't give the combo many breaks tonight. Thought you might be hungry."

"I am." Pablo gave a short laugh. "Even the thought of one of Mama G's conch and caper sandwiches makes my mouth water."

I hurried back to the Frangi, filled a tray with two sandwiches, a heap of chips, and a soda. When I returned, Pablo still sat at the snack bar. I offered him the tray, and he reached for it so eagerly I wondered how long it had been since he'd last eaten a real meal.

"What can you tell me about Dad's death? Can't find much in the *Citizen.* Start from the beginning. Start from the time you

189

discovered him in the water."

I hated the retelling. It came close to making me relive the scene. He asked no questions and made no comments until I finished my story. I expected him to demand more details, but he brought up more practical matters.

"So where is Dad's body now?"

"The medical examiner still holds it."

"I need to talk to the police, to the medical examiner, to a funeral director."

"You needn't be concerned about funeral plans. In your absence, Brick, Threnody, and I have agreed to claim Pablo's body and plan the funeral — if that's all right with you. If not, you can step up and help us, or you can take charge at any time. We didn't know how to get in touch with you. We were acting out of respect and kindness to our friend — and to you."

Someone rapped on my door while Pablo and I sat talking. "Need any help, Rafa?" Kane asked when I opened the door. Jessie glared at Pablo without speaking, but his hands at his sides curled into fists. I told myself I wasn't afraid of Pablo, but I appreciated their concern and appreciated knowing that they were aware of Pablo's presence in my suite.

"Thanks, guys. Everything's fine here.

We'll be in touch soon."

Kane nodded and then headed for the elevator with Jessie following close behind. Pablo said nothing about the interruption. He waited until Kane and Jessie had time to reach the ground floor, then he nodded to me and headed for my door and the elevator.

"Hola, amigo," Mama G called to me when I returned to the Frangi as if I'd been away a long time. "I be packing my willow basket and heading home. Don't like the looks of things here — Pablo, barging in like that. Sullen. That's what he be, sullen. And Jessie. He be angry. Mama G no like sullen. No like anger in people."

"Pablo might have seemed sullen," I said, "but he wasn't barging in. He does work here, you know."

"Now and then." Mama G scowled. "Maybe we no need his kind anymore. On again. Off again. Got no band I can depend on."

"I really like playing drums," Dolly said. "Kane and Brick always fuss about me having to pinch-hit for Pablo, but I don't mind." Dolly laughed when we continued to look at her in astonishment. "You know by now I'm no fancy drummer like Pablo, but years ago on my sixteenth birthday, I

191

ran away from home. No job. No place to sleep. But I lucked out in Miami. Bobo Bongo and her all-girl band were playing at a club on Collins Avenue. Bobo Bongo and her Sweethearts of Swing. She needed a drummer to fill their contract for a gig requiring nine musicians on the bandstand. She had only eight. I joined them then and there."

"For the night?" I asked.

"Right," Dolly said. "And for the next night, too. Bobo taught me how to keep a steady beat on the bass. She hired me on the spot — helped me apply for membership in the musicians' union."

Except for the part about playing drums, Dolly could have been telling my own story. Was she making fun of me? Did she know about my running away from home as a teenager? No. For the most part, Mother and Cherie had been able to hush up my escapades. Dolly had lived in Key West only a short time. She couldn't have known.

"I played with the Sweethearts of Swing for the summer," Dolly said. "Did all right, too. Kept that band going and earned some bucks I needed."

"We'll keep you in mind as our steady substitute drummer," I said. "We need to give Pablo some room, need to give him a chance to play if he wants to."

"I can keep a steady beat on the bass. That's important for the dancers. And that's about all I did tonight. But I know how to flam-a-diddle, par-a-diddle — soft fancy stuff on the snares and the small cymbals. Bobo Bongo taught me a few drumming rudiments while I played with her band."

"Hola, amigo!" Suddenly Mama G smiled and slapped Dolly on the back. "I talk to Pablo about you flam-a-diddling on his trap set. If he say okay, you be what Rafa says — a steady sub." She gave a short chuckle. "Think I could play drums myself if I had to."

I hid a laugh. "Pablo says everyone thinks they can play drums. Says he found out it's harder than it looks."

"Flam-a-diddle, par-a-diddle," Dolly said. "I got a knack for it."

Before Mama G could say more, Dolly swooped onto the patio dance floor, batted her eyes at Brick, and began helping him extinguish the torches ringing the dance floor. A breeze freshened and the torch flames grew broader and higher. They reminded me of shimmering dancers autographing the night sky with their names of fire. Brick picked up a large aluminum candle snuffer and began walking the perimeter of the area, snuffing out each flame. For a moment the scent of sulfur hung in the air.

Threnody and I started carrying trays of glasses and coffee cups from the patio to the kitchen. We had stepped back toward the sink and the dishwasher when we heard Dolly scream.

EIGHTEEN

"Help! Someone help me! I'm on fire!"

I dashed from the kitchen in time to see a torch flame igniting Dolly's flowing sleeve. Threnody gasped in horror. When Brick saw flames licking Dolly's blouse and then curling upward to singe her hair, he threw himself at her. Ripping the burning blouse from her body, he flung it onto the floor, stomping it. At the same time he pulled her toward him and wrapped her in a deep embrace that smothered the sparks burning her bra. I smelled the pungent odor of singed hair and silk.

For a moment Dolly relaxed in Brick's arms, then she stiffened and stood clinging to him, refusing to let him go.

"Quick, Threnody. Grab a glass of water. Douse her hair. I'll grab a towel from the kitchen. We'll wrap her in it." I dashed inside. When I returned with a towel, Threnody stood immobile.

"I think he did that intentionally," she whispered to me, still holding a water glass and staring at Brick.

"Surely not." Ignoring her, I ran toward Dolly and Brick, pulling them apart and wrapping Dolly in the towel. "Come to my suite, Dolly. Let us see how badly you've been burned. We may need a doctor."

"And you can wait where you are." Threnody's voice held a steel-gaff coldness as she glared at Brick.

Dolly wept, near hysteria while I tried to calm her and lead her from the dance floor to my suite. At last Threnody came to life and followed us.

"Help me support her while we get her to my guest room," I said. "We'll help her lie down there while I get some ice cubes and salve. I didn't see any deep burns on her skin, but I'll apply ice, then check again more carefully for injury."

By the time we settled Dolly in my guest room and I found ice cubes, a bowl, and some salve, she managed to sit up and dry her tears to a mere sniffle. I wondered if Brick still stood where Threnody had ordered him to stand. I squelched a grin.

"I'm o-okay, R-Rafa," Dolly said. "No b-burns — except for my blouse and bra. I'm sorry for causing so much trouble." She blew her nose into a tissue I pulled from the sequined caddy on the bedside table. "You go ahead and close the Frangi. I'll be okay."

"Plenty of time to do that later. Or maybe Brick will close up tonight." I applied ointment to her reddened skin. "You relax and we'll talk about this in the morning. I'm glad you weren't badly burnt, Dolly, and I'm sure you didn't intend to cause trouble. Accidents happen. Try to relax now and get some sleep." I brought her a satin gown and a robe, waiting nearby while she slipped into the gown and then into bed.

Dolly dropped to sleep almost immediately. Leaving a nightlight on, I closed the door and left her alone. During the time I spent soothing Dolly, my mind had been bursting with questions. Had Threnody been right? Had Brick deliberately torched Dolly's blouse? Had he been trying to play hero? Again, I remembered Kane's words. Did Brick really have that much of an "eye for the ladies"? Had he used a fire to get a more personal look at Dolly? I could hardly believe that. I told myself the whole thing had been an accident. But Threnody's jealous reaction made me wonder if such instances happened often when Brick was around.

It was after midnight before Threnody and Brick left. I kicked off my sandals and sat enjoying the cool touch of terrazzo underfoot when a call came over my intercom.

"Ma'am. Henri here. Pablo Casterano is at the front desk, asking to talk with you. Shall I send him up or away?"

"Please send him up, Henri."

Why had Pablo returned? I wasn't afraid of him, yet I welcomed having Dolly in the next room, welcomed having Henri aware of Pablo's presence in my suite. I waited at the doorway until Pablo stepped from the elevator, not wanting him to ring and waken Dolly. After I invited him inside, we sat in the living room. I didn't pull the mini-blinds across the sliding glass door to the balcony. Anyone could look in and see us — anyone who happened to be up five stories and was interested in looking.

"Thanks for letting me come up again, Rafa. But my mind won't rest."

"I won't ask you where you've been these past weeks." I sat on the couch and he sat in the chair to my left. "But we've missed you and we're glad to have you back — on a permanent basis, I hope."

"Tell me more about Dad. I realize now I need to know more." Pablo jumped right to the topic uppermost in his mind. "I have to know more. I'm sorry you had to be the one who found him. But who do you think murdered him?"

"I've no idea. Thought maybe you could give me some clues." I shuddered as I told him of Chief Ramsey's Q&A session at the police station. "The chief will want to talk to you, Pablo, since you're Diego's next of kin. He asked about your whereabouts, but none of us had any answers."

"I suppose you'll tell him I showed up here tonight."

"If you ask me not to, I won't volunteer the information, but if he asks if I've seen you, I'll speak the truth. And you may be interested to know that there were plain-clothes cops at the Frangi tonight."

"I didn't notice."

Now I wondered about the pack of tarot cards Pablo laid before us on the coffee table and began to feel uneasy here with him — this homeless man who believed he could find answers to life's important problems with a deck of strange-looking cards.

"Tarot cards sometimes reveal much to me, Rafa. The origins of tarot are veiled in the mists of time. I don't expect the cards to shout out the killer's name, but they do speak to those who listen and seek answers.

They offer miracles of psychological insight. Many times the cards allow me a look into my own soul."

"I'm not putting down tarot, Pablo. I believe people find what they're looking for. Seek and ye shall find. The answers may be in tarot or in the Bible. They may be lost in history or found in some vast universal intelligence. But I firmly believe that answers to human questions can be found."

"Thank you for not laughing at me, Rafa. I believe the cards can emit mystic powers and esoteric wisdom. Oh, when I'm on-island, I sometimes read fortunes for tourists on Mallory at the sunset celebrations. But when I'm alone, I lay out cards for myself — for serious study."

"I hope you're right about the tarot, but I need to share a secret with you — a secret Kane disapproves of."

"Kane disapproves of many things, including me. So what's your big secret?"

"I'm doing a covert investigation of your father's death. In many ways, all of his associates are suspects."

"And Kane objects to that?"

"Feels I might ruin my future chances as a serious writer by getting involved as an amateur in a murder investigation."

"It's something to consider, Rafa. The

Good Ole Boys on the Key West police force and the elected citizens on the board of commissioners may not welcome an amateur detective no matter how covert. Dad probed deeply into local politics. But tell me who you suspect as his killer and why. What are your thoughts? And how can you be sure I'm not the guilty person?"

"There's an honesty about you that inspires my trust, Pablo. How can I suspect a guy who honestly gets psychological insights by reading and studying the tarot and sometimes seeing into his own soul?"

I went on to discuss each of Diego's associates and to speculate on each one's motive for wanting Diego out of the picture. I spoke of everyone except Kane. I could hardly bear to admit that Kane had a motive for murder, let alone admit that he might be Diego's killer.

"Why are you willing to get so involved in this case?" Pablo asked. "You have good reason to run the other direction."

"I'm willing to do all I can to help find your father's killer because your father was my friend. And maybe I'm thinking of myself, too. Someday I plan to write novels, perhaps mystery novels. Working on this case will provide primary research into a murder."

"So good luck to you," Pablo said after I finished. "If I get any hot leads, I'll share them with you. I want to find Dad's killer, too. Don't want any of the locals looking my way and imagining guilt written on my forehead."

"You could help your image on the island by showing up for work here every night. How about it? We need you. You know that."

"I'm making no promises, Rafa, but I'll *try* to show up."

"I'll appreciate your trying. And where are you staying tonight?"

"Around."

"I could order a room made up for you here at the hotel."

Pablo stood. "Sorry. I appreciate your offer, but no."

Pablo stood, stuffed his tarot cards into the pocket of his jeans, and strode toward my door and the elevator. I stood, considering calling him back, but my telephone rang. I ran to answer it, then stopped. Was I ready to face another dead line? Refusing to wimp out at the sound of a telephone, I answered and heard Threnody's voice, so low I knew she must be whispering.

"Rafa, may I come talk to you now? Are you free?"

NINETEEN

I recognized anguish in her voice. "What is it, Threnody? Of course you may talk to me. What's up? You sound frightened."

"Tell you when I get there."

"I'll ask the desk clerk to send you right up."

"No. No. Please meet me at the front entryway — under the Mermaid. I'll pick you up and we'll find a place where we can talk in private. Okay?"

"Sure, that's okay, but why all the secrecy?"

"I'll explain later."

I started to say more, but she'd hung up. I stood listening to the dial tone for a few moments before I replaced the receiver in its cradle. The wind outside had picked up and I reached into my closet for a sweater, wondering where Pablo would sleep tonight. I tried to push him from my thoughts. Impossible. Did he have a key to Diego's private apartment at Brick's marina? Or would he be sleeping under a palm on the beach? I pulled my sweater more tightly about me as I visualized the beach-at-night scene. How did those homeless guys keep warm? How did they avoid fire ants? Maybe Pablo might check in at a homeless shelter. At least he'd be safe at a shelter. And warm. Key West nights can grow very damp and chilly before dawn.

I grabbed my key ring, locked my door behind me, and took the elevator to the lobby. A full moon shone against the croton hedge almost like a beacon, and I stood in the shadow of the mermaid sculpture until Threnody arrived in her Caddi convertible. No headlights. Top up. She braked to a silent stop and a frisson of unease crawled up my spine when I considered getting into the car with her, destination unknown.

I forced myself to swallow most of my misgivings and eased onto the passenger seat, inhaling the gardenia scent that wafted around us and clung to the leather upholstery. For an instant neither of us spoke. The moment my car door slammed, she pulled away from the curbing and headed toward less-populated streets near the viaduct before she drove on toward Smather's.

Once we reached the beach, we saw a plethora of empty parking places lining the boulevard that separated South Roosevelt from a wide sidewalk and a retaining wall. Threnody parked across the boulevard from the slots reserved in the daytime for food and drink vendors and their vehicles. The police considered this lane a legal parking area, although it lay on an almost deserted path full of ruts, an area darkened by the shade of palms and untrimmed Australian pines.

"Threnody, what's up? Give. Why all the secrecy?"

"I didn't want anyone to see me return to the hotel tonight."

"I saw nobody around. We could have talked in my suite or downstairs beside the pool."

"Nobody in your suite but you *and Dolly* right?"

"Yes, but Dolly was sound asleep. Threnody, do you really think Brick caused her accident tonight?"

"Let's walk to one of the tiki shelters on the beach." Threnody left the convertible and as soon as I joined her, she locked the doors with the click of her car key. "I'll be sure nobody can overhear us there."

Sand blown from beach to street gritted

underfoot, and once we'd climbed the retaining wall steps and reached the deep mounds on the beach, grit seeped into my sandals and stuck to my toes. An onshore breeze carried a living sea scent that competed with Threnody's gardenia cologne — an unusual but interesting mixture of aromas. I stumbled over an abandoned ball as we walked past a volleyball court and stepped onto the concrete base of the nearest tiki shelter. Moonlight peeked through holes in the palm-frond roof, scattering silvery coins onto the rough picnic table.

"You think your car's bugged? You think . . ."

"I'm not sure what I think, Rafa. That's one reason I wanted to talk to you. The car may be bugged. I don't know how to tell. Brick's sly and likes to keep close track of my activities. If I as much as look at another man, he lets me know about it. Yet he feels free to flirt with any and every woman he sees — says the ladies enjoy his attention. If I protest, he assures me his outgoing personality brings us business."

"He may be right."

"Or he may be making it big-time with Dolly. To please Brick, I pretend to like Dolly, but don't you resent that crazy wannabe poet flirting with Kane?"

"Sometimes," I admitted. "But Kane isn't interested in Dolly or her poetry, and all her flirting makes her look foolish."

"So forget Dolly — for tonight, at least. She's not what I drove here to talk to you about, Rafa."

"So what's bugging you? You're making me very curious — and nervous."

"I want to ask you to help me investigate Diego's murder."

I made no effort to control my surprise. "Why me? Be real, Threnody. Why me? I'm no detective."

"But you're deeply interested in Diego. You were going to write one of your columns about him. Didn't you tell me that? You've already done some research on his life in Cuba, his life here. Somehow all that knowledge can help us find his killer."

"I don't think so, but . . ."

"And you and your family were his friends, right?"

"Yes, but . . ."

"Then I'm asking you to help me investigate his death, not as a detective, but as a private citizen. I've come prepared to bribe you." She laughed as if that were a joke. "Two grand for starters. But I don't suppose money will change your mind."

I laughed too. "No. Of course not. But I

might help you just to be on the side of justice — to fight the pain of injustice. A good man lies dead and his killer walks free. That's injustice!"

Maybe someday I'd write a novel that would point up that theme. Maybe someday I'd be brave enough to give up writing my column for the *Citizen,* strike out on my own as a novelist. But not yet.

"I didn't come to you for a lecture, Rafa. I want you to help me find Diego's killer. In Chief Ramsey's eyes, we're both persons of interest. Do you realize what that means? Either of us could find a murder rap laid at our feet. But if we work together and find the killer, that can't happen."

"Who do you suspect as the murderer, Threnody? You have reason to point your finger at someone?"

"I'm not pointing at anyone yet. I have no idea who killed Diego. That's why I want you to help me in a covert investigation. I've brought cash to back up my request. We'll need money."

Threnody pulled a thick envelope from her shoulder purse and thrust it toward me. When I didn't reach for it, she opened the envelope flap, pulled out some greenbacks. I still didn't reach for it.

"I don't know, Threnody."

"You know you want to work on the case. I've sensed that since early this morning in Chief Ramsey's office. So I'm offering the retainer to give you some extra motivation. I want us to work together. What do you say? If we solve the case, it would be good publicity for you when you break out as a novelist."

"You give a good reason for me to help you, but why are you so interested in finding the killer? In your case, the answer could fall very close to home."

"You mean Brick or Jessie, of course."

"Yes, that's what I mean. Not that I'm ready to accuse either of them, I'm just talking possibilities. Why do you want to risk finding a killer that might turn out to be a family member?"

"Because I don't think it will turn out that way. The killer could be Dolly — who saw Diego alive very close to the time that the police found him dead. It could be Pablo, his next of kin. It could be Kane, who wrote all those fiery letters."

"But it's worth two grand for you to find out. Why?"

"I have to know because in my mind I don't think either Brick or Jessie was involved in Diego's death. And I don't want this homicide to turn into a cold case, a case with no killer found and punished."

"I wouldn't want to see that happen either."

"A cold case wouldn't matter to tourists who come and go from the island, but a cold case would be remembered forever by the locals. The locals would be suspicious of someone, and they would gossip among themselves, probably blaming a member of the Vexton family. I can't live with that, Rafa."

"I can understand that."

"We have to work fast." Threnody leaned forward. She pushed the envelope closer to me. "The first few hours following a murder are crucial to the investigation."

"The police are working on it."

"I want more than that. I want us to be working on it, too."

Waves murmured against the shore while I thought more about Threnody's proposal. Waves seldom splash and roar in Key West. A reef a few miles offshore slows them down. Right now I felt like those waves — murmuring and slowed down, slowed almost to a stop but not quite. I picked up the envelope that Threnody slid toward me and tucked it into my shoulder bag.

"I'll work with you, Threnody. And having

some money to work with will certainly help."

"I'm so glad. You'll never know how glad. Now, please tell me where you think we should start the investigation. Tell me if there's anything I can do to help — anything that won't give away the fact that we're investigating."

"For starters, I'll tell you that I've already started working on the case."

"In what way? And how?"

I told her about getting a piece of the blue line and about being unable to find similar line here on the island.

"We'll find that line somewhere," Threnody promised. "It's a good starting point. I'll help you look for it."

"So far, I haven't an idea of where else to start looking." I wasn't about to tell her of the blue line aboard Kane's boat. I had no intention of trying to incriminate an innocent man, and I felt almost sure Kane was innocent. Almost.

"Let's go now," Threnody said. "I told Brick I needed a few things from the twenty-four/seven grocery, but he'll be suspicious if I'm away too long. I've insisted that Brick, you, and I meet at the marina early tomorrow morning to discuss Diego's funeral. Chief Ramsey had no objection to that plan.

211

I'm hoping you can be there around eight."

"What about Pablo?"

"Of course we'll include Pablo — if we can locate him."

TWENTY

Early Monday morning I didn't disturb Dolly, knowing she needed some extra rest. We'd discuss last night's accident in more detail later. I tried to make myself believe it was an accident in spite of Threnody's take on it.

I drove to Vexton's marina and parked in a visitor's slot next to Threnody's Caddi. For a few moments I walked along the planked decking in front of the chandlery enjoying the salt taste of the sea air and absorbing the ambience of the area. Crafts of all kinds bobbed in their slips — sailboats, cruisers, runabouts. Two captains shouted greetings to each other, revved their motors, and managed no-wake exits toward open water in spite of their obvious eagerness to bait their hooks and wet their lines. The stench of gasoline hung in the air.

Brick's crayon-shaped dock pilings discouraged most water birds from perching.

Today I smiled as three pelicans and two gulls left their calling cards on the sterns and motors of docked boats while they perched nearby waiting for handouts.

After squinting into the glare of sun on sea, it relieved my eyes to step into the dimness inside the chandlery. Where was everyone? I could have rung the bell for attention, but instead I speared a hotdog from the countertop mini-grill, wrapped it in a bun, added mustard. Hotdogs might be falling off the tip of nutritionists' pyramid of healthful foods, but I felt no guilt while I enjoyed the salty spiciness of one of my favorite foods.

"Morning, Rafa," Threnody called, stepping from a doorway at the back of the store. "We're going to meet here in Brick's office."

"May I bring you a hotdog?" I pointed to the grill.

"No thanks. My stomach balks at hotdogs before noon."

"But mine doesn't." Brick grinned and stepped onto the selling floor. "Bring me one, okay? Catsup, please. No mustard."

I wondered if anyone ever disobeyed Brick's commands. I laid my hotdog on a napkin beside the grill while I fixed one for him and carried it into his office.

"Thanks, babe."

Stepping into Brick's office was like stepping back in time. Posters from past decades decorated the walls. The seventies? The eighties? *Star Wars. Arthur. Casa Blanca.*

"Have you learned when the ME and the police will release Diego's body?" I asked, pulling my thoughts to the present.

"Probably sometime today," Brick said. "I told both the police and the medical examiner I'd claim the body and pay any fees involved."

"So shall we plan the funeral for tomorrow?" Threnody asked. "Tuesday? Maybe tomorrow afternoon?"

"The sooner the better," Brick said.

"What mortuary will handle the service?" I asked. "We'll have to schedule a time that suits the mortuary. A time and a place."

"I'll check the mortuaries," Threnody offered. "I think Tisdale's has a crematory. We'd want that, wouldn't we?"

"I think so," I said. "Maybe we should ask Pablo about that."

"Only if he drops around," Brick said. "I know of no way to reach him this morning. Get prices as well as availability, Threnody."

"Of course." Threnody grabbed a telephone directory and turned to the yellow pages. "Maybe a mortuary will offer a chapel for their services. Or do you think we should hold the service in a church? Diego was Catholic, wasn't he?"

"I wonder how big the crowd will be," I said. "Diego may not have had many family members in this country, but he had lots of friends from Key Largo to Key West."

"And there'll be the curious," Brick said. "Either of you ever attended services for a homicide victim? Unless we plan private services, some people may attend out of curiosity."

"Don't think Diego would have wanted private services," Threnody said. "He doted on his friends and acquaintances. I suggest an open funeral in a large church for his service."

"St. Paul's, perhaps?" Brick asked. "How cool would that be?"

"That's Episcopal, not Catholic."

"May I offer a suggestion?"

We all looked up, startled, when Pablo spoke from the doorway. Brick rose from behind his desk, but Threnody and I remained seated.

"Come in, Pablo." Brick pulled up another chair, easing it between Threnody and me. "We're planning Diego's funeral. Of course, if you want to take over, you're more than welcome to do so."

Pablo remained standing behind the chair Brick offered. "Thank you. I don't want to take over the planning of Dad's ceremony, but I'd like to be a part of that planning. Dad and I had been estranged recently, but . . . but . . ."

Pablo's eyes grew moist and I thought he might break down, but Brick came to his rescue.

"We understand, Pablo. We understand. Threnody and I certainly know how difficult it is for parents and children always to be in agreement, to keep their relationship on an even keel."

"We're glad you showed up last night at the Frangi and approached us here this morning." Threnody scooted her chair back to make more room for Pablo should he decide to sit beside us.

Pablo eased into the chair, and Threnody continued speaking.

"We're pleased to have your input on planning Diego's service. We had tentatively decided to hold it tomorrow afternoon. If we call the *Citizen* today we may be able to get an announcement in tomorrow's paper. Of course, we'll arrange for radio and TV announcements. We'd like your input on the place for the service as well as for the burial spot."

"Care to share your feelings?" I asked. "Under the circumstances, I feel sure you and Diego never discussed these matters."

"Right. Never."

"So what do you suggest?" Brick sat again behind his desk. "Threnody mentioned the Tisdale Mortuary."

"That'd be fine with me." Pablo leaned forward in his chair. "Dad was never much for attending church, so I'd suggest an outdoor service."

"Do you have a location in mind?" Brick asked.

"When I was a child, Dad and I spent many pleasant times in Bayview Park. We called it Jose Marti Park because it's the place where Marti organized revolutionists to help defeat Spain's hold on our homeland. Maybe we could arrange an outdoor service at Bayview."

"Sounds like a good idea," Threnody agreed. "We could check out that plan with the proper officials. Since Diego served as a councilman, our getting permission to use the park should be no problem. Would you like to go with me to make those arrangements?"

"Yes. I would like that, and maybe we can also discuss plans for some music. Would you sing, Threnody? Dad and I always liked to hear your voice. Would you do 'Amazing Grace'? That was one of the few hymns Dad knew."

"I would feel honored to sing," Threnody said. "Perhaps we can arrange for a portable organ or piano and a pianist to play in the background before and after the service."

"And the burial?" Brick asked. "If you go along with the cremation plan, we could scatter Diego's ashes in a place of your choosing, Pablo. Perhaps at sea?"

Pablo shook his head. "After our escape from Mariel, Dad's never been fond of the ocean. I think he'd like to be buried in the Key West cemetery. It's another spot we frequently visited when I was a child. Strange place to take a kid, right? Maybe. Maybe not. Dad liked to study the inscriptions and the art on the tombstones. That cemetery's still in use, isn't it?"

"Yes," Brick said. "I'm sure it is."

"So let's see if we can buy a burial plot there. Some people think a burial at sea has an ethereal appeal, even a glamorous appeal. But I've never felt that way. I'd like to see him laid to rest in a spot where I could place a hibiscus blossom on his grave marker now and then."

Brick stood. "So why don't you and Threnody secure a mortuary and get permission to hold the service in a secluded area at Bayview? Due to Diego's Cuban heritage, we should have no trouble with the authorities in control of the park."

"That's fine with me." Pablo looked at Threnody, who nodded in agreement.

"Pablo, I suggest that I go to the cemetery officials and make arrangements for burial there," Brick said. "As a respected business-man, I think they'll agree to sell me a suitable plot at a reasonable price. Rafa, why don't you join me? Two business people may get a better deal than one."

"I have plans for the morning, Brick, and I know you'll be able to make the necessary arrangements at the cemetery."

Brick shrugged and nodded in silent agreement.

I didn't care to bargain over the price of a burial plot, nor did I care to join Brick. No way did I intend to fall into the category of one of the "ladies Brick had an eye for." I owed that to myself and to my covert partnership with Threnody.

I left Brick's office glad to hurry back to my car, but was surprised to see Kane sitting on the passenger side waiting for me. We exchanged a deep kiss before I spoke.

"Great to see you here, and I hope nothing's wrong at *The Buccaneer*."

"Nothing wrong that I know of." Kane grinned. "But there's a murderer at large. Remember? I like knowing where you are and that you're safe. Hope you don't mind that I thumbed a ride over. Figured you'd be here."

"Come on, Kane! I won't have you playing protector. Makes me nervous."

"And your planning to investigate Diego's murder makes me nervous. Very nervous."

To tell him I wasn't going to investigate would be a lie. To tell him I would be circumspect in my investigating would break my promise to Threnody. I chose my words carefully.

"We all need to do whatever we can to bring Diego's killer to justice."

"Leave it to the police, Rafa. You could blackball yourself and your future career in Key West by nosing into this case."

"We've been over this before. Discussion closed." I started the car.

"Where are you going now?"

"Going to drive by Bayview Park. Pablo suggested we hold Diego's service there. I'm not totally sure where it is."

"Hang a left out of the marina and you're headed right toward it. It's on the corner of Truman Avenue and Jose Marti Drive. A

221

beautiful area. Pablo's made a good choice. Look!"

I looked, but not at Bayview Park. The small parking area at a tourist information office had an empty slot and I pulled into it. Bayview Park lay half a block or so behind us, and we stepped from the car for a better look at the vast expanse of grass bordered by palms and seagrape trees. A small monument stood in the distance, but we couldn't see it clearly. Perhaps a likeness of Jose Marti, I guessed. Three boys ran across the grass flying kites until one of them fell, lay still for a moment before he struggled to his knees, then lay down again.

"Look, Kane. He's hurt. But no. He's getting up. Guess he didn't break any bones. Probably turned his ankle."

"Maybe stepped into an owl's burrow. Guess he's okay. He's chasing after his friends. Didn't even lose hold of his kite string."

"Burrowing owls? Never heard of that before. Florida owls don't live in trees?"

"Some do. Some don't. Many times conservationists rope off areas where the owls live in the ground — especially if they have young."

"And when do they have young?"

"I don't have the statistics on that. Want

to look it up? The city might refuse to let anyone schedule a funeral in the park if it's going to disturb the owls."

"That's not my problem. Pablo and Threnody were going to try to make arrangements to use the park — or at least some area of the park. Brick's to arrange for a burial plot at the cemetery."

"And what was your assignment?"

"I don't have one. I planned to return to the hotel, check on Dolly, and see if everything's going smoothly at the Frangi."

"Expecting trouble?"

"No. But I wanted to make sure Dolly's okay after the accident last night. Want me to drive you to your boat?"

"No, thanks. Just let me out at the next corner. I'll run into Fausto's for a few groceries, then I'll jog on to *The Buccaneer.*"

"You'll have things to carry. I'll wait and drive you to your boat slip."

"Thanks, Rafa, but not this time."

I let him out at Fausto's and drove on to the hotel.

TWENTY-ONE

I parked in my usual place behind the hotel. Sun sparkled on a few drops of dew still clinging to the scarlet poinsettia plants that ringed the fence around the pool. A coconut thudded to the ground near the gate, and another splashed into the pool. The lingering aroma of frying bacon that wafted from the hotel kitchen reached me as I left my car. Walking to poolside, I grabbed a dip net and fished the coconut from the pool and carried it to a trash can before I took the elevator upstairs to my suite.

"Dolly? Dolly, are you ready for some breakfast?" Crossing the carpet to the guestroom, I rapped lightly on the door. No response. I rapped again. "Dolly? Dolly, you okay?"

The door opened so quickly, I stepped back in surprise.

"I'm up, Rafa. And I'm okay. But we need to talk."

I peeked inside my guestroom. The bed lay in a tumble of pillows and sheets. It looked as if she might have thrashed about all night. But she was up and dressed in the silk jumpsuit I'd laid out for her.

"Sorry if I've overslept a bit this morning."

"You deserved to sleep in this morning after what happened last night. I didn't come to hurry you back to work. I came to check to see if you're okay."

"I'm fine. Skin's a little red in spots, but no pain. None at all."

"Let's see your hair. How's it look?"

Dolly pulled a hairbrush from the pocket of the jumpsuit and ran it through her hair.

"Hair's okay. I had to trim off a few scorched ends here and there, but for the most part I don't think anyone can tell."

I motioned toward a bedside recliner, but Dolly remained standing.

"Your upper arms. Push up your sleeves. Let's see all of your arms. I hope there aren't any blisters."

"No blisters. None at all. I tell you, you're a good nurse, Rafa. My elbows are a bit tender to the touch, but I massaged lotion on them and I'm feeling fine."

"I'm very relieved about that, but perhaps you should see a doctor to be sure everything's all right — no chance of any infection. I could call my doc. I'm sure his receptionist would put you on fast forward to see him if I asked."

"No doctor, thank you. My blouse and bra are ruined, but I have extras and I can order replacements from Burdine's in Miami. I know they carry my brand."

"Please be sure to send me the bill. I know Mother carries fire insurance. Now that it's daylight, I'll take a careful look around the Frangi. There may be some fire or smoke damage that we overlooked last night."

"I'll go with you and help you inspect. You're right. In all the excitement, we might have overlooked some destruction."

I led the way from my guest room and Dolly followed. The Frangi smelled of smoke, and I raised the side curtains to allow more air to circulate. After we made a thorough inspection, we sat at one of the glass-topped tables.

"The fire was an accident, wasn't it, Dolly?" I stared into her face, forcing her to meet my gaze.

"Why, Rafa! Of course it was an accident. What else could it have been? I was trying to help Brick extinguish the torches and I got too close to one of the windswept flames. Nobody was to blame. Unless you

226

blame me for carelessness."

"Nobody is blaming you. Nobody."

"Maybe Threnody. I saw her scowl at me. I heard you tell her to get something in the kitchen, but she didn't move. She seemed angry and she stood there scowling."

"I doubt that you really remember that. How could you recall or even notice such a small thing when your hair was about to go up in flames?"

"I can't answer that. People remember strange things in times of crisis, and I do remember Threnody scowling. Sometimes I think she doesn't like me."

"She wouldn't hire you to help clean their mansion if she didn't like you and your work." I wanted to tell her that she might make brownie points with Threnody if she stopped flirting with Brick. But now was no time for that.

"Dolly, I'm glad — relieved that you're okay. If you need more rest, do take the day off. I feel sure the Vextons will agree to that, too."

"I'll work as usual."

I tried to change the subject. "Have you made any decision about your poem? You going to buy some copies of the vanity book?"

"I haven't decided yet. If everyone knows

about the kind of a scam that makes writers think they're professional when they're not, I might say no. I don't want people laughing at me."

"I think that would be a good decision, Rafa. If you keep writing and submitting your poems, they will find their place in legitimate venues. I like your poems — especially the ones about cats."

"Thank you, Rafa. I appreciate knowing that. But enough about me. What about Diego's murder? Police have anything new to say this morning?"

"All Diego's friends are 'people of interest' at this point. Some weren't at our morning meeting." I told her about the tentative funeral plans.

Dolly looked at the floor and spoke softly. "There's something I didn't tell Chief Ramsey at yesterday morning's meeting."

"What's that?" I tried for a casual tone, but now I held my breath.

"I know I'm a person of special interest because I was the last one to see Diego alive."

"The chief knows that. What didn't you tell him?"

"I didn't tell him that before I saw Diego that evening, I heard him and Pablo arguing."

"Where were they?"

"They were inside the chandlery, but their voices carried to me. Very loud. It would have been hard not to have heard them. It surprised me because at that time I didn't know Pablo was back on-island."

"What was their argument about?"

"Money. Their talk didn't make a lot of sense to me."

"You sure it was Diego and Pablo talking?"

"I'm positive I heard Diego and Pablo arguing. Diego told Pablo he'd given him enough money. Told him it was time he began looking for a job, began supporting himself instead of hanging out with a bunch of beach bums."

"I'm sure Diego's words weren't what Pablo wanted to hear."

"Right. Pablo shouted that he would choose his own friends. That he didn't need Diego's help. He shouted that he'd hang out where he chose to hang out, that he didn't need Diego's input on that, either."

"What then? Did you actually see Pablo?"

"Yes. Just a glimpse of him. I didn't let on that I'd heard the argument because I couldn't see either of them as they spoke, but I heard Pablo walk from the chandlery. You know how shoes scrape on sand. I heard him, but I didn't turn to look. And I didn't let on that I'd seen him. From the corner of my eye, I saw Pablo."

I smiled. "Not the right time then to make your presence known."

"Right. I went on sipping tea and musing about the poem I wanted to write. I don't believe either Pablo or Diego saw me, and I think their argument spoiled my concentration."

"You're probably right. But why didn't you tell Chief Ramsey about that?"

"I guess I didn't tell because Pablo scares me."

"Intentionally scares you? I mean . . . I mean, do you think he might have killed Diego?"

"I'm not pointing a finger at anyone, Rafa. Nobody. But Pablo always has scared me. He never smiles. I like to smile at people because most of them smile back. But Pablo? No. When I've tried smiling at him, he looks past me as if he hasn't even seen me. I always wonder why he's so grim."

"You're more afraid of him since Diego's death?"

"Right. I didn't want to tell everyone in the chief's office I'd heard the argument. Didn't want Pablo to find out. Didn't relish giving him reason to take out one of his death wishes on me."

"This story will come out sooner or later. You might want to consider making it sooner by going to Chief Ramsey and telling him what you've just told me."

Dolly said nothing, but she shook her head and her eyes said, "I don't think so."

TWENTY-TWO

"Rafa? Rafa? Are you home?" Threnody's voice on the intercom snapped me to attention. "Got good news."

"I'll be right down, Threnody. We need to talk."

"I'll be out front in the Caddi."

Minutes later, even with her convertible top down, the scent of gardenia traveled with her. Her smile told me of her morning's success with Pablo.

"I've brought sustenance, Rafa." She held up a box from Pier House. "Got time for a mushroom salad? Portabello with garlic and feta cheese?"

"Wonderful, Threnody. Why don't we drive to Mallory and enjoy a picnic beside the sea?"

"My thoughts exactly."

The dock and the harbor were close by and Threnody wove through the heavy midday traffic, turning onto the bricked alleyway that led to the parking lot. At this time of day we had our choice of parking places. An on-shore breeze blew in from the Gulf and we found a bench close to The Wreckers sculpture and began enjoying both the breeze, sun glinting on sea, and our salads.

"Threnody, the blended flavors of portabello, feta cheese, and garlic sum up my favorite taste of Key West."

"I agree — until I remember how much I love grouper fillets and coconut shrimp. But let me tell you about my morning. I talked to the owner at Tisdale Mortuary, and by hiring extra workers Mr. Tisdale managed to schedule Diego's outdoor service at mid-afternoon tomorrow — Tuesday."

"That's good. I have my cell phone with me. If we call right away, maybe we'll be in time to get a notice in tomorrow morning's *Citizen.* And what about Bayview Park?"

"Pablo can turn on the charm when he wants to. Too bad he doesn't want to more often. He talked to the mayor and received permission to schedule Diego's service at Bayview. He chose a secluded place behind the Jose Marti statue with its flags and fern plantings and far from the tennis courts and the Truman Avenue traffic."

I followed a bite of salad with a sip of pina

colada Threnody had included in her lunch box.

"Pablo had the mayor in his pocket the moment he mentioned Diego's name and their father–son relationship. Three o'clock. No time limit. And under the special circumstances, no charge."

"That's great news, Threnody. Hope Brick had success at the cemetery. Wish we knew for sure."

"Guess we can do the newspaper notice without including the burial information. It would be embarrassing to mention the cemetery and find out later that a plot won't be available."

"Should we make the call to the newspaper right now? Or maybe it'd be more effective if we drove to their office and made our request eyeball to eyeball."

Threnody laughed. "I'm for that. The office is only a few blocks from here on North Roosevelt."

"Everything's only a few blocks away on this rock. That's another one of my favorite things about Key West."

We stuffed our picnic leavings into the Pier House box, deposited it in a trash barrel, and left the dock. When we reached the *Citizen* office, we both went inside where low ceilings captured and held the scent of newsprint and fresh ink. Three women sat at desks, their eyes focused on computer screens. None looked up until Threnody cleared her throat and coughed.

One plump woman wearing a rust-colored tank top and a gathered-at-the-waist skirt rose, stepped toward the counter that separated us, and listened to our plea. Her name tag said Dot Dumple.

"You expect to get this notice in tomorrow morning's paper? Such material should have been in our hands yesterday afternoon at the very latest." Dumpling scowled, spoiling the sweet image she first projected.

"Surely you can make an exception for this special funeral," Threnody said. "Unusual circumstances. A homicide victim. We made arrangements for his service as soon as we could. Had to get the go-ahead from the police and the medical examiner before we approached the mortuary people and the Bayview Park official — the mayor."

"I'll see what I can do," Dumpling said. "One moment, please."

As she turned to leave us, Threnody sighed and called after her. "We're willing to pay a late fee. The notice won't be of interest to anyone on Wednesday."

We paced the waiting area, listening to the hum of the AC and the distant clatter of a typewriter. At last Dumpling returned.

"We'll get it in for you tomorrow. No late fee necessary. Shall I write the details for you or do you want to do it yourself?"

"Please do it for us." Threnody jotted the facts on a green sticky note Dumpling offered. "And send any bill to Brick Vexton at the Daiquiri Dock Marina."

"And thank you so much," I added. "We're most appreciative." We turned to leave the office when Dumpling called to us.

"Ladies?"

Threnody turned to face her. "Yes? Is there something else you need?"

"What about a more detailed obit? We might not get it in tomorrow, but we could get it in on Wednesday. For sure."

Threnody and I stared at each other for a moment. "We haven't had time to write the obituary yet," I said. "We'll work on it and get it to you soon."

"Thank you," Dumpling called. "Dot Dumple. That's my name in case you want to call the obit in. Or you can email me, ddumple@aol.com."

"Thank you," I called over my shoulder as we left the office. "We'll be in touch."

"Pablo will be in touch," Threnody corrected. "He knows more about Diego's past life, his family, than either of us. Suppose he can write?"

"I'm guessing he can. But will he? That's the question."

"Okay, I appoint you, Rafa Blue, a committee of one, to get an obit from him."

"Guess I can't refuse. I'll talk to him tonight — if he shows up. Otherwise, I don't know how to get in touch with him."

Threnody drove me back to the hotel and then went on to take care of the small details connected with Diego's service. I sometimes enjoy working outdoors, and today a few palm branches had fallen near the entryway and I pulled them to the trash can near the alley, dropping them there for the yard man to break into short segments and fill the can for pickup.

Twice as I worked, I saw Detective Lyon drive past the hotel. I didn't wave to him, nor he to me. It shouldn't have surprised me that the police placed The Blue Mermaid under surveillance, but I thought they could have been more subtle. Lyon drove an unmarked Crown Victoria that almost shouted "here-come-de-cops."

At midafternoon I was still thinking about asking Pablo to write Diego's obituary when the phone rang and I picked up.

"Hello?" No response. "Hello? Rafa Blue

speaking." Still no response. I banged the receiver into its cradle, almost sure now that someone was trying to frighten me — maybe the same person who caused my balcony fall. When Kane stopped by a few minutes later, I said nothing about the dead-line calls. We sat beside the pool discussing Diego's funeral arrangements. Kane waved to Detective Lyon on another of his passes by the pool. Lyon didn't return his wave.

"Kane, let's walk to the graveyard. I want to see the burial spot Brick chose for Diego. It's such a personal thing. What if Pablo doesn't like it? Do you suppose he could change it at the last minute?"

Kane hesitated. "You been to the graveyard before?"

"Of course I've been there — but not for ages. Guess I've never had reason to go there. Dad was buried at sea."

"The locals refer to it euphemistically as the Cemetery. It's not my favorite place, but your wish is my command. Let's go." He gave a short laugh. "It bothers me that all the burial vaults are above ground. Back home, we bury people in the ground."

"Some visiting dignitary once called the above-ground vaults white-washed hope chests." I stepped into the hotel lobby and picked up a tourist guide to the cemetery and handed it to Kane.

He shuddered and then glanced at the brochure. "Guess the place is open daily — at least from sunrise to sunset, according to the info here." Leaving the hotel, we headed toward Angela Street at the edge of Old Town, a street little more than a one-way trail in places. Kane read snatches from the brochure.

"Says here that city officials established the cemetery in eighteen-forty-seven. Hmmm. I've seen graves that date before that."

"How can that be?"

He pointed to an inside page in the brochure. "The original graveyard was closer to the lighthouse, but city fathers moved it to its present location years ago when a hurricane passed through, disinterring many graves. Now, all the bones rest in above-ground vaults."

We reached the graveyard almost before I realized it. White hot. Treeless. Many flowering shrubs. "Egrets, Kane. They're drifting about among the vaults like white ghosts." I took his hand as a chill feathered along my spine.

"You think *this* is spooky! You should pass by here at twilight when mosquito hawks swoop and dive for their suppers. Their *piskk-piskk* chirps can curdle your blood."

We stopped to read the epitaphs on several gravestones. Most said "Beloved Mother" or "Always in our hearts." Kane pointed to one engraving that said, "I told you I was sick."

I hesitated over another man's stone. "Always dreamed of being someone. Still dreaming." I wondered if he had been a writer. I could identify with his thought.

"Wonder where the caretaker is." I inched closer to Kane.

"We should have called ahead if you expected to talk to him."

"I did jot down his phone number and I have my cell phone. If we could talk to him right now, maybe he could direct us to the spot Brick chose for Diego's cremains."

"Go ahead and give it a try, Rafa. If he keeps regular office hours, he should still be on duty."

I pulled my cell and the caretaker's number from my pocket and keyed in the digits. The phone rang only twice before he spoke.

"Key West Cemetery. Adrian Diaz speaking."

"Rafa Blue here, Mr. Diaz. I'm inquiring about the location of the burial plot Brick Vexton chose this morning for Diego Casterrano. I'm at the cemetery now and I'd like to see the burial place if that's possible."

There was a brief pause before Adrian Diaz cleared his throat and spoke again. "Miss Blue, there must be some mistake. I'm acquainted with Brick Vexton, but I haven't talked with him any time lately, and certainly not today."

"He's made no burial arrangements?"

"No, ma'am. None. Perhaps he changed his mind and chose some other cemetery. However, we have several plots available should he call me today."

"Thank you, sir. I'm sorry to have bothered you."

"No *problemo.*"

Mr. Diaz broke our connection and I stood looking at Kane dumbfounded. "I wonder what changed Brick's plans. At our meeting this morning, Pablo suggested having the burial here and we all agreed. But maybe Pablo changed his mind. He might not have seen the place since childhood days. Perhaps he came to look it over and found that it didn't seem suitable to him."

"Wonder if Pablo hired a band to play the dead home."

"Kane! Well, I guess people still do that sort of thing. I've read about it in the paper."

"Only sometimes. I borrowed a snare and

241

played with a funeral band a couple months ago."

"Pablo didn't say anything about a funeral band. But he did agree to let Brick make burial arrangements."

"Guess everyone knew that except Adrian Diaz." Kane grabbed my hand. "Let's get out of here, Rafa. The sun's dropping low and I've always thought this's one creepy place."

I followed Kane down Palm Avenue that bisected the cemetery and once outside the gates, we hurried toward The Blue Mermaid.

Twenty-Three

"Kane, why do you suppose Brick failed to secure a burial place? I wish now I'd insisted on coming here with him."

"He invited you to do that?"

"Well, yes. But I didn't want to."

"Don't think it's anything to worry about. Brick will find a burial spot somewhere that pleases him and that would have pleased Diego."

"Don't understand his thinking. According to Mr. Diaz, there are plots available for purchase."

Kane shrugged. "Maybe he thought that laying Diego to rest in this graveyard would make his grave all too visible at this time."

"And we're supposed to keep him invisible? Be real, Kane."

"No matter who dies, curiosity seekers want an inside scoop on the details of the death. When the deceased's a homicide victim, it makes some people even more curious."

I turned toward the hotel. "I've read that criminals sometimes return to the scene of their crime. And later, maybe even to the burial place of their victim."

"I'm guessing the police will probably be scrutinizing the crowd at Diego's services tomorrow."

"I'll be doing the same thing, Kane. Won't you? Maybe all the 'people of interest' will be on the alert."

"If the killer attends the funeral, I think he'd be so nervous he'd throw up, or maybe jump up and leave. Think that's what I'd do — or want to do."

"Don't think either of those things will happen. Whoever killed Diego is too tough-minded to show any reaction."

Kane linked his arm through mine as we left the cemetery. We turned our backs on the ghostly egrets still wandering among the burial vaults. Thank goodness we were too early for the mosquito hawks!

"There's another thing that might have changed Pablo's mind about securing a burial plot here," Kane said. "This graveyard gets lots of media publicity — newspapers, magazine articles. Maybe Pablo didn't want to see Diego's vault featured in the next tourist brochure. Not only are those folders available at the welcome center in Old Town, but also in welcome centers from Miami to Key West. And of course they appear in racks at the airports."

"You may be right about that. I wouldn't want my dad's grave featured on a tourist's brochure. But couldn't Pablo sue the brochure company for invasion of privacy?"

"Don't have an answer to that one, but Pablo would have to make that decision." Kane began walking faster and I matched my pace to his, eager to leave the graveyard behind us. "We can quit speculating on Brick's intentions because I'm going to ask him for an explanation tonight when he arrives for work."

When we reached the hotel and went directly to the Frangi, Mama G shouted her usual greeting.

"Hola, amigos!"

"Hola," we responded.

"I arrive early with my sandwich fillings. Will help you make the sandwiches — if need be. Brought chopped eel and caper filling. Brought escargot and feta cheese filling. Brought . . ."

True to form, Mama G spouted orders to everyone within earshot. She reminded me of a mechanical toy someone had wound too tight.

245

"I'm outta here," Kane said. "See you later. Gotta secure my boat for the night and get dressed before I come to work."

"Kane!" Mama G shouted to Kane, who turned to leave. "Need you to taste the fillings."

"Your sandwich fillings are always delicious, Mama G." Kane continued striding toward the elevator. "Save me a ground conch and pickle, okay?"

Mama G's face flushed with pleasure at hearing Kane's compliment, and the elevator door closed behind him before she found presence of mind to call to him again. Pablo arrived just then, distracting her even more.

"Rafa," Pablo said, "I plan to play with the combo tonight if you still want me to."

"Is my band," Mama G said, stepping forward and standing between Pablo and me. "I am band leader you should be asking."

"So I'm asking both of you on bended knee — but remember, I own the trap set." He knelt to emphasize his words. "May I play with the combo tonight?"

"*Si. Si.*" Mama G looked at me. "He be welcome, right?"

"Of course, Mama G and I want you to play, Pablo. Will your presence be a steady thing from now on?"

Pablo hesitated only a moment before he nodded. "Yes. From now on a steady thing. Count on me. You can tell Dolly you won't need her on drums anytime soon. Right now I plan to check over my trap set — see what she may have done to it."

"Dolly Jass take good care of drums," Mama G said. "No need you worry about that. She be a careful person."

Ignoring Mama G's words, Pablo took a step toward his trap set as he patted his shirt pocket. "Need to see if the drum heads are in good condition. I've brought my tuning key in case the heads need to be tightened."

"Good idea," I said. "I don't know much about drum heads, but let me know if you think I can help."

"Thanks, Rafa."

As Pablo stepped onto the bandstand and began tapping on the drum heads, tightening them, and then checking the contents of his music folder, I heard Brick and Threnody arriving in the elevator down the hall. I began planning the questions I'd ask Brick concerning my encounter with Adrian Diaz at the graveyard. But before Brick and Threnody reached the dance floor, Mama G began blowing on her conch shell. No time now to ask anyone anything.

How could she do this to us? I needed to change into evening clothes. Couldn't she see that we wouldn't be ready for guests for an hour or more? Nobody had lit the patio torches, and the sandwiches hadn't been made and arranged on serving plates. We weren't ready to admit patrons. Pablo stepped down from the bandstand, shaking his head and smiling for a change.

"She doesn't get any better, does she?" He nodded toward Mama G, whose face had grown crimson from her blowing efforts. "She says her first number's always 'Row, Row, Row Your Boat,' but she could fool me."

With effort, I kept a straight face. "I don't recognize the tune either, but I guess recognition doesn't matter. It's the wailing noise that helps draw a crowd." I nodded toward the hallway outside the Frangi entrance. Couples, some in poolside cover-ups and others in evening finery, were beginning to arrive. Two women peeked through the entryway, curious to see the source of the weird noise, eager to know what was happening or what was about to happen next.

"I'll light the torches," Brick shouted, barely making himself heard above the eerie clamor of Mama G's conch shell. Pablo stepped back on the bandstand and rechecked his trap set, tightening a couple more snare drum heads before he stepped onto the dance floor and turned to help Brick. No time to talk with Brick now. I wanted his undivided attention when I instigated our conversation. I seized the moment to rush to my suite, change into my hostess attire, rush back to the dance floor.

By the time I returned, torch flames like giant-sized party candles undulated toward the sky and for a few moments the smell of lighter fluid hung in the air. Dolly left the kitchenette and her sandwich preparation, but when she saw the flames, she backed away, perhaps remembering last night's fiasco in extinguishing the torches.

Due to the Frangi's impromptu opening and our rush to make sandwiches, greet patrons, and serve refreshments, almost two hours passed before I found a quiet moment to talk to Brick between combo numbers. Was it my imagination, or had he been avoiding me?

"Threnody tells me she and Pablo made the necessary arrangements for Diego's service at Bayview tomorrow afternoon."

Brick nodded and paused while a patron stepped between us to pay for a sandwich and a soda. "I've been checking on things at the chandlery. Jessie's preparing it for a small reception following the service. Had some of the dock hands shove motors and reels of line aside so he could set up chairs and a refreshment table. Don't know how many people might plan on attending."

"How thoughtful of you to offer your place of business. Pablo must be most appreciative."

"Yes. He is. I've also asked one of the dock masters to serve coffee, and Mama G will be supplying sandwiches — pulled pork. I spoke to her and insisted on nothing more exotic. She and I have an agreement about that. No escargot. No pickled conch with capers. Just sandwiches suitable for a quiet and dignified funeral reception."

"Brick, I'm concerned. Kane and I walked to the graveyard this afternoon." I forced myself not to shudder at the memory of the egrets wandering among the vaults. "I talked to Mr. Adrian Diaz, the man in charge of the place. He said nobody made any arrangements with him for Diego's burial plot. What happened to our morning's plan? Did you have a problem?"

"Well, you could see how crowded the graveyard is, Rafa. Mr. Diaz told me there were no plots available at this time."

"You mean the graveyard is totally full? What will the grieving families do in the future?"

"It's only full temporarily," Brick said. "At least they couldn't get a spot ready as soon as tomorrow afternoon."

"What did Pablo and Threnody have to say about that?"

Brick looked across the room at Pablo's trap set, then paused a moment. "I haven't given him that news yet. But not to worry. I talked to Mr. Tisdale at the mortuary. He said they will hold the urn, the ashes, until we decide on the proper place for them. It's a service Tisdale's offers free of charge."

"Then I'll stop worrying. It's something we can take care of later. Glad there's no problem."

Maybe no problem with the funeral service and reception, but I had a problem with Brick's lies. Adrian had said there were plenty of open plots. He said he hadn't talked with Brick Vexton.

Twenty-Four

The evening at the Frangi passed smoothly. Threnody sang "Harbor Lights," the signature opening number before the combo took over, playing sets of five tunes, and then taking a brief break. During one of their intermissions, Pablo motioned me aside — a poor time for me, since the break minutes were times customers wanted to chat with me and ask questions about the hotel and Key West. But Dolly stepped forward to relieve me and Pablo stood aside, letting me lead the way.

When we reached a far corner of the room, he pulled out a chair for me. I sighed, relieved to sit and relax for a few minutes, but Pablo's straight-as-a-fly-rod posture put me on edge.

"What is it, Pablo? Got a problem with your drums?"

"No problem there. I need to talk to you about Brick — and Dad."

"What about them?" I felt wary of anything he might say.

"They were at odds, you know."

I knew Kane's version of the future hotel-management disagreement between Brick and Diego, but I wanted to hear Pablo's version, too. People seldom saw things in exactly the same way.

"Brick wanted to expand the Vexton business." Pablo squirmed a bit, but didn't relax his rigid posture. "He owns some land behind the chandlery, and he wanted to build a hotel. Probably still wants to."

"Seems that could be a good idea," I said. "Key West is growing. There's probably a demand for more tourist rooms — especially for big events like Fantasy Fest and Hemingway Days. Brick may be wise to be looking to the future."

"Brick felt sure that another hotel would do a good business. The problem lay with Dad."

"Diego tried to tell Brick what to do?"

"More like what not to do. Dad's position on the council gave him subtle ways of influencing other council members in matters concerning the ROGO."

"The building permits."

"Right. It can be very difficult to get any kind of a building permit in the Keys unless

253

the council agrees to it. I heard talk about a guy who had to wait several months just to get a permit to build a pine housing for his air conditioner. Got no way of knowing whether that's true, but Brick felt Dad was causing a delay in Brick's name moving up on the ROGO. Brick wanted Jessie to manage the hotel once it was built. Dad wanted to be named manager. That was the problem."

"And you think Brick's feelings may have escalated into a disagreement that led to Diego's murder."

"It's a possibility, Rafa. I wanted you to know this because I'm aware that you're investigating Dad's death and . . ."

"Hold it right there. What makes you think I'm investigating?"

"Don't look so surprised. You're not going to deny it, are you? You, as well as several of Dad's friends, are 'persons of interest' to the police. I see you as the kind of woman who wants to fight crime as well as one who doesn't want to feel the finger of guilt pointed in her direction."

Pablo's words rang with more truth than I wanted to admit. Sometimes the best defense in this case would be an offense — especially in view of Brick's lie. I gave it a try.

"You could be right about bad blood between Diego and Brick over the ROGO and a new hotel, but you must have shared your dad's feelings. A new hotel with Diego in charge would have a trickle-down effect. One day it might drop more dollars into your pocket, right? Perhaps you and Brick also were at odds. Instead of working up a case against Brick, you'd better be watching your own back."

Pablo stood abruptly. Without mentioning any weakness in my logic, he strode back to the bandstand and picked up his drumsticks as Mama G sounded a piano glissando, her signal to start the music again.

To all outward appearances, the rest of the evening passed smoothly. I could only guess at what might be going on in Pablo's mind. Dolly made no offer to help Brick extinguish the patio torches. Pablo and Kane pushed tables and chairs into place before leaving for the night. Of course, Kane had seen Pablo and me talking during an intermission. I knew he must be curious about our conversation, but he asked no questions. I offered no explanation.

The next morning I blinked sleep from my eyes and reached for the ringing telephone on my bedside table.

"It's in, Rafa! It's in!" I recognized Threnody's voice but not the importance of her message.

"What's up, Threnody? Something wrong?"

"Sorry it's so early, but I knew you'd want to know. Diego's funeral notice made it into today's *Citizen*. In addition to that, Brick called the local radio station and we heard the announcer break into the morning news to make a special report on the time and place for the service and the reception this afternoon."

"Tisdale Mortuary is taking care of all the details?"

"Right. They'll have plenty of folding chairs set up, a dais and mike for the minister, and an electric piano for background music."

"It might have been nice to have asked Mama G to play."

"The mortuary furnishes a pianist, but I plan to sing *a capella*. I think that's most effective for an outdoor service, and it eliminates the problem of finding time to rehearse with an accompanist."

"Hope they've assigned us a place where traffic sounds won't drown out your voice."

"They have. I checked it out yesterday afternoon. No problem there. All Brick and I have to do is to be there a half hour or so early to greet the mourners as they arrive. You're welcome to help us with that duty if you care to."

"What will you wear? For once, Dolly's poet's outfit will fit the occasion. But I'm stumped. I seldom wear daytime dresses. Don't think I have any that would be suitable — just casual pants and tees."

"Nothing wrong with casual. Just add a silk scarf and some subtle jewelry."

"Could be okay," I agreed, "but my hotel evening clothes won't do. That's for sure." I sighed. "I won't even consider borrowing a daytime dress from Cherie's collection of Diors and Pradas. No matter what my choice from her closet might be, she'd never let me forget how tasteless it was once she found out. And she'd make it a point to find out. I suppose I could wear something black — maybe a pant suit. I have a couple of those."

Threnody laughed. "Don't get in such a dither. Why don't you come over to my place and we'll choose something in my closet. I'll be glad to lend you an appropriate dress if you decide against a black pant suit."

"You're very kind."

"Sometimes I'm invited to sing at club meetings. I have some daytime dresses that are suitable for any special occasion. You're welcome to borrow one. Can you come on over now? I'll surprise you with a new recipe I made yesterday. Would love to have your opinion while we chat a bit — maybe about your investigation. Then we'll look at the dresses."

"Give me a few minutes, okay?"

I left cleaning instructions for Dolly on the countertop, and twenty minutes later I arrived at the Vexton mansion. Threnody stepped onto the veranda to greet me.

"Come on inside. I hope you like macaroons. That's my new recipe."

"Wonderful. I love macaroons. But Threnody!" I grinned and stifled a laugh. "Have you ever looked closely at this baluster beside the veranda steps?"

Threnody paused to scrutinize the balusters. "What do you mean? I see them everyday, of course."

I pointed at one baluster and stepped back, laughing. "At first I saw only the heart-shaped cutouts in the gingerbread design. Then when I take a closer look, I see whiskey bottle cut-outs set between the hearts."

"Right." Threnody nodded. "I've noticed them. Brick says some carpenter created this baluster during prohibition days. Maybe as a joke. Maybe as an advertisement for his bar. Most people don't take time to notice the bottles. You have an eye for detail — a good thing in an investigator."

I gave a lingering glance at the baluster and then at the graceful brackets decorating the porch columns. "Threnody, some day I'd like to take a walking tour and study Key West's gingerbread-trimmed homes."

"Give me a call and I'll join you. Brick's always been interested in the past and he knows a lot of baluster history. They weren't all designed by ships' carpenters whiling away boring time at sea. Talented wood-workers of the land-oriented variety have always worked in Key West — some still do."

I followed Threnody inside to a glass-topped table in her kitchen that overlooked a small garden of hibiscus bushes, pink, red, gold — and all in bloom. She rapped on the picture window to frighten a small green iguana that sat nibbling on a pink blossom. The creature disappeared into the shrub-bery and I peered after it into the greenery while Threnody prepared to serve our breakfast snack.

She served steaming cups of green tea, then in moments, she returned to the table carrying a silver salver of French-style macaroons in green and lavender. "I made these yesterday — just practicing, but I think they're still edible today."

"Threnody! How beautiful! Tell me about them. I've never seen any like these before."

"Special recipe from a friend in Paris. The lavender ones have a raspberry rose flavor and the green ones — Sicilian pistachio."

I took a nibble from a lavender macaroon, almost hating to spoil its shape. "Delicious as well as beautiful, Threnody. If I were into baking, I'd ask for the recipe."

"Maybe Kane would like to try it. He's a good cook and I know he likes sweets."

We sat for a few minutes enjoying the macaroons and the tea until Threnody leaned forward.

"Rafa, have you discovered anything of interest in your investigation?"

I licked a macaroon crumb from my finger. "Not much time for investigating so far. But I did learn that the type of blue line binding Diego's feet is no longer manufactured for today's market. I checked several chandleries. None carried anything similar."

"Where do you suppose it came from?"

"That's one thing we'll need to find out." I wanted to tell her about the compartment lid on Kane's boat. But no way. At least not yet. I refused to do anything that might point a finger in Kane's direction. We might

need to learn more about the former owners of *The Buccaneer,* but I could think of
no logical reason to give Threnody for doing that. But if that rope on Kane's boat
had been there since he bought the boat, a
former owner might be able to reveal more
about its source. If one of the former owners lived on Big Pine Key, maybe another
one might live somewhere in Key West.

"Last night Pablo told me about the hard
feelings between Brick and Diego — the
hotel idea, the ROGO."

Threnody nodded. "I know about that.
Guess that's one reason I want you to
investigate — to help keep Brick in the
clear."

"I think we need to talk personally to each
'person of interest' and get more in-depth
information on their alibis. I can do that,
but I'll have to work carefully in order to
avoid everyone knowing we're investigating."

"We?" Threnody raised an eyebrow.

"Yes, we. I want you to help me however
you can."

We had almost finished our macaroons
and tea before Threnody spoke again. "Let's
forget investigating for now. Dress-up time."

I helped carry our dishes to the dishwasher, then followed her up a curving

staircase to a bedroom where she had laid out three dresses for my inspection.

"We're about the same size, Rafa, except for you being a little taller. I think any of the three will fit you, so take your choice. Better try them on."

After a half hour or so of trying on the dresses, I chose one, plainly designed and forest green in color. Threnody smiled and slipped a garment bag over the dress.

"Redheads always choose green, don't they?"

"It's ingrained into us in childhood."

Taking the garment bag, I headed downstairs and to my car, with Threnody following me to the veranda and waving farewell. After I turned from the Vextons' lane onto Eaton Street, I noticed Detective Lyon behind me in his unmarked car.

TWENTY-FIVE

Although I didn't need groceries, I stopped at Fausto's and picked up some coffee. That must have put Lyon off course. Or maybe he hadn't been following me. Could have been my imagination. I drove around Old Town for several minutes until I was sure I didn't have a tail. Back at the hotel, I hurried to my suite with my borrowed dress. Dolly turned off the vacuum and picked up a dust cloth when I stepped inside.

"Any calls?" I asked.

"Just one." She unplugged the vacuum and wrapped its cord around the handle. "Kane called just a few minutes ago. I offered to take a message, but he declined. Didn't say what he wanted."

"Thanks. I'll give him a call after I hang up Threnody's dress. Want to see?" Dolly nodded, and I removed the garment bag and showed her the plain green shift. "I have the string of pearls and the drop earrings

Daddy gave me years ago, so I guess that solves the problem of what to wear to the funeral."

I shoved some extra clothes Kane kept at my place farther to one end of my closet before hanging Threnody's dress beside them. When Dolly went to Cherie's suite to work, I phoned Kane. "Dolly said you called."

"Right." Kane's voice always sounds low and sexy over the telephone. I like that in a man, and I waited for him to continue. "Want to do lunch? Margaritaville?"

"Thanks, Kane, but not today. Have a few details to attend to around here before Diego's service this afternoon. Maybe another day."

"Fine. Just thought you might need something to do to take your mind off the funeral for a few minutes."

"Very thoughtful of you, Kane. I appreciate the invite. And I have a question for you." Why had I said that? Was I really ready to ask questions?

"So give. What do you need to know?"

"What were the names of the guys who owned your boat before you bought it? I know you told me, but I can't remember them now."

"Sure. Let's see. There was the guy who

went back to Iowa, then Red Chipper. And before him, Snipe Gross, who bought it from Bucky Varnum. But what's the deal? Why the sudden interest in former boat owners?"

"I have my reasons, but I don't want to talk too much about them over the phone right now."

"Think your line might be bugged?"

"Who knows? I'm not sure my fall from the balcony was an accident, and I'm taking no chances on the security of my phone line. Maybe I'll take you up on that lunch invitation after all. But let's do Margaritaville when fewer tourists are on-island. There's a big cruise ship docking today and Duval Street restaurants will be overflowing. Why don't I pick up sandwiches and sodas? How about a lunch on the beach?"

"Fine with me."

"I'll stop by for you in a few minutes, okay?"

"Okay. Now you've really aroused my curiosity."

"Ten minutes, okay?"

"You got it."

Kane was waiting on the dock when I arrived. Leaving *The Buccaneer* bobbing on the blue-green water, I drove us to Smather's. We found a metered parking place and I bought hotdogs and sodas from a vendor parked at the curbing. After we climbed a short flight of stairs to the sand, Kane helped me spread a blanket near a volleyball court that wasn't in use.

"Okay, so what's too important to discuss over the phone?" Kane bit into his hotdog and rolled his eyes in pleasure.

For a moment I hesitated, then I spoke softly. "Kane, I know you don't want me to investigate Diego's death, but you know I'm going to."

"Glad you're ready to be upfront about it."

"In addition to investigating, I'm going to ask for your help and tell you why I needed the names of those former boat owners."

"Give."

I took a big swallow of soda before I began. "You remember the line that some-one tied to Diego's feet? Blue line."

"Hmmm. Of course. Hadn't thought any more about it. What's your thinking? I didn't see anything unusual about it."

"I think it's the same kind of line that's on the compartment lid under the mattress in your bunkhouse. Chief Ramsey let me take a snip of the line binding Diego's feet. I showed it to some boat supply stores here on the island and learned that such line hasn't been available for a couple of decades. An old man named George who runs a tackle shop told me that, and I think he knows what he's talking about."

"That bunkhouse compartment was on the boat when I bought it. Any of the former owners might have put it there."

"We need to learn more about that line. One of those former owners might have the information we need. Once we find out where that line came from, we may be able to locate more of it. And that could put us closer to finding the killer."

"And maybe put you closer to getting into big trouble. Forget it, Rafa."

I pretended not to hear his comment. "Will you help me find Red Chipper? I think you said he lives on up the highway on Big Pine Key."

Kane hesitated, making me uncomfortable. What if he refused to help?

"That's a long shot. A very long shot."

"Kane, you're a person of interest to the police. You've written several opinion-page letters about your working waters disagreement with Diego and the county officials. If the police go snooping around on your boat, they might notice that under-the-mattress compartment and see the blue line."

Kane grinned and finished his hotdog. "So

you're going to protect me from myself by finding the killer before the police search my boat."

"Something like that," I admitted. "It's the only plan I can think of for starters."

"Rafa?" The question in his voice made me look directly into his eyes. "Rafa, you don't think I killed Diego, do you?"

"Of course not. No way." My voice held more certainty than I felt. Not Kane. Not the man I loved. I believed Kane innocent, but under the circumstances, I needed to prove his innocence to myself and to the world before I'd feel completely sure.

"Rafa, a person is innocent until proven guilty in a court of law."

"That sounds good, but under our legal system, sometimes people don't really believe that. You have a better chance of avoiding prison if you can prove yourself not guilty."

Kane stood, tapped his wristwatch. "We'd better be going. By the time we dress and drive to Bayview, it'll be time for you and the Vextons to greet the mourners."

"You'll help me investigate, won't you?" I asked as I folded our blanket.

"Maybe if I say no, you'll give it up and let the police do their thing."

"Don't count on it. I'll take you back to

your boat now. But do think about what I've said."

"How about picking me up later? I don't want to arrive at a funeral in a work truck."

"Sure. Will do. Dolly might want a ride, too. Doubt if she'll want to pedal her bike to a funeral. But then you never know."

"She'll probably write a poem about it."

TWENTY-SIX

Kane and I ended our impromptu picnic at odds with each other. I drove him to *The Buccaneer* with not only his denial of help but also with his warning about the dangers of my intrusion into the police investigation. On the way to the hotel, my thoughts whirled. Now, more than ever, I wanted to investigate Diego's death. I needed to prove to myself that Kane was innocent.

Threnody had given me a retainer and wanted to help. It irritated me that Kane wanted me to keep my distance from any investigation on my part. Was he worried about my safety and my future as a writer, or was he concerned that what I might learn would lead the police to him? The police had given me a snip of blue line to work with. Surely they have guessed that all the "persons of interest" were in various ways involved in their own covert investigations.

"Want to ride to Bayview Park with me?"

I called to Dolly who was leaving the hotel as I arrived.

"Yes." Dolly grinned at me. "No bike ride today. I planned to take a Maxi-taxi, so thanks for your offer."

I looked at my watch. "Let's leave in a half hour or so. Promised Kane to give him a lift, too."

I showered then ran a brush through my hair that tended to kink in all directions if I didn't tame it with styling gel and hairspray. Threnody's shift brought out the green in my eyes and I never objected to that. The dress must have been long on Threnody, but on me it fell at knee level. I added my pearl necklace and earrings then slipped on white sandals.

Onward. A glance at the Prius told me Dolly already sat waiting for me in the back seat. Once underway, I felt like a cabbie driving a fare until we reached the dock and Kane dropped onto the passenger seat beside me. He gave me a wolf whistle and my face grew hot.

"Nice rag, Rafa."

I grinned, trying to forget our differences for the time being. I didn't bother to tell him the dress was a loaner from Threnody. For a few moments on Duval Street, a trio of moped riders traveling three abreast cut ahead of us, forcing us to follow at their speed for a few blocks before a cop put an end to their game. They then rode in single file, laughing at us when they turned the next corner. Once on a clear route to Bay-view, we drove several blocks before we turned and headed toward the visitor's parking lot.

"Wow!" Dolly exclaimed. "Look at that white canopy. Tisdale's must not have noticed there's not a cloud in the sky."

"Guess it's to shade us from the sun." I parked beside Threnody's Caddi, locked my car, and we walked toward the canopy.

"Looks as if the mortuary workers have done a good job," Kane said. "Dais for the minister, plenty of chairs, an electric piano and a piano bench."

"Threnody told me she planned to sing *a capella*." I noted the white wicker table bearing a ceramic urn decorated in swirling seascape shades of blue and green. Diego's ashes? My body stiffened at the sight of the urn, and my mind flashed to Brick's office and a yellowed poster showing Peggy Lee holding a mike, her blond hair shining above her obsidian evening gown as she sang "Is That All There Is?".

The scent of gardenia snapped me back to the present when Threnody approached us. "What's your opinion?" she asked. "Think they've set up enough chairs? Supposed to be over a hundred."

"I've no idea of how many people may arrive," I said. "Everything looks lovely. Tisdale's did a good job."

"I thought one of us could stand at the end of the back row of chairs to greet people and pass out these folders." She gave me a folded obituary that I eased into my purse. "Brick will oversee the parking at the visitor's lot, point guests to the canopy, and then join us before the service begins."

"Fine with me."

When a few mourners began to drift toward the canopy, Kane sat beside Dolly in a back row. A good observation spot, I thought. Dolly pulled a small notepad from her purse and held a ballpoint at the ready. I sighed. Couldn't she even attend a funeral without composing a poem?

Pablo took a chair at the center of the front row, directly in front of the urn. I watched him carefully for signs of guilt. What were signs of guilt? I tried to forget the question. The minister approached from the sidelines, taking a seat next to Pablo. A fair-sized crowd sat waiting for the service to begin. Chief Ramsey arrived. Alone. From the north. Threnody greeted him, and he chose a chair in the back row, far from Kane and Dolly. In a few more moments Detective Lyon drove his unmarked car into the visitor's lot, parking near the exit. He strode toward the canopy at a quick pace until he stumbled, almost fell, then regained his balance and continued walking at a more sedate pace. An owl burrow? Must have been. We exchanged weak smiles before he took a seat at the end of the second row.

Guests filled the chairs quickly, remaining silent as the pianist played a prelude, a medley of hymns. Diego's favorites? Or did he have favorites? Were Cuban hymns different from American hymns? Maybe Pablo had chosen the selections. Or maybe the pianist. In addition to my close associates, I knew many of the guests through my work at the newspaper and through having given many speeches up and down the Keys for writing workshops — nonfiction, of course. But these were not people I mingled with socially. I left the social mingling to Mother and Cherie.

I needn't have concerned myself about what to wear. Guests arrived in various modes of dress. A few of the men wore casual jackets, slacks, and shirts without ties. Others wearing jeans, tees, and deck shoes looked as if they'd come straight from the docks. Except for Threnody and me, few of the women wore dresses. Silk pant suits were the garment *du jour.* Had these people called each other ahead of time to plan their costumes?

Jessie Vexton took a chair on the end of the third row as if planning a quick escape route. Soon after that, the minister rose from his seat beside Pablo and went to his place behind the dais. Threnody claimed a seat beside the pianist. I used that as my cue to slip into a chair beside Kane and Dolly.

Dressed in a collared white robe tied in front with a golden sash, the minister nodded to the crowd. "Ladies and gentlemen, let us bow our heads as we offer our silent prayers for the soul of our lost comrade."

We bower our heads.

Following the prayer time, the minister cleared his throat. "And now, if you've brought your Bibles, you may turn with me to the following scriptures that were some of Diego's favorites." I heard wind flutter the pages as he opened his large Bible with gilt-edged pages protected by a white leather cover. I imagined the scent of leather.

Kane leaned toward me and whispered. "I don't see anyone opening Bibles. Didn't know we were supposed to bring Bibles."

"Hush." I frowned.

The minister read three passages of scripture. After closing his Bible he offered a short eulogy, telling of Diego's life in Cuba, his legal passage to Florida, the loss of his wife. After those facts, he related more about Diego's present-day success in learning English, working at the Vexton marina, and gaining political notice resulting in a seat on the esteemed board of commissioners.

"In closing, I'd like to invite any of Diego's friends who care to, to share with us a few words concerning your thoughts about this man."

A mourning dove called into the silence while we waited, but nobody stepped forward. I knew, had Mother and Cherie been present, Diego would have had two to speak in his favor. Since nobody approached the dais, the minister nodded to Threnody, and sat again beside Pablo.

The pianist sounded a single pitch and Threnody began singing.

"Amazing grace, how sweet the sound . . ."

Before she could continue, everyone looked forward, hearing a flutter of wings when a small brown bird perched on the blue-green urn. An owl? In attack mode? Nobody moved. Threnody continued her solo, ". . . That saved a wretch like me . . ."

Now the minister rose and stepped toward the urn, flapping the end of his golden sash at the bird until it flew toward the top of the canopy. I thought it would be frightened into leaving us. Wrong. With another rush of wings the owl dived and perched on the speaker's dais.

". . . I once was lost, but now am found . . ."

Again the minister flapped his sash at the owl. This time the bird left the dais and circled overhead for a few seconds before it flapped toward Jessie Vexton. Hovering above him for only a moment, it dive-bombed him. Standing, Jessie raised his arms to protect his head while he fled across the park toward his car.

". . . Was blind, but now I see."

With dignity Threnody finished her song and sat again beside the piano as if nothing unusual had happened.

"I'm outta here." Kane rose and started to leave. "That bird may know something the rest of us don't know."

"Ladies and gentlemen." The minister stepped forward. "I apologize for this very unusual intrusion. I think our uninvited visitor has departed, so please, let us continue with this service." Tightening the sash at his waist, he took his place again at the dais. In the distance, everyone could hear Jessie bang his car door, rev the engine, and burn rubber as he sped from the park.

Acting as if he hadn't noticed this additional noisy intrusion, the minister raised one arm and addressed the crowd. "Before we bow our heads for a final word of prayer, I want to extend Brick and Threnody Vexton's invitation to each of you to stop by their marina and greet Pablo and your friends as you partake in sandwiches and coffee."

"I'm not greeting anyone over sandwiches and coffee," Kane said, his words audible above the minister's prayer. "I'm outta here."

"You rode with me, remember?" I whispered.

"I'm walking back."

We both hushed until the prayer ended, then Dolly followed Kane and me to the end of our row of seats.

"I don't mind walking home, Rafa. I think you and Kane need to talk — in private. I don't intend to go to the Vexton reception."

"Are you going to it, Rafa?" Kane asked.

"Not at the moment. Dolly, I'll drive you home, then I'll take Kane to his boat."

"What does 'not at the moment' mean?"

Kane asked.

"Kane, I think the meaning's clear enough. I'm not going to the Vexton dock right now, but that I might stop by later. Please excuse me while I say a few words to Pablo."

Pablo stood next to Threnody as I approached him. Threnody eased toward the minister when she became aware that I intended to talk to Pablo. I welcomed the privacy.

"Pablo, it was a beautiful service and I think Diego would have been pleased."

"Pleased to be dead?"

"No, of course not." His crude words caught me off guard. Had this man murdered his father? Were his words intended as a cover-up of some kind? "I mean, I think Diego would be pleased to know that he had the respect and good will of his fellow citizens. And I do want to apologize for the bird's intrusion."

"The owl."

"Yes, I suppose it was an owl. Anyway, I'm so sorry the creature chose today to make an appearance."

"According to my interpretation of the book of tarot, the owl selected its rightful place at the rightful time. I expected it."

"Pablo! I don't understand."

"Let me remind you that tarot was written long ago. In Diego's universe, in my universe, owls sometimes carry messages from the beyond. The wise do their best to interpret those messages."

"What is your interpretation?"

"I do not care to reveal my interpretations."

And I didn't care to press Pablo any further concerning his interpretation of the owl's appearance. To each his own. Maybe he hoped people would think him crazy in case he needed that for a defense tactic later.

TWENTY-SEVEN

Giving Dolly the VIP treatment, I drove her to the hotel portico, waiting while the uniformed doorman welcomed two passengers exiting from a black Lexus. After they turned their car over to a valet, Dolly slipped from the car and waved a farewell. After that, I drove Kane through the hustle-bustle of tourists to Land's End Village and the harbor walk.

"Sure you don't want to attend the reception?"

"Very sure. See you tonight at the Frangi — and thanks for the ride."

As I approached Mallory Dock after leaving Kane, the *Sea Princess* sounded its departure whistle and tourists flooded the street. They swarmed toward the cruise ship from all directions, caring little that they blocked traffic, treating the street as it were a sidewalk laid especially for them.

Patience. Patience. Dad's wise words from

my childhood did a slow rerun through my mind as I waited. *Always remember that the tourists are the ones who put the tinkle in our cash registers.*

Sometimes I tended to forget Dad's words, but this afternoon I relaxed and braked the Prius. I couldn't help smiling at pudgy men wearing new Sloppy Joe tees and at chic women carrying bags revealing they had patronized Banana Republic and Coach.

I eased slowly through the streets toward Daiquiri Dock. As usual, parking places were at a premium, but Diego's reception was a come-and-go affair. I waited when I saw a car filled with guests leaving, and I eased into the slot they left. After locking the Prius, I strolled toward the chandlery.

"Need your boat, Miss Blue?" a dock master called to me.

"Not today, thanks." I wondered who they'd found to take Diego's place, and how this man had learned my name so quickly.

Shading my eyes from the afternoon glare of sun on water, I walked on inside the chandlery. I won't say it looked like the reception hall in a church, but workers had shoved boats and motors, display ads, and rolls of nautical line aside. In their place a banquet table clothed in white lace held a punch bowl and a choice of crystal cups at one end. At the other end lay an assortment of napkins and plates on either side of a platter of sandwiches. Pulled pork.

Tisdale's had done well at setting up the reception, but nothing could mask the odor of diesel fuel wafting in from a recently started boat motor. Perhaps they could have silenced the not-too-distant sound of someone boring a hole in a very hard substance with a jackhammer, but none of the guests seemed offended by the smells or the sounds. Perhaps the lingering taste of barbecued pork blotted out other sensory perceptions.

Although Mama G wore a spotless white uniform while she ruled over the refreshment table, she had not given up her Birkenstocks or her tendency to spout orders.

"Be free to help yourself," she called to the lineup of guests. "Enjoy. Pulled pork sandwiches. Sparkling papaya juice be in the punch." When one guest hesitated over the sandwich platter, Mama G leaned forward, winked, and spoke softly.

"Have special conch and capers sandwiches for those who might have allergy to pork." From under the table she produced a smaller platter of her favorite Cuban sandwiches.

"I'd like a conch and caper sandwich, please," I said, grinning at her.

Brick saw this, and although he glared a Mama G for a moment, he shrugged and ignored her breaking her promise to Pablo concerning sandwich fillings.

As the crowd began to thin out, I eased toward Brick, deciding to ask him a few questions. He might have some answers that Kane refused to discuss with me. I took care not to arouse his suspicions. Everyone expected columnists to ask questions, didn't they?

"Good work, Brick. I think Tisdale's did a fine job with the funeral service as well as with the reception."

"Agreed. I think it pleased Pablo, too."

"Brick, maybe you can help me."

"Be glad to. In what way?"

"I'm planning to write a column about Kane. Although it's not to be a surprise, so far I haven't mentioned it to him."

"Think he might object?"

"No. I think he'll go along with it, but in addition to his facts, I need the thoughts and feelings of other local citizens. And since you know the local boating people, you're a logical one for me to approach."

"Glad to help if I can. A few quotes would give me some welcome publicity, right?"

"You flatter me, but yes, it might. Lots of people read my column. It wouldn't hurt to have your name appear in it."

"So what do you need to know?"

"Since the 'working water' problem has been under community discussion recently, I thought readers might welcome some insight into the life of a working shrimper. A commercial fisherman."

"That sounds like info you could get from Kane with no problem at all."

"You may be right, but I'd like to know more about *The Buccaneer* and I thought you might be able to tell me more about that boat since you've known lots of boaters and their boats."

"Might not be able to help you there. Kane's owned the boat since I've known him. Don't know who owned it before that."

"Kane mentioned Captain Red Chipper as one captain who had owned the boat. Did you ever know Captain Chipper?"

"Well, yes. I did meet him years ago. Don't think he lives in the Keys any longer. I heard once that he'd moved to the Carolinas."

"Drat. I'm sorry to hear that. I wanted to actually interview some of the former boat owners. That would add depth and interest to my column. Lots of people are interested in the history of ships and boats."

"Sorry I can't help you there. I've only owned this marina a few years, compared to the number of years *The Buccaneer*'s been around. That craft has a long history."

Brick pulled his cell phone from his shirt pocket as if in a hurry to make a call. I didn't intend to let him get away so easily.

"Do you know how long it's been around? Got any dates I can relate to?"

"Can't really say." Brick looked toward the door. "Rafa, please excuse me. I see an old friend getting ready to leave and I'd like to say a few words to him before he goes."

"Of course, Brick. But keep me and my column in mind. If you remember anything else about the former boat owners, give me a call, okay?"

"You've got it, Rafa."

Threnody startled me when she came up behind me.

"Not flirting with my husband, are you?" she asked, laughing.

"Trying to, but he wasn't interested. You're the one I really want to talk to."

"What's up?"

"I want to get going on our investigation."

"Our?"

"Yes. *Our.* I'm going to need all the help I can get, and Kane's being very uncooperative. He wants me to leave all investigating to the police."

"You got a lead of some sort?"

The reception was slowly drawing to a close, and the Tisdale workers began clearing away the table and chairs. Threnody drew me aside.

"Tell all, Rafa."

"You mustn't repeat what I'm about to say, Threnody. Promise?"

"Promise."

"This involves Kane, and I don't want the police to start investigating him."

"You have reason to think they might?"

"They shouldn't, but, yes, they might." I told her about being on *The Buccaneer* and seeing the old blue line that matched the line around Diego's feet.

"Where did Kane get it?"

"It came with the boat when he bought it. We need to find out where the previous boat owner got that line. Knowing its history might put us closer to the killer. Kane says a captain named Red Chipper once owned the boat. Kane told me Red Chipper still lives in the Keys. I talked to Brick about it. He said Captain Chipper moved some time ago, but he didn't seem too sure of that."

My mind whirled. Had Kane lied to me about Red Chipper or had Brick lied? Maybe neither one had deliberately lied.

Maybe neither was absolutely sure, neither having a real need to keep track of Red Chipper. Or maybe the captain had moved without either of them being aware of it.

Threnody led the way to Brick's office and we searched the phone book. No Chippers listed.

"Dead end here, Rafa."

"Look up Snipe Gross. Kane told me Captain Chipper bought *The Buccaneer* from Snipe Gross."

I waited while Threnody flipped to the G listings. In minutes, she looked up smiling. "Hey! I've found Snipe Gross. Strange name and the only one listed. He's in Marathon. Maybe he's the guy we need to talk to."

"I'll key in his number. Talk to anyone who answers." I pulled my cell phone from my shoulder purse. Threnody read the number to me and I hardly had time to punch it in before a male voice answered.

"Hello. Hello?"

I made no response.

"Hello? Gross residence. Hello?"

I broke the connection, feeling a bit guilty because I knew how I hated a dead line.

"We know he's home." I replaced the cell in my purse. "We have his address from the phone book. Let's go see him. A phone call would only warn him something's up. A surprise call would be more effective."

"Right." Threnody shoved the phone book back into the drawer where she found it. "Too late today. Let's go first thing tomorrow morning. We can call again to be sure he's home."

It sounded like a good plan until we left Brick's office and headed to the front of the chandlery. Mama G came striding toward us, her Birkenstocks snapping against the concrete floor at every step.

TWENTY-EIGHT

"Rafa! Rafa! Need help."

"Of course, Mama G. What can I do for you?"

"Car won't start. Need ride to hotel. Spend too much time here preparing for this party."

I didn't bother to tell her this reception in honor of Diego could hardly be considered a party.

"Of course, Mama G. Let me help you with your things. Maybe Brick or one of the dock masters can start your car. In the meantime we'll go on to the Frangi."

"Sandwich makings in refrigerator. I think ahead. I plan for tonight. Early this morning I plan for tonight."

"We appreciate your thoughtfulness. My car's out front, so we can go whenever you're ready." I followed her to the small area behind a sales counter where she picked up a cooler of sandwich fillings.

Jessie stepped from an office behind the counter.

"I'll carry the cooler to the car for you."

I spoke for Mama G, who seemed even more surprised than I at seeing Jessie. I said nothing about his abrupt flight from Diego's funeral. "Thanks, Jessie. We'd appreciate that."

Before our short drive to the hotel I called the bell staff office, asking for help in unloading the cooler. With the fragrance of barbecue sauce wafting about her, Mama G sat stiff and straight in the passenger seat of the Prius like a dignitary being escorted to a place of honor. I couldn't argue with that. Much of the Frangi's success depended on Mama G's sandwiches and her ability to keep a trio of musicians performing on the combo platform each evening.

Once we reached the Frangi, I snapped on the lights. A faint fragrance of frangipani barely masked the scent of the cleaning crew's lemon oil. We stood aside while a bellhop set the cooler in the kitchen.

"Is there anything else I can help you with, Mama G?" I asked after the bellhop left.

"*Nada. Nada.* Thank you for ride. *Muchas gracias.* Mama G no like asking favors."

I left Mama G scurrying about in the small kitchen while I went to my suite, slipped from Threnody's dress, and dropped onto my bed for a brief rest. This long day wasn't over yet. I had wanted to talk more with Threnody at the marina, but Mama G's request for help intervened. When my cell rang, I thought Threnody might be calling me.

I jumped up and headed for the bedside chair where I had dropped my purse — and phone.

"Hello." No response. "Hello? Who's calling, please?" Still no response. I closed the phone, holding it and waiting to see if it would ring again.

It didn't, so I stretched out on my bed, relieved that we'd located Snipe Gross, yet wondering about the strange call. Few people had access to my cell number. Close friends and business associates. I set my alarm clock, thinking I might nap for a few minutes before I geared up for a night of greeting guests.

My mind hazy with sleep, I jumped startled when my cell rang again. This time I'd placed it under my pillow. Groping for it, I answered after only three rings.

"Hello." No response. "Who's calling, please?" Another dead line. I turned the phone off, irritated and upset at the person playing phone games with me. I eased the phone under my pillow and tried to drop off to sleep again, but once alerted, my mind refused to drop into relax mode. Turning the phone on again, I tried to call Threnody. No answer. Surely she'd had time to get home from the marina.

I started to close the phone again when it rang. I hesitated. Why give the prankster another chance? But curiosity overcame caution.

"Hello."

"Hello, Rafa Blue."

I didn't recognize the voice. Male? Female? I couldn't tell. Androgynous. It could be either. "Who's calling, please?"

"A friend calling with a friendly warning. Watch your back tonight in the Frangipani Room. Your life is an hourglass. The sands of time are dropping one by one. When the last one drops, you're a dead woman."

When I broke the connection, my hands shook. Dry breath snagged in my throat. I waited to see if the caller would try again. After a few minutes I closed the phone. I'd been a fool to answer that last call. I rose and paced. What to do? Someone had threatened my life. I knew I should call the police. But no. I refused to run scared. Surely this threat related in some way to the call to Snipe Gross. But how could that be?

Can cell phones be bugged?

Dusk veiled the sky and I pulled the draperies across my picture window. Although I had no appetite, I ordered an entrée from room service. On most evenings, that was my custom and I adhered to it. I hoped my secret caller would notice and think he/she hadn't frightened me. After the tray arrived, I set it on my coffee table, dropped onto my couch, and clicked on the TV. Watching the evening news was a poor way to relax.

When someone knocked on my door, I froze.

"It's me, Rafa," Kane rang my bell and then called through the door. "They let me come up unannounced. You home?"

"Just a minute, Kane." I stalled, trying to sort out my feelings, to hide my panicky thoughts. Could Kane have been my secret caller? I mustn't let him know about the threatening message. I'd keep it a secret between the caller and me. I took three deep breaths, releasing each one to a count of ten. That helped calm me. Not entirely. But the deep breathing helped.

I slipped into a robe before I opened the door to let Kane step inside.

"You doing okay, Rafa?"

"Of course. And you? I missed you at the

marina this afternoon."

He enfolded me in a deep embrace and I didn't struggle against it. I melted into his arms and we exchanged deep kisses as he pulled me even closer. I felt much of my fear dissolve in the safety of his warmth and his nearness. When at last we eased a few inches apart, I looked into his eyes, knowing he would never threaten me. No way. Not Kane. I smiled.

"I really did miss you at the reception, Kane, but Tisdale's had the event well under control. I'm guessing over a hundred people stopped by. Mama G reigned in glory, providing sandwiches, urging everyone to enjoy seconds."

"I would have made it if I could. The engine parts I needed came in, and I spent the rest of the day working on the engine, tinkering with the new parts."

"Good." I forced my voice into steadiness. "Then you're ready to go on another shrimp run? How long's it been?"

"Too long. I have a crew ready to go out Thursday or maybe Friday at the latest, but I wish you'd spend a day on the water with me tomorrow. I need to give that motor a thorough test."

"Why me, Kane? I'd be no help if something went wrong, if for some reason the motor malfunctioned."

"I'm not really worried about my fixit job, but I never go on a shrimp run using new repair parts without testing them on open water first. The real reason I want you along's because I love you, Rafa." He kissed my earlobe. "I like having you near, and I also want to entice you away from Key West for a few hours. You need to get your mind off Diego's death and his funeral. You need to distance yourself."

"And I'm thinking you're also wanting to make me forget about investigating Diego's death. True?"

"That, too, may be behind my invitation, but not entirely. Humor me, okay? We haven't spent a day on the water in a long time. Please say you'll come with me." He pulled me close again, dropping kisses along the back of my neck before he stood back and met my gaze. "I'll pack our lunch. I'll take us out near the reef for some trolling. See what we can catch. Weather's supposed to be great tomorrow. And only a bit of wind. That spells calm seas."

"Guess I can't say no to an invitation like that. What time do you plan to leave?"

"No later than eight o'clock. That okay with you?"

"Sure. I'm an early riser."

Kane kissed me as if to seal my promise. I hoped he couldn't read my thoughts. He had no way of knowing of Threnody and my tentative plans for tomorrow. I hoped we wouldn't have to cancel them. Maybe Kane would decide not to stay on the water for the full day.

TWENTY-NINE

Before leaving for the Frangi, Kane decided to exchange the coat he wore for one he kept in my closet. No problem. Can people give themselves high fives? Maybe not. But the minute Kane left my suite and headed for the dance floor, I congratulated myself for keeping my threatening call a secret. I might have felt safer had he known, but he would have insisted on telling the police. No way did I need that.

I tried to call Threnody to tell her about the snag in tomorrow's plans. Still no answer. I glanced at my watch. Almost time to begin our evening. Threnody never arrived late. My news could wait until I saw her in the Frangi.

Although I felt frazzled and would rather have spent the night huddled in bed, I forced myself to dress. Knowing Kane would be there to protect me during the evening helped me conquer my fear of the unknown dangers that might lie ahead.

My favorite work costume, an off-the-shoulder gown in black, suited my mood, but I lightened the dress, if not my mood, with platinum earrings and a single-strand diamond necklace. The four-inch heels on my strappy sandals would lift me above the crowd.

Never regret being tall. Dad's words did a rerun through my mind. *Enjoy every inch of it. Women will envy you. Men will admire you. Stand straight and enjoy. Never regret being tall.*

I tried to heed Dad's words as I locked the door to my suite, tucked the key into my bra, and walked to the Frangi. Kane and Brick, looking resplendent in their white jackets and black crew necks, shared the task of lighting the torches while Dolly in her poet's blouse took care to keep her distance from the flames. Mama G stood beside her piano calling orders to Pablo and Jessie, who took pride in ignoring her and doing as they pleased. The scene reminded me of a cameo from a movie I'd seen many times before tonight.

Threnody hurried toward me, wearing a sequined tank top over a wispy skirt that skimmed a scant inch above her knees. I spoke before she could say anything.

"I've accepted Kane's invitation to go boating tomorrow."

"How could you! Time's getting away from us. You could fish with Kane any day of the week."

"Couldn't turn him down without revealing our plan to approach Snipe Gross. Have you called him again to set up an appointment?"

"Not yet. Thought we should take our time, plan our approach carefully. But we need to see him tomorrow, Rafa. Can't you put Kane off?"

"No. I really can't do that, Threnody." I told her about Kane's new motor parts and his need to give *The Buccaneer* a trial run before finalizing plans with his shrimping crew. "Once he's on a run, he has to pay his crew whether they're dragging nets or stalled somewhere tinkering with a stubborn motor."

"You humor that guy too much."

"I'll see to it that I'm back at the hotel by two o'clock. No later."

"Marathon's over an hour's drive from Key West." Threnody looked at her watch. "And that's if traffic moves fast forward and if there's no snarl on Seven-Mile Bridge."

"Okay, ladies." Brick smoothed his beard as he approached. "I see guests gathering in the hallway. Mama G's about to blow her conch shell. Prepare to smile."

"Sure, Brick," I said. "I'm always prepared to smile."

Threnody started to say something, but Mama G's rendition of "Row, Row, Row Your Boat" drowned out her words. She shook her head and settled in a chair near the bandstand while I approached the arriving guests with smile in place. Could one of these strangers be my secret caller? I couldn't help wondering. And worrying.

After Threnody's opening ballad and the combo's first five numbers, Mama G called a short intermission. Without hurrying, Threnody approached me.

"I can call Snipe Gross from your suite. Give me more privacy than calling from here."

"Good idea." I gave her my door key. "If we could set a late afternoon time to talk with him — say four or four-thirty, we could make it home by five-thirty or six with no problem. The meeting with him shouldn't take long — unless he's a talker, unless he gets carried away with his story."

"Maybe we should invite him to meet us over a light supper somewhere."

"Better not plan on that." I didn't want to meet with Captain Gross or any other

301

person I didn't know well. But I couldn't explain that fear to Threnody without telling her about the threatening call. "Maybe we could take him a small gift to thank him for his time and willingness to meet with us."

"What kind of a gift, Rafa? That's a hard one. Candy? He's an old man, right? Maybe he's diabetic. How about a book?"

"A book would be good. Unless he has macular degeneration. But I don't have time to go shopping."

"Let's pretend he has perfect eyesight. I'll pick up something while you're fishing with Kane. But first we have to call this guy, to see if he'll be willing to talk to us."

"Go. You have my key. Go call him before it gets any later." I tapped on my watch. "Don't want to wake him up — put him in a bad mood for starters."

"Right. I'm on my way."

"What'll you say to him?"

"I've been thinking about that. You're a writer. That much's true. I can tell him you're interested in history — boat history."

"Good idea. That's true, and I think he'll be flattered at our questions about his old boat — questions that only he can answer."

"Okay. I'll go for it." Threnody stood and started to leave, peering down the hallway toward my suite. "Talk to you soon, with any luck at all, maybe the next intermission."

"Deal." I stood and began mingling with the guests once more, trying to keep close to Kane without making my intentions obvious. The combo played three more sets of tunes before Threnody returned and threaded her way to my side.

"Any problems?" I asked.

"Nobody answered at first. But I kept trying. He finally picked up."

"So give! What did he say?"

"You were right. He was flattered to have our attention and he agreed to talk with us. I suggested a four-thirty meeting, and he said he'd expect us around that time."

"Wonderful. Great job. Now let's avoid talking together any more this evening. Brick seems to be keeping an eye on us. Don't want him asking questions."

"Right. No way do we want that. But there's one more thing we have to take care of."

"What's that?"

"We have to get police permission to leave the island. Remember?"

"I don't think so, Threnody. Chief Ramsey didn't say anything about asking permission to leave. He said we should let him know if we planned to go off-island. I listened carefully to his order. There's a difference between asking and telling. I don't think he can restrict us by refusing us permission to leave Key West."

"Hope you're right, and I'm going to let you check that out. Your turn. I've talked to Snipe Gross. You can talk to Chief Ramsey. You found Diego's body. You're of more interest to him than I am."

I smiled and nodded in case anyone was watching us, but I hated being reminded of that truth. "I'll call his office first thing in the morning. Don't think I have to talk to him personally — just let someone in his office know of our plans."

"Think someone will want to know why we're going to Marathon?"

"Anyone asks, I'll say we're going to a dress sale. I think Anthony's often advertises a sale. Not an event Chief Ramsey would care about."

"Nobody who knows you will believe you shop in Marathon."

"Okay, so we're going to dinner and a movie."

"Dinner's okay, but no time for a movie if we plan to work the Frangi tomorrow night."

"Maybe *you* should make the call, Threnody, if you think I'll say the wrong thing."

"No thanks. That one's all yours. Talk to you later. We need to fine-tune our departure plans."

"I'll drive," I said.

"Good deal. That way Brick can't check on our mileage."

"He does that?"

Threnody shrugged. "Only when I take the car out of town."

I didn't comment. But I was learning more about Threnody's life than I cared to know. She and I were becoming friends and I wondered why Brick felt a need to check her car's mileage. Didn't she resent that? My protective feelings toward her surprised me.

THIRTY

The evening passed uneventfully. After Kane and Brick extinguished the torches ringing the dance floor, Kane made arrangements with Mama G to make sandwiches for our fishing trip the next day.

"Lobster sandwiches, please. None of your aunt's weir— er — unusual recipes, okay? How about minced lobster with a touch of capers?"

"Be okay with me," Mama G said, but her elaborate shrug showed her disapproval of his choice.

"And how about a couple pieces of Key lime pie? You do make pies, don't you?"

"It be very late to be making pies tonight. But for you, I do it."

"Thanks, Mama G. You're a doll."

"Humph!" Mama G replied. "You no need doll. You need a wife. A wife who cook."

"Wish you'd speak to Rafa about that.

Maybe I can convince her while we're on the water tomorrow."

"Lucky you," Dolly said with a sigh as she looked at me. "I'd like to spend a day on the water."

"Didn't know you liked to fish," I said.

"I don't. But what a chance to be alone with the sea and the sky and to let the elements inspire me to write poems. Maybe poems so unique, so deep, that someone would publish them."

"Maybe someday I'll take you out in *The Bail Bond*, Dolly."

"And maybe I'll agree to go with you if you'd promise to write a column about me as a Key West poet."

"A poet who sells her creations for a dime apiece?" Kane laughed.

"Laugh all you want," Dolly turned her back and headed for the kitchen, calling over her shoulder, "Someday I'll be famous. Someday."

Kane grinned at Dolly's back before he walked me to my suite. I was tempted to invite him to stay the night, because I loved him, because I welcomed his nearness, and also because I welcomed the protection and comfort his being near me would offer. But no. It was past midnight and I knew he'd have to rise before dawn in order to get *The*

Buccaneer ready for our outing.

Before seven on Wednesday morning, I talked with an officer at the police station. She made note of Threnody and me leaving the island later in the afternoon, and returning before the Frangi opened that night. She made no objection to our plans and that was that. No questions. No problems.

After a quick breakfast of oatmeal, orange juice, and a precautionary Dramamine pill, I dressed for the day. Layers. DKNY swimsuit first in case the day grew hot and we decided to swim. Tank top with shorts over the swimsuit. Crew neck over the tank. A Banana Republic hoodie on top of the other shirts, then matching ankle-length fleece pants.

Regardless of the hokey look, I tugged on a pair of purple ankle socks before I shoved my feet into purple beach Crocs. I could already imagine Kane laughing. But I dressed from experience. Nothing worse than feeling chilled in the early morning hours of a fishing trip. Easy to remove layers when the sun began bearing down. Easy to pull off socks.

I'd started to leave my suite, then I turned back and stuffed the snip of blue line Chief Ramsey had given me into the pocket of my hoodie. Maybe Kane was right. Or maybe the two lines weren't a true match. And maybe I'd have a chance this morning to take another look at the under-mattress compartment on *The Buccaneer.*

After stopping at my storage locker in the hotel basement, I grabbed my spinning rod and reel and thrust them into the back seat of the Prius. Little traffic this early. Few tourists out and about. I had no trouble finding a parking place near Kane's dock. A light on-shore breeze left the bay waters millpond smooth, but the stillness increased the ever-present fishy stench that wafted about the dock. I could understand why the commissioners persuaded others to vote to close the working waters to the shrimp fleet. But I never mention that to Kane.

Gray gulls rose from their perches on the security line bordering the catwalk, screaming protests when I disturbed them by hurrying along the swaying planks toward *The Buccaneer.* Kane stood waiting, wearing only faded swim trunks and deck shoes. My mind whispered *Brrrr.* I didn't give voice to the mental comment.

"Yo!" Kane shouted a greeting before offering a hand to steady me while I stepped over the gunwale, making no comment about my socks in Crocs. We exchanged brief kisses that might have merged into something more interesting had a nearby captain not sounded a toot on his boat horn. When we stepped apart, I noted the compact pile of gear behind Kane in the wheelhouse.

"Wonderful morning, Kane." I clamped by teeth together to stop their chattering.

"Got everything we need. Fuel. Bait — both shrimp and ballyhoo. Sunscreen. Water. Sodas. Lunch. You still like lobster sandwiches?"

"My favorite." I hoped the Dramamine would kick in before lunchtime.

"Mama G delivered them and the Key Lime pie before seven. That woman's something else."

The motor throbbed smoothly as Kane executed a no-wake exit from the bay and then headed for the blue water west of Key West.

"Thought we'd try trolling on our way to the reef."

"Fine with me." Sometimes I white-lie a little. I consider trolling a silly hit-or-miss way of fishing, believing that trollers enjoy a day on the sea more than they enjoy serious fishing. And even if I manage to snag a fish while trolling, it's unlikely I can boat it before some larger shark or 'cuda sees it as breakfast and zeroes in on it, leaving me to reel in a dangling fish head. Ugh! Shades of Hemingway's *Santiago*.

I preferred backwater fishing — casting to a target, a permit or a bonefish. Even a 'cuda. Gram taught me to cast years ago, but I knew Kane couldn't safely take this boat into the back country. We'd go aground in the shallows.

We were barely out of sight of Key West when the steady hum of the motor changed from a *purrr, purrr, purrr* to a *brrr-thump-thump, brrr-thump-thump*. Little wisps of smoke began rising from the motor and I smelled burning oil. Scowling, Kane stopped the boat's forward motion, reversed it. The same no-purr sound repeated itself. *Brrr-thump-thump. Brrr-thump-thump.* The wisps of smoke disappeared, but the burning oil smell increased. I moved until I stood upwind of it.

Kane cut the motor and radioed to a captain at Harbor Walk Dock that we were in trouble, giving our position but requesting no help — yet. I knew how much having to report a possible need for help wounded Kane's ego. But the wound was too shallow to put our safety in danger.

"Drat it, Rafa. I had that motor working smooth as my wristwatch yesterday. What the hell!" He opened a gigantic toolbox, dragged it to the motor, and began clang-banging with pliers and wrenches. "Don't be scared. I'll get it running smoothly again. We're in no danger. We'll be on our way in a few minutes."

"I'm not scared, Kane. You know your way around boats and motors. Take your time."

I believed Kane. Being stranded for a while didn't scare me. If he didn't get his motor working, he knew plenty of tow services in Key West that would rescue us. My chief worry concerned yesterday's threatening phone call. I felt safe here at sea with only a balky motor to give trouble. My second worry concerned getting back to the dock in time for Threnody and me to make it to our appointment with Snipe Gross.

"Anything I can do to help? Hold a wrench for you? A pair of pliers?"

"Thanks, but I can handle it. Try to relax and enjoy the view. It should take me only a few minutes to get us going again."

Sensing that my peering over his shoulder might be bothering him, I retreated toward the bow. I watched Kane for only a few minutes longer before I saw this as my op-portunity to take another look-see in the bunkhouse. While he worked deftly in greasy motor parts, I slipped to the bunk beds, raised the mattress on a lower bunk. No blue line. Sand-colored line. Maybe I picked the wrong bunk. Lifting the mattress on the other bunk, I saw the same thing. New line held that compartment lid in its slot, too.

Dropping the mattress back into place, my mind whirled when I walked on to the bow to think. Had Kane heeded my warning and changed the line to protect himself in case Chief Ramsey or Detective Lyon ordered a thorough search of the boat? Or had he changed the line to cover his own guilt in Diego's murder?

Maybe I'd played right into a killer's hands by agreeing to this day on the water — alone with Kane. But no. I tried to reason that fear from my thinking. Lots of people knew Kane and I planned to be out trolling in nearby waters today. Threnody. Brick. Dolly. They'd heard us making plans. Mama G had delivered sandwiches to Kane this morning. And just a few minutes ago, Kane had radioed our position to potential helpers. I felt ashamed of myself for having suspected him.

Kane wouldn't have told anyone our exact position if he planned to kill me. I tried to believe that. But what if I fell overboard? What if I had an accident? A fatal accident?

THIRTY-ONE

Kane worked with the motor for over an hour with no success before he threw the wrench and pliers into the toolbox, cut the motor, and radioed for help, giving *Sol Salvors* our exact position and the exact time. Static garbled the response, and Kane shouted our plight and position again.

"They'll be here, Rafa. They're dependable. I've used their service before."

He felt more sure of their having heard our message than I did. If we couldn't understand their response, how could we believe they had heard us? I corked my concern as Kane grabbed his tools again and started working on the motor.

Sometimes it's hard to tell when you're changing position on the water, but we were drifting and Kane had been working close to two hours now. We were getting closer to some outlying islets. The water around us had changed from deep blue to a sandy brown and I could make out mangroves surrounding the islets.

"Kane. Look. To your left. We've been drifting."

Kane looked, and before he could say anything, our hull scraped against sand. He jumped up, grabbed an emergency paddle from its caddy on the portside gunwale, leaned over the side, and tried to push us free. No luck. The crunching against sand stopped. We were aground — one of a seaman's greatest embarrassments.

"Damn!" Kane thrust his whole weight against the paddle and the sound of splintering wood required no interpretation.

"Hey, no problem, Kane. The water's really shallow here. We'll just go overboard and push the boat free."

"You ever been grounded before?"

"No. I've only sailed with Gram and Dad. They both knew their way around the flats and how to avoid sandbars. They both understood the changing of the tides. But this water only appears to be about waist deep."

"Right. The water's shallow, but the bottom is deceptive. It looks firm, but once we're overboard we'll sink in to our waist — or worse. I'll give the radio another try."

This time the static made it clear to both

of us that we were the only ones who heard Kane's voice.

"We'd better go overboard and try to push the boat free. Or maybe the tide will come in and float us into deeper water."

Kane shook his head. And pointed to a tide chart. "If we're where I think we are, the tide's going out."

"Maybe someone will pass this way and see us."

We scanned the horizon, but saw no boats in sight. I waited no longer. Skinning from my many layers of clothes, I dropped them in the wheelhouse, hoisted myself over the gunwale, and jumped into the sea. To my surprise, Kane didn't follow my lead. Instead, he ran to the boat's stern and lowered a small motor. My hopes surged then dropped. The motor barely reached the water.

"You didn't tell me we had an auxiliary motor!" I shouted.

Kane splashed into the water beside me. "That motor won't help get us into deeper water."

"Then why lower it?"

"It'll give you something to hang onto while you try to climb back to the deck. Keep lifting your feet. Try not to sink any deeper into the muck." Kane offered me his hand and tried to pull me closer to the motor.

I felt water touching my knees, my crotch, and then my waist. When I tried to lift my feet, I felt myself sinking deeper. I clutched his hand and then got a grip on the motor.

"Hoist yourself up and onto the boat and then turn and give me a hand."

My grip on the motor was so unsure I almost fell back into the water, but I managed to pull myself up while Kane pushed on my bottom.

"Up. Up. You can do it, Rafa."

Right. I managed to get aboard. My lungs burned as if I'd swallowed a man-o-war, and I fought for breath while I turned, leaned over the gunwale, and offered Kane a hand. The boat shifted position, but he managed to tug himself onto the motor and then aboard.

We both stood clutching the gunwale and feeling the sandy slime drip from our legs onto the clean deck.

"My fault, Kane. All my fault. I apologize. You were right. We shouldn't have gone overboard."

"Could have been worse. We're still alive. The sea allows a person a few errors, but no real mistakes."

"Thank heaven the sea called this mishap

an error."

Slipping, sliding, and dripping slime, Kane made his way back to the wheelhouse, grabbed a line, and tied it around the bail of a bucket. Then after tossing the bucket over the side, he hoisted it in full of sea water. We washed ourselves and then sluiced the deck before we dropped down to rest.

"What now?" I asked after almost a half hour passed.

"Guess we'd better stand up and hope someone sees us, realizes we're in trouble. I'll get my emergency kit and hoist a distress flag."

We stood for a while and I got a second wind. "Guess there's no reason why I can't do some fishing while we're standing here awaiting rescue."

"Go ahead. I'll try the radio again."

Once more, the radio didn't work. I grabbed my rod and spinning reel. After baiting the lure with a piece of dead shrimp and wiping my fingers right on my DKNY swimsuit, I threw a long cast.

"Not a fish in sight, Kane. No helpers. No fish. What kind of an ocean is this, anyway?"

"What about that dot off in the distance to your right? Fish?"

I looked where he pointed. "Right. A fish. And it's coming my way. Looks like a black-tip."

"Have at it."

I moved in a way that kept my shadow from falling on the water. I waited. Yes, a black-tip. I waited. When I made my cast, the lure landed right at the shark's mouth. He snarfed it, I fought to keep the rod tip up, and the battle began.

"Good cast, Rafa."

I hardly had breath to answer. "Gram was a great teacher."

"You've told me before. For two years she thought fishing was more important than school."

I let the shark run, then I reeled it in a bit. Let it run again. We played that game for over a half hour, before the black-tip gave up and came to the boat. I'm always overwhelmed by the beauty of any fish. The black tip on this shark's dorsal fin set off its silvery scales, the creamy white of its underbelly. I stood admiring it so long, Kane took the rod from my hand.

"Want me to bring it aboard?" he asked.

"No way. I'm a catch-and-release person. Gram taught me that, too. Since I caught it, you can release it."

"I'm going to boat it first." Kane ran to the wheelhouse and returned with camera, tape measure, and gaff. "There's a black-tip tournament going on and this fish might win you a prize."

He pulled the shark onto deck and thrust the leader into my hand. "Now hold it high, and hold the tape at its nose with the numbers toward the camera. This will be proof of your catch."

I followed instructions and in moments the fish was back into the sea, lying stunned and quiet. I wished I could lean over the gunwale far enough to grab its tail and swish it through the water to help it survive. In moments, I knew the shark needed no help. It turned and streaked toward the horizon, its silvery body glinting in the sunlight and then disappearing first into the shallows and then into deep blue waters.

We'd been so engrossed in the shark scene that we hadn't noticed the bright orange boat approaching.

"*Sol Salvors*!" Kane shouted. "They did hear us." He stood waving as if they hadn't already spotted us. In moments the captain tossed a line to Kane who secured it around a prow cleat. In moments we were afloat again and headed back toward Key West. Slowly. Very slowly.

"It'll be a long ride." Kane opened the cooler. "Might as well enjoy Mama G's lunch."

And that's what we did until Kane broke the silence growing between us. He took my hand, squeezing it while he looked into my eyes.

"I love you, Rafa. You know that and believe it, don't you?"

"Yes. I do know and believe. And I love you, too." I'd have sealed my words with a kiss had the salvage captain not been peering over his shoulder now and then and grinning at us.

"Our love can't grow while there're secrets between us. Level with me, Rafa. What happened in your family to cause your parents to allow you to drop school and live for two years with your grandmother on Big Pine?"

I intended to share the story with Kane — at a time of *my* choosing rather than his. I'd like to avoid thinking about that time in my life, but Kane deserved better from me than secrecy. Maybe this was as good a time as any to talk about my past. I had the slight advantage of catching Kane at a time when his confidence in himself and *The Buccaneer* hung at low ebb. If he hadn't already heard about my past and preferred to pretend innocence, I'd rather have him hear the whole story from me than from the local gossips.

Thirty-Two

The odor wafting from the salvage boat motor, the slap of the sea against *The Buccaneer,* and the whirl of my own thoughts tended to throw me off balance, but I grabbed a deep breath and began my tale.

"Okay, Kane. I regret this part of my past. The foolish things I did still embarrass me and I hate talking about them — hate the memory of them. If you can't forgive and forget, I'll understand. Please remember that all this happened long before I met you and that it has nothing to do with our present relationship."

Kane squeezed my hand. "I'm ready to forgive and forget. Been ready for months."

I grabbed a deep breath, almost tasting the salt in the sea air as I stared at the horizon. Sometimes focusing on the place where sky meets water helps settle my mind as well as my stomach.

"I ran away from home when I was thirteen." My throat ached, and for a few moments I couldn't continue my story.

"Lots of kids run away from home, Rafa, or at least they think about running away. It's no big deal as long as they return to their parents with nobody getting hurt. You appear unscathed to me."

"Physically, perhaps. But not mentally. I'll never be the same, never forget my foolishness."

"Maybe you need to forgive yourself before you can accept forgiveness from others."

I stared at the horizon for so long, Kane spoke up again. "If the subject pains you so, I'm sorry I asked you about it. Maybe I should ask your forgiveness for prying."

I began the story again. "I ran away from home at age thirteen. I'd bottled lots of hurts inside me — some real, some imaginary, I'm sure. I was convinced my parents loved Cherie much more than they loved me."

"They tell you that?"

"Only by their actions, never their words. I once overheard Mother tell Gram that kids were like waffles — the first one seldom met expectations. I never forgot those words. I arrived two years before Cherie. Even at that young age, I resented all the attention she received as the new baby. Gifts arrived — for Cherie, none for me. People came to see the new baby. Nobody came to see me."

"Sometimes adults are thoughtless." Kane nodded and waited for me to continue my poor-little-me story.

"As we grew older, I began to understand why Mother and Dad preferred Cherie to me. Cherie was petite and beautiful. I stood tall, awkward, and homely, towering over Cherie by several inches, although we were only two years apart in age.

" 'Be proud of your height,' Dad would say. 'Shoulders back. Head up. You'll never see stars looking down.'

" 'Stop slumping and slouching,' Mother would say. 'You'll never be beautiful if you act ugly. Stand up straight.'

"How I hated standing up straight. I towered over everyone in my class — even my teacher, even Roger Wiltis, the junior high school basketball star. Kids teased me by secretly adding my name to the first-of-the-year basketball sign-up sheet for boys. Everyone laughed at that, but I never saw the joke."

"School years can be tough," Kane said. "Nobody could understand why a boy like me, born and raised in the corn country of Iowa, wanted to be a commercial fisherman and live on a houseboat."

"You always wanted that?"

"Yes. I did. As a special treat, my grand-father enrolled me at age ten in a six-week session at sea camp — right on Big Pine Key. I fell in love with the ocean and its creatures. And today I'm living my dream. I graduated from Iowa State, but someday I may go back to college here in Florida and study to be a marine biologist." He nodded toward the tow boat and gave a pretend laugh. "But forget my dream for now. This's your story."

I grabbed another breath and continued. "I couldn't take the put-downs, both from my parents as well as from Cherie. Mother always compared my grades to Cherie's higher ones. Cherie always laughed at my jeans and tees and tried to get me to dress like she did — stuff straight from the pages of *Glamour*. And the kids at school tormented me, too. I won't say my friends at school, because I felt I had no friends. Everyone called me a loner. I never wanted to be a loner. I wanted everyone to like me. But few of my peer group did. Peer group. That's who my counselor said I didn't fit in with — my peer group.

"So one day I'd had enough of home, school, and Key West. I packed a small bag of jeans and tees, swiped one of Cherie's sleek dresses in case I *had* to dress up. Taking two hundred bucks that I'd been hiding in my underwear drawer, I boarded a bus for Miami. I knew nobody would notice that. Our family traveled in Lincoln Town Cars and Dad's private plane. Don't think Cherie even knew the location of the bus station. I didn't leave a note. In my mind, I dreamed my family might think I'd been kidnapped. I dreamed they might care that I was gone."

"Miami!" Kane exclaimed. "A big city for a thirteen-year-old. Where did you go? What did you do? You're lucky to be alive."

"I walked the streets for a while. The bus station area looked dirty and seedy. I walked a long ways and stopped at a nice-looking hotel. The room rate was seventy-five dollars a night for a single. I knew then my two hundred wouldn't last long. I found a less expensive hotel, The Pla-Mor, not nearly as good looking as the first one, and I booked two nights. I could pay and have a little eating money left over.

"The hotel had a bar and lounge, and after I unpacked, I took the elevator to the lounge to eat dinner. The only item on the menu I thought I could afford was the deep-fried shrimp appetizer. I didn't want to run out of money, so sitting at the bar, I ordered a margarita, price two dollars, because I thought that a sophisticated thing to do and a thing I could afford."

"Nobody questioned a kid ordering a margarita?"

"I didn't look like a kid. I coiled my hair on top of my head, used lots of eyeliner and lip gloss, and wore Cherie's black slinky shift — sleeveless and barely touching my knees. And even at age thirteen, I towered over lots of men. Cherie would have been proud to know her lessons in grooming and wearing the 'right' clothes were paying off. Before long a guy joined me, sat beside me on the next bar stool, smiled.

" 'You look hungry,' he said.

"When I didn't reply or return his smile, he ordered two shrimp dinners. I ignored him. When the shrimp dinners arrived, he motioned for the waiter to set one of them in front of me. I wanted to get up and leave, but my stomach growled, reminding me I hadn't eaten since breakfast — hours ago. And this guy looked nice enough. I began by tasting one shrimp. I didn't stop until no shrimp or anything else remained on the plate. I still remember that shrimp dinner as the best meal I ever ate. I haven't eaten shrimp since. After the meal, one thing led to another. We spent an hour or two drinking more margaritas and dancing, until he invited me up to his room."

"Were you used to drinking?"

"Of course not. Nor dancing. That night I stumbled a lot, trying to follow his lead. At home, sometimes Cherie and I would sneak some booze from our parents' liquor cabinet. Not enough to make us drunk. But that night at the Pla-Mor Hotel, I began to feel sick. I tried to excuse myself to go to the ladies' room, but Mike — his name was Mike Wilson — Mike took my hand and said, 'Come along with me.' And I did.

"All I wanted to do was to lie down and sleep. And I did that, too. I knew I shouldn't, but how could a guy so nice and generous and caring be bad? No way, I told myself. When I woke up in the morning Mike was gone. Oddly enough, my suitcase was on the luggage rack beside the bed. I dressed quickly and opened the hotel room door. Mike had been thoughtful. He had placed a DO NOT DISTURB sign on the doorknob to the room. I dressed in jeans and tee, hurried to the lobby, bought a Key West *Citizen,* and carried it back to the room. Our room? I wasn't sure whose room it was. It didn't matter. I was alone. I read the *Citizen* carefully, expecting to see headlines about my disappearance. Nothing. Nothing on the front page or any other page. I sat there crying until someone knocked on the door and called out 'room service.'

"I peeked through the peephole at a uniformed employee carrying a tray covered with a white napkin. I opened the door and accepted the tray. Even with a still queasy stomach, I downed omelet, toast, orange juice. I stretched out on the bed again and didn't wake up until I saw Mike standing over me smiling and offering me a bouquet of daisies."

"And one thing led to another," Kane prompted.

"Right. You can guess the rest of the story. I fell in love with Mike Wilson. He told me he loved me. He told me this room was his hideaway and he asked me to share it with him. And I did. Since my folks didn't even care enough about me to put a 'missing girl' notice in the local paper, why should I even consider returning to Key West?"

"You stayed with this guy?" Kane sounded unbelieving. "How long did you live with him in that hotel room?"

"Too long. But not as long as you might think."

"What's that supposed to mean? Even one night was too long. Did he rape you?"

"No. The sex we had was consensual. I fell in love with him. Can you forgive that?"

Kane didn't answer. His face grew red. His hands balled into fists. Then he spoke through lips that barely moved.

"Forgive who? You, in spite of your height and sophistication, were still a kid — a juvenile. He led you astray. This guy used your innocence to lure you to him. In olden days, people would say you fell in with evil companions. There are laws against men like Mike Wilson, Rafa. They're called pedophiles."

"I know that now. But the story gets worse and since you insisted on hearing it, I expect you to listen to all of it."

Kane didn't try to stop me.

"I didn't leave that hotel room for three days. When I looked through the peephole at the next person who knocked on the door, I saw a woman carrying a baby. I thought she was lost and had knocked on the wrong door. I opened the door to help her. She called me a slut, a whore, and several other names before she told me she was Mrs. Mike Wilson — Mike's wife.

"Kane, you can't imagine how I felt. I had been sleeping with another man's wife. I was the 'other woman' breaking up a family. Maybe Mrs. Mike Wilson spoke the truth. Maybe I was a slut and a whore. Ever since meeting Mrs. Wilson I've wondered if I am corrupt. But how could anything that felt so good be so bad?

"She called me a few more names before she left me standing alone. It took me only a few minutes to pack my bag and leave. Mike had left me money and I had no compunction against using it. I took a taxi to the bus station and caught a bus to the Keys, getting off at Big Pine Key where Gram lived. She welcomed me with open arms, not having known I'd gone missing since my folks had hushed it up.

"Once Gram called Mother, she and Dad came running to Big Pine, pretending forgiveness, eager to sweep the whole episode under the rug before anyone else heard about it. Dad had hired a private detective to try to find me, but they had told nobody I had gone missing. Since I'd left no message and since they'd heard nothing from a kidnapper, Dad said they figured I'd run away and would return home as soon as my money was gone. Dad confessed that he'd run away as a boy, as if it would make me feel better.

"Gram agreed to keep me for a few weeks, until the gossip blew over. Mom said I'd always be punished for my sins. Gram

331

argued with her. She said that sometimes people aren't punished for their sins. They're punished *by* their sins, and that she wasn't going to stand by and let that to happen to me.

"Dad invited me back home. Mom said no way — at least until they learned for sure I wasn't pregnant. I had no real desire to return home. So that's how I happened to spend two years with Gram, who thought lots of things were more important than going to school. Mom fabricated a story about me studying abroad and Dad finally insisted that I return home."

"Then what? At fifteen, you could hardly pick up where you left off in junior high. Nor could you join your former classmates in high school."

"Right. But I managed to earn a high school diploma — GED. Then I really did go abroad to study. Switzerland. France. England. I loved Europe and I studied languages as well as English literature and composition. The family, mostly my dad, of course, persuaded me to return home. I had missed the freedom of the Keys. As a young adult, I saw Big Pine Key and Key West from a different angle, and I thought I'd prepared myself to write a book. That was my dream. So far a column in the *Citizen* is as far as I've come in achieving that dream. But I haven't given up on it. I've mentioned it to you before, and it's still a major goal that I try to work on daily."

"Some story. Some life you've had."

"And having heard it all, you can still bear associating with me?"

THIRTY-THREE

For a few moments Kane didn't reply. Then he stood. Although the guys on the salvage boat no longer watched us, Kane pulled me to my feet and along behind him into the wheelhouse. He responded to my sordid tale with kisses instead of words. And I responded in kind. I felt a freedom and a cleansing I hadn't known since I was thirteen.

"If I ever meet the guy who took advantage of you in that Miami hotel, he'll be sorry," Kane said.

"What about forgive and forget?" I smiled as I met his eyes on a level. "Haven't I just proved it's a good plan?"

Kane didn't have time to answer. Our rescuers were maneuvering *The Buccaneer* to his dock. He walked aft to greet them, to thank them, to pay them, and sign some papers. He secured the boat, and I took that as my cue to gather my clothes and fishing gear. I stepped over the gunwale with a minimum of assistance and jogged toward my car.

Time enough for "thank yous" and "so sorrys" when we met at the hotel tonight. A discussion I had dreaded lay behind me. Moments I still dreaded lay ahead of me. If we wasted no time, Threnody and I could keep our plans to approach Snipe Gross. I keyed Threnody's name on my speed dial.

"I'm back," I said when she answered. "Are you ready to go? I can shower and be ready in fifteen minutes."

"I'm ready. I'll call Snipe Gross again to be sure he's home. If he isn't, we'll worry about that later. Have a good day on the water?"

"Tell you about it later. I'll pick you up in a few minutes."

I showered and tugged on a clean pair of jeans and a tee, feeling my Keys-casual outfit would help ease our way into the meeting with Captain Gross. Moments later, Threnody stood waiting on her veranda and slid onto the passenger seat beside me. She wore chinos and a white shirt. Good choice.

"He answered his phone," Threnody said. "I told him you were a writer seeking information on old boats, and he seemed willing, maybe even eager to talk with us. Told him we'd be there in an hour or so. I even found clippings of some of your old columns to take along for show and tell. Wanted to be able to prove that you are who I said you are."

"Good thinking." I eased through heavy traffic to the highway and then headed for Marathon. "Got his exact address?"

"Right here." She waved a card. "He lives in a mobile home park — oceanside as we leave Seven Mile Bridge. Pelican Park. Should be easy to find."

"What sort of questions are we going to ask?" I intended to keep our conversation focused on Snipe Gross rather than on my fishing trip with Kane. We needed to think carefully about what we planned to tell him, or to ask him. And also because I didn't want to reveal all to Threnody concerning my threatening phone call. No point in alarming her. I'd be safe enough with her away from Key West this afternoon. Nor did I want to talk about my day with Kane. It's usually better to let a boat captain tell his own version of going aground, his own take on a repair that didn't quite work. Threnody didn't push me for information. She and I had grown close during the past few weeks of working together at the Frangi, and especially during the days since Diego's death. I felt guilty at keeping so many secrets from her. It didn't occur to me that she might be keeping secrets from me, too.

Once we crossed the Boca Chica Bridge, the traffic thinned and we made good time — as good as any driver could make and keep within speed limits that changed every few miles, varying between forty-five and fifty-five mph.

"How are we going to approach him about the blue line, Rafa? That might be tricky. Did you bring a piece of it with you?"

"It's in my shoulder bag. I've practiced a casual speech about looking for matching line for some craftwork I've started."

"Good idea. Hope he goes for it."

We passed Cudjo Key, Ramrod, Summerland. Then I slowed as we reached Big Pine.

"Something wrong?" Threnody asked.

"There's a strict speed limit on Big Pine. It's the home of the National Key Deer Refuge. Anyone hitting one of those miniature deer is in big trouble." As if to mark my words, a brown creature no bigger than a Boxer or a Rottweiler dashed in front of our car. Tires squealed and seat belts tightened as I braked. The driver behind me blasted on his horn. The yearling ran across the highway unscathed then walked on, intent on deer business. We breathed again.

"Glad I don't live on this Key," Threnody said.

"It's really a great island. My grandmother has lived here all her life. She recently moved from her stilt home on a woodsy avenue to a ground-level house in Pine Channel Estates. Got tired of climbing twenty-one steps to her front door."

"Doesn't she worry about hurricane water flooding her home?"

"I suppose the concern is there, but she seldom mentions it. Impending hurricanes allow people plenty of time to evacuate to safer places."

"Pine Channel Estates sounds very up-scale."

"It's not all that upscale, and that's not the reason she moved. She wanted to live on a clean canal that's less than five minutes from good fishing waters. She's getting older. She was lucky to find a ground-level house for sale."

"Lucky until the next hurricane hits," Threnody said. "She may end up wishing she'd stayed in her stilt house."

"Guess she's willing to take her chances. Like Snipe Gross. He's in a mobile home park. Hurricanes aren't kind to mobile homes."

The only traffic light between Big Pine and Marathon flashed green as we approached, and we continued on past the state park, Duck Key, and then onto Seven Mile Bridge. As a kid, I used to check our car's odometer to make sure the bridge measured seven miles long. It did. And after a few crossings, I stopped checking on it.

At the end of the bridge a cop sat in a patrol car on the side, ready to nab anyone who failed to heed the sudden thirty-five mph speed limit. I heeded it, and we turned into the first mobile home park we came to — Pelican Park.

"Number two-oh-six." Threnody read from her note card.

We drove along narrow lanes separating several rows of silver-colored mobile homes before we found two-oh-six. We had slowed to a near stop when an old man wearing navy slacks and a chambray work shirt stepped from his double-wide onto a small sheltered patio and motioned to us. His baldness shone in the waning sunlight until he picked up a navy yachting cap trimmed with gold braid from a table, slapping it onto his head.

"Rafa Blue? Threnody Vexton?" He leaned toward our open car window, and when we nodded, he motioned us to a parking slot big enough for one car. Seconds later, he pulled a bicycle propped on a kickstand aside so we'd have a little more room, grinning at us as he did so.

"Welcome, ladies. I've been watching for you. Don't have a lot of company these days. You're an event."

After shaking hands with our host, we followed his lead onto his patio, taking the plastic chairs he offered. To my surprise, the chairs, cushioned in a green and white awning-striped fabric, felt comfortable.

"Thank you for your willingness to talk with us," I said.

Threnody reached into her shoulder bag and pulled out a small folder of clippings, thrusting them toward him.

"I've brought some of Rafa Blue's published columns," Threnody said.

"They're samples of the type of column I'd like to write about your old boat that my friend Kane Riley now uses in his shrimping business."

Captain Gross scanned the clippings before he looked at me. "What is it that you want to know?"

"Whatever you want to tell us, sir," I said. "Human interest stuff with maybe a few dates thrown in here and there."

"Bought the boat from Captain Bucky

Varnum in nineteen-eighty," Captain Gross said. "The boat showed lots of wear. Varnum had used it as a water taxi in the Mariel Boatlift. Took me a while to make repairs, but after I cleaned it up and gave it a little spit and polish, I used it for years. Worked out of Key West Bight alongside dozens of shrimpers. Made a good living, too. That's when the Singleton family owned the shoreline around the bight. Of course, after old Henry passed on, those in charge of his estate sold the bight to Key West."

Once we got Captain Gross talking, I wondered if we'd be able to get him stopped. Sometimes I took notes. Sometimes I just listened. His tales never bored me, but I knew we needed to be starting home soon, and so far I'd mentioned nothing about the blue rope. I pulled my snip of line from my shoulder bag and dangled it before him.

"This is off the subject, but have you ever seen this kind of line before?"

He peered at the line, then he carried it inside his home, returning a few moments later with a magnifying glass.

"Eyes aren't what they once were," He said. "Seems to me there was a coil of this type of line aboard that shrimper when I first considered buying it. But I don't remember seeing it later. It's just old nautical line. You want to put that information in your article?"

"You can never tell what readers may find interesting," I said. "I've been looking for some cord this color for a craft project I've been considering. You have any of that line left?"

Gross shook his head. "Afraid not. Don't remember seeing it on the boat again once I bought it. Want to see some pictures of the old craft?"

"Sure," I said.

"Got some snapshots in an envelope inside. Let me get them for you. Before and after shots. Before I fixed it up. Then after the repair job."

Before we could stop him, Captain Gross stepped into his trailer. After several minutes he returned with the pictures. "Don't know whether you could use these to illustrate your article, but if you can, you're welcome to them."

Threnody leaned close to me so we both could see the pictures. I traced the ship's bell with my finger.

"What happened to the bell?" I asked. "It's in the 'before' shot, but not in the 'after' shot."

"Varnum wouldn't part with the bell," Captain Gross said. "Sentimental, I suppose. If you're interested in the pictures, take 'em with you. But send them back when you're through with them. Someday I plan to organize them into a scrapbook. Someday. Someday when I get bored. Trouble is, I never get bored."

We managed to draw the interview to a close. I tucked the blue line back into my shoulder bag and Threnody dropped the envelope of snapshots into her bag.

"We'll get the pictures back to you in a day or two," I promised. "And we thank you for your time and patience in talking to us. I'll send you a copy of my column when the *Citizen* publishes it. It may be a few weeks. I work ahead of deadline."

"I'll be looking forward to seeing it," Captain Gross said. "Talking with you has been my privilege."

I backed the Prius carefully from its tiny slot, and in moments we were headed on our way to Key West.

"Threnody! That bell. Take a good look at the picture that shows that bell. I think we're both thinking the same thing."

"Right. It looks like the same bell that's hanging on our front veranda."

"But how could that be?"

343

"Well, you know how Brick likes old stuff. He could have picked up the bell at a flea market, an antique shop."

Threnody pulled the snapshots from her bag and thumbed through them until she reached the one showing the bell. Finding a small flashlight in her bag, she focused its beam on the bell.

"What do you think, Threnody? Is it the same bell? A similar bell? Or what? If we weren't on Seven Mile, I'd pull over and take a look."

"I can't be sure, Rafa. Old brass bells look a lot alike. The size could be different. The etchings around the bell's rim could be different. I've never really studied that old bell at the mansion."

"Let's take a look when we get back."

But when we got back and I drove Threnody to the mansion, Brick heard my car and came to the door. He stepped onto the veranda and dropped his cell phone into his shirt pocket before he waved a greeting. Threnody laid the envelope of snapshots onto the car seat then she left me to greet Brick. Turning back toward me, she called over her shoulder.

"Thanks so much for the trip to Marathon, Rafa. Too bad we didn't find anything at Anthony's."

"Better luck next time," I called, giving Threnody a smile and Brick a casual wave.

Thirty-Four

Brick irritated me with his checking-up on Threnody. I wondered why he didn't trust her, why he kept such a close check on her comings and goings. Had she stepped out on him sometime in the past? I smiled to myself. Seemed to me it might be the other way around. I drove the short distance to the hotel quickly, eager to get Snipe Gross's snapshots to a bright light and a magnifying glass. Yet, what would I be able to tell without the bell at hand? And what difference did it make if the bell in the snapshot was the same bell now in place at the Vexton mansion? Lots of people buy old bells to give their homes a Keesy look. Gram had one roped to the banister of the steps at her old stilt house.

Our trip to Marathon had been to find information on the blue nautical line. From that standpoint, the trip had been a fiasco. I hated knowing my search for similar blue line had failed. Kane might not say I told you so, but that's what he'd be thinking. I also hated having to phone him because I knew I should tell him about the threatening call I received yesterday.

After returning to the hotel and parking my car in its usual slot, I locked it, dropped the key into my shoulder bag. I should have taken time to return my fishing rod to my hotel locker, but weariness caught up with me. I'd do it first thing tomorrow. I prized that rod and reel, but nobody would steal them tonight from my locked car. I was in no mood to do details that could wait until tomorrow. With luck, I'd have time to take a careful look at the snapshots and maybe get a few minutes of rest before the Frangi opened for the night.

I carried the snapshots to my desk then hurried to the refrig for a glass of guava juice before I searched for my magnifying glass. For once, I found it in my desk drawer right where it should be. I saw nothing unusual about the bell. Brass. Weathered by years of salt air. In the picture, it looked as if it might measure about twelve inches in diameter. It could have been the bell from any ship, from any decade. Nothing special marked it as an artifact from Bucky Varnum's water taxi in the 1980s. I studied the etchings around the bell's rim. Anchor. Pirate's flag. Anchor. Pirate's flag. The design repeated itself.

I sighed and dropped the snapshots into my desk drawer. If I wrote the article I planned to write about Kane, I could mention his old shrimp boat, and I might be able to use one of the snapshots to illustrate my writing. I should do that. Snipe Gross would be expecting it. And he deserved it, considering the generosity he showed Threnody and me this afternoon.

Taking no chances of falling into a deep sleep, I set my bedside alarm for one hour and I slept so soundly during that hour that I had trouble remembering the day, the place, the time when I awakened. I jumped up, splashed cold water onto my face, and toweled it off before I peered into my closet, shoving Kane's coat aside. What to wear. What to wear. That problem wouldn't have bothered Mother or Cherie, that's for sure.

Tonight I slipped into a sleeveless crimson top then pulled on a black silk skirt that flowed around my ankles. Strappy sequined sandals looked very glamorous once I retouched the scarlet polish on my toenails. Past time for a pedicure. Far past. But the last few days had offered little time for frivolities like pedicures.

"Rafa?" Kane called as he rang my door-bell. "Rafa?"

I opened the door quickly and almost fell into Kane's arms. He stepped inside and closed the door before we kissed.

"You look gorgeous, Rafa."

"Because I knew you'd notice if I didn't," I teased. "You look pretty neat yourself. But enough compliments. How's your boat? What was the problem? And did you get it fixed?"

"One question at a time, woman. And we'd better head for the Frangi before Mama G storms right to your suite to get you."

And that's what we did. We were the last to arrive before guests began to leave the elevator and head our way. The torch flames undulated in a gentle breeze. I recognized Threnody's subtle gardenia scent and smiled at her as she came closer. Kane started to tell me about his boat motor, but the sound of Mama G's conch shell made him shake his head and wait. When she stopped blowing, Brick headed our way. I wanted to talk to him but when he and Kane began discussing motors, I welcomed the chance to draw Threnody aside where we could speak without being overheard.

"I know Brick's bell at the mansion is the

same one in Snipe Gross's snapshots, Rafa. I memorized the etchings around the bell's rim. I said nothing to Brick about it. Didn't want to have to answer any questions. But I think it's a strange situation."

"Maybe not so strange. We both know Brick prowls antique shops and flea markets. And sometimes stuff like that appears at auctions. That bell could have belonged to several people before Brick owned it."

"Of course, you're right. But something about the situation gives me the creeps. Had the bell been left in place, it might now belong to Kane."

"It's the blue line that matters, Threnody. The blue line. We learned nothing more about that."

After Threnody sang her opening song, I busied myself talking to our guests, seeing that they were comfortable and enjoying their refreshments. Threnody helped Dolly in the kitchen. A lady sitting near the combo stand motioned to me and when I reached her side, she asked for a margarita, blended, salted rim. Making my way through the dancers to the kitchen, I waited while Dolly prepared the drink.

When I picked up a serving tray, set the margarita on a napkin in the center of the tray, and prepared to leave the kitchen,

Dolly stepped forward.

"I'll carry it to her," Dolly said. "You're supposed to smile and greet, not carry trays."

"I'll do this one, Dolly. The woman was very nice, and I think a little extra attention will please her."

I kept the tray and turned toward the dance floor, hoping to edge around the inner perimeter and serve the margarita without disturbing the dancers. I almost reached the woman's table. She turned to smile at me when suddenly I tripped over a foot in my path. The tray crashed to the floor. Glass shattered. Then I lost my balance and fell on top of the spilled drink and the broken glass. Who had tripped me? Accidentally? On purpose? The threatening call replayed in my mind. I tried to study the people nearby, but their faces blurred. Strangers. Pain shot up my leg.

Mama G saw my plight. She kept the combo playing, hammering out a loud piano tune with lots of thumbnail glissandos in an effort to keep attention focused on the combo rather than on my clumsiness. Stabbing pain froze me in place. Kane came to my rescue, trying to help me up. Now blood mingled with margarita added more slipperiness to the floor.

People at the nearby tables jumped to their feet. When Dolly rushed toward us with towels to mop up the spill, I noticed two women trying to brush margarita from their gowns with napkins. A man stood behind each of them, helping them to their feet and hurrying them from the Frangi to the hallway. Had one of those women caused me to trip? Why were they hurrying away?

Once I regained my footing again, I looked down at a long rip in my skirt. Would the fabric hide most of my injury? Blood trickled from my knee to my ankle.

"Oh, her skirt!" a woman exclaimed.

"It's ruined," another said.

"Ripped on one of those stiletto heels," a third chimed in.

I wanted to tell them to hush, that I wasn't badly injured.

Threnody came running to help Dolly mop up the spill, but I saw no reason for my fall. I remembered feeling a foot in my path.

"Help's on its way." Kane supported me as we left the Frangi. "Can you make it to your suite? Or think you should stay here?"

"I can make it. I'll be okay in a minute or two. Don't call for help."

"Too late. The desk clerk downstairs

alerted one of the hotel guests — a doctor. He's coming right up."

"Drat, Kane. I don't need all that fuss."

"Threnody and I think you do need all that fuss — as you put it."

Once Kane and Threnody helped get me settled in my suite, the doctor arrived. Plump. Bushy haired. Kindly eyes. Hotel robe pulled on over . . . maybe over nothing. I couldn't tell for sure. *Did he always carry his medical case when he traveled?* I wondered. His words and actions assured me that my cuts were superficial, but there was no way of easing my mental anguish without including Kane in the conversation.

"Superficial cuts," Dr. Plumply said. "Keep them lightly bandaged until tomorrow. You'll be fine. Take it easy tonight and get plenty of rest."

I thanked him for his help, but I doubt he heard me. For him it was far past yawn time. He left before anyone could protest or pay him for his call.

I felt rattled and off balance, and now I knew I had to tell Kane and Threnody about my threatening call.

And that's what I did.

"Rafa, you know you should have told Chief Ramsey the minute you broke off the connection with the caller. He might have had a way to trace the call. Police can do things ordinary citizens can't do."

"Give me a break. I felt safe on our boat trip. I felt safe on our trip to Marathon. I planned to call Ramsey first thing in the morning — really I did."

"You waited too long before making that call. I'm not leaving you alone here tonight." Kane plopped down in an easy chair as if he intended to sleep there all night.

"I told Brick I'd stay here with you tonight," Threnody said. "Once the Frangi closes for the night, he'll drive home without me. Maybe both of us should stay, Kane."

"Out! Out! Both of you. I'm going to be fine right here — alone. No need for anyone to stay with me." I sounded braver than I felt. Ever since I fell from my balcony, I doubted the penthouse security system. But I'd keep my door locked. Nobody could enter without my permission.

"I don't like the idea of your staying here alone," Kane said. "I'd invite you to spend the night on *The Buccaneer,* but I doubt you'd adjust to one of those hard bunks."

Threnody spoke up before I could answer Kane. "If you don't want me to stay here with you, Rafa, at least come with me after the Frangi closes. Spend the night at my place."

354

My reaction to that idea must have shown on my face. Threnody spoke again before either Kane or I could protest.

"There's a spare room at the mansion, Rafa. Don't know what it was used for in the past. Maybe a maid's quarters. It's unsuitable for a guest room. But it has a lock in place — an old-fashioned hasp on the inside of the door."

"No point in causing you a problem," I argued. "I'll be fine right here."

"Brick and Jessie are driving to Miami tonight. They'll check into a hotel so they'll be there for a business meeting first thing in the morning. You'd be doing me a favor if you'd come over, Rafa. I dislike spending the night alone. It's a creepy place after dark — guess that's why it's one of the stops on the Key West ghost tours."

Kane laughed. "Good try, Threnody. Since when did you start believing in ghosts? Those after-midnight ghost walks are strictly for tourists who want a good story to tell the folks up north. Believe me. Some of the tales may be true, but I'm guessing others have grown with embellishment."

"Okay, you two. I'm perfectly okay for staying here alone tonight, but I've read that ghost tour booklet. Whether they're true or untrue it'd be nice for Threnody to have some company tonight."

Kane shrugged when I started packing a small overnight case. "Your choice, Rafa. I won't force myself on you, but remember this. You do have my name at the top of the list on your speed dial. If anything causes either of you the least worry or fright, call me. Deal?"

"Deal!" Kane glanced at his watch. "Be quittin' time in another hour or so. Get some rest, Rafa, and keep your door locked until the Frangi closes."

THIRTY-FIVE

Once Kane left and I'd packed my cosmetics, a for-emergencies-only sleep shirt, and a change of clothes, I was ready to leave my suite. Threnody moved to an easy chair and turned on the TV.

"What's going on?" I asked. "If you'd rather spend the night here, I can arrange for that, but . . ."

"No. We need to go to my place, but I want to give Brick and Jessie plenty of time to pack their essentials and leave. Don't want to see them again tonight — and maybe have to answer questions."

So we waited a few more minutes before we stepped into the moonlit night and I flung my overnight case onto the back seat of the Prius. We left, passing the swimming pool as we headed for the mansion. I'd never been to the third floor of Threnody's spacious home, and I hoped the climb wouldn't cause my leg to start bleeding again. After we drove down the lane and turned onto the Vexton property, I stopped at the front door, but Threnody spoke up.

"Let's use the back door, Rafa. Your car will be out of sight there. No need to advertise that you're spending the night here."

I parked where she suggested beside her Caddi, seeing Brick's car nowhere in sight. Nor Jessie's. Good. I peered up at a window on the third floor. "That the spare room?"

"Right. We seldom use it. Use only the second-floor guest rooms. Saves everyone a climb."

"I could stay on the second floor if it's more convenient for you."

"No. I promised you a locked room. You'll find a hasp inside the door of the third-floor room. Tonight I'll sleep up there, too, in the tiny alcove right across a narrow hallway from your room. There's a louvered door and a daybed there. If you need help during the night, you can call me. I'll be close by."

I parked the car and we both got out. Moonlight made the night almost bright as day, but Threnody hurried ahead of me to snap on a porch light. When I turned to get my overnight case from the back seat of the car, the dome light flashed on again and I saw my fishing rod on the floor. Drat. I should have taken care of it when I came in earlier this afternoon.

"Come on, Rafa." Threnody opened the back door and reached around the jamb to switch on a light in the kitchen. "What's the problem?"

"No problem. But do you have a water hose back here someplace?"

"Rafa, it's late." Threnody returned to my side. "Why do you need a hose? What we both need is some sleep. Come on. Let me carry your bag."

From the light on the porch, I saw a garden hose coiled near the porch under a spigot that jutted out from the house. "This'll only take a minute. I forgot about my fishing rod. It's still in the car and I need to hose it down. Shouldn't have left it this afternoon coated with salt water. It's my favorite rod."

"You can wash it off in the morning. One night isn't going to make any difference."

I knew Threnody might be right. But my personal rule required me to take care of fishing tackle immediately after I finished using it. Gram gave me this rod, my favorite, years ago. I turned on the hose.

"Okay," Threnody called. "Have it your way. Can I help?"

"No, thanks. I'll be finished in a sec, then

I'll prop the rod against the porch and let it drip dry."

Threnody laughed. "Sure you don't want to towel it down and put it to beddy-bye in a velvet case?"

I knew she was joking and being a bit sarcastic, but I did wish I could towel the rod dry right then. However, I pretended otherwise and followed her into the house. The spic-and-span kitchen opened into a breakfast nook where we'd enjoyed macaroons. A small table sat with dishes and silver in place, ready for use in the morning.

"Want anything to eat before we settle down for the night — the rest of the night, that is." She looked at her watch and yawned.

"Thanks, but no. Let's get to bed."

Threnody carried my overnight bag and I followed her upstairs, listening to the creaks and groans of the seldom-used steps, feeling the old treads dip to the center. When we entered the third-floor bedroom, Threnody unfolded a luggage rack and laid my bag on it before she flung open a window to admit a light breeze.

"Shut it in a few minutes, if you feel too cool, Rafa. We keep this floor closed most of the time. It needs to air out, but the bed's made and ready for use. Guess I have Dolly

360

take care of the beds like you take care of your fishing tackle. Want them to be ready at a moment's notice — even this one."

Pine paneling covered both the walls and the ceiling of the room, giving it a special charm of its own, charm that no wallpaper or paint could match. Once Threnody closed the door, I dropped the bolt hanging from a chain through the hasp, changed into my sleep shirt, and eased onto bed. Both the mattress and the pillow felt soft and comfortable. I tried to relax.

After such a long, hard day, fishing with Kane, talking with Snipe Gross, working and falling at the Frangi, I thought I'd drop off to sleep immediately. But no. I lay there staring at the ceiling, listening to some night bird calling into the silence. Mourning doves. Do they mourn at night? I didn't count sheep. Instead, I counted the many questions still plaguing my mind concerning Diego's murder.

The blue line tying Diego's feet matched the blue line on Kane's boat. The blue line on Kane's boat had disappeared. A normal thing, right? A normal thing for Kane to get rid of anything that might tie him to Diego's death.

Much as I tried to forget my plunge from the balcony, it loomed in my mind, preventing sleep. Someone had deliberately called me, intending for me to fall — to my death. Had the laundry ladies not been working on the laundry room balcony two floors below, I might not be lying sleepless tonight. Who wanted me out of the way? I shuddered when I thought of the threatening call I'd received and then my fall in the Frangi tonight. Someone thought I was getting too close to exposing Diego's killer. But how could that be? Tonight I felt as far from knowing the murderer's identity as I did the morning after I found Diego's body in the sea. Pablo? Kane? Brick? Jessie? I refused to add Threnody and Dolly to the list.

Putting those memories from my mind, I thought again about the bell that had once been on Kane's boat years ago, the bell that now hung at Brick's front door. Was that a clue to the killer's identity, or was it merely a result of Brick's fondness of antiques? I wished now I'd asked him where he got the bell. Many times he liked to tell the history associated with his artifacts.

Too many puzzles. Too few solutions. Just as I felt myself beginning to fall asleep, I heard a car door slam. On my Prius? On Threnody's Caddi? I bolted upright. No mistake. The sound had carried through the open window. I eased from bed and tiptoed to the window. My car keys glinted in the moonlight that fell on my bedside table where I'd left them before I turned out the lamp. Nobody could get in my car. Maybe Threnody hadn't locked the Caddi. I peered out the window, looking down at the two cars.

Nothing moved. No sound broke the quiet. Even the night bird remained silent. What had disturbed it? *Watch your back.* Words from the telephone threat did a rerun in my mind. Tonight I translated them to *watch your car.* In all the fuss about hosing down my fishing rod, maybe I forgot to click on the door lock.

I continued to watch. I continued to hear nothing. But I had to know for sure that I'd locked my car doors. Key West is noted for attracting a high population of the world's homeless. I didn't want any of them sleeping in my car — or Threnody's.

Easing to the bedside table, I picked up my car keys, padded back to the window, and pushed the lock button. The lock clicked. The car's lights flashed for an instant. So! I had left it unlocked. But maybe the lights would flash even if I pushed the lock twice. I'd never found reason to think about that. I pushed the unlock button and heard the door unlock, saw the lights flash. Then I locked it again. No matter that I hadn't had the emergency button repaired. The sound of the lock and the flash of light should scare off prowlers.

In reading books, I always laughed when the story's endangered heroine stepped into some dark and dangerous place where she was almost sure to be accosted, raped, or killed. Now I contemplated playing the part of the endangered heroine in my own story. I needed to creep downstairs, step into Threnody's backyard, and make sure both cars were okay — and locked.

No. I wouldn't be so dumb. I'd wake Threnody. After I told her what I'd seen and heard, we'd go downstairs together to check on our cars. Threnody would want to make sure her car was locked.

I undid the hasp, stepped into the narrow hallway, and approached Threnody's alcove. The breeze caused by the opened door molded my sleep shirt to my body. No time now to think about sleep shirts. I tapped gently on the alcove door, wanting to make no noise that might carry outside and alert an intruder. No response.

Although I hated to, I knocked louder. Hairs rose on my nape and I only waited a few seconds before I turned the door knob, opened the door.

No Threnody. The bed lay empty, yet I'd heard no one leave the room. No footsteps on the creaky stair treads. Had I fallen asleep unaware I'd been sleeping and dreaming? No. I couldn't believe that.

"Threnody?" I whispered. No answer. Maybe she'd gone to the bathroom.

"Threnody?" I spoke louder, but still no response.

Now, unmindful for the need or silence, I hurried on down the stairs, forgetting about my injured leg. When I reached the kitchen, I snapped on a light. No Threnody. I opened the back door.

Silence. Not even a mosquito hummed in my ear. No dove mourned.

"Threnody?" Again, I whispered her name. Running to my car, I jerked on the driver's-side door. Although I'd just locked it from upstairs, the door opened and the dome light flashed on. Glancing into the back seat, I stifled a scream.

THIRTY-SIX

"Threnody!" Forgetting any need for silence, I shrieked her name, then clamped my jaws, gritted my teeth, squelched screams.

Threnody lay facedown with her head on an old pillow I'd thrown into the back seat that morning before going fishing. For a few crazy moments, I thought she might be sleeping in my car. Wishful thinking!

Her long satin gown clung to her upper body wrinkled and twisted, revealing skin from buttocks to ankles. The slipper from her left foot had dropped onto the floor of the car. The right slipper remained in place. Her long hair lay splayed over the pillow and onto the car seat. At first I didn't notice the length of blue line double-wrapped around her throat.

Pulled tight.

Knotted.

Tail ends falling down her back, peeking

from under her hair.

I wiped away tears, although I hadn't realized I was crying.

Blue line. I couldn't see her face, nor did I want to. Like Kane, I'd watched too many *Law and Order* reruns. I wanted to remember Threnody as she looked earlier tonight at the Frangi.

My squelched screams gave way to a more urgent need to vomit. I choked back the bitter gorge rising in my throat. Heat flooded my face at the same time my fingers and toes grew icy cold. I wanted to back away, to retreat from the scene, but I couldn't force my feet into action. Vomit flooded the carpet of my car, then trailed in yellow/brown strings to the seat cover. I wiped my chin on the tail of my nightshirt.

In my heart I knew Threnody lay dead, yet she might be alive. I remembered thinking the same thing about Diego a few days ago. He might have been alive. Since Diego's death, Threnody and I enjoyed strong bonds of friendship. I had to make sure there was nothing I could do to help her. Maybe I could loosen the garrote around her neck. Why had she come to my car? Who had done this to her? Who had left her like this?

Once reality began to pierce my brain, near panic set in. Where was Threnody's killer? Was I next on his list? In spite of my gut feeling, my gut desire to put distance between myself and Threnody, I eased onto the back seat beside her body, closed and locked the door, and then leaned forward to push the button that would lock all the doors.

"Threnody?" I spoke softly at first, as if I might wake her from needed sleep.

No answer. In my heart I hadn't expected a reply.

"Threnody." I spoke louder, waited a few seconds, and then in the next moment I shouted her name and shook her shoulder. "Threnody! Threnody! Speak to me."

Although I hadn't touched my car key, the door locks clicked and someone opened the driver's-side door. Who? At first I couldn't tell. Friend? Foe? He wore jeans and a tank top, and he kept his face turned from me.

"We're going for a little ride, Rafa."

Pablo! When had he found my car key? When? How? Before he could start the engine, I opened the back door wide, stepped onto the ground, and began to run. Where to go? I headed around the house. Maybe I could hide where he couldn't find me. Hide where? At first I saw no place to hide. Then I spied a palm thicket at the side of the house and slipped under some low-hanging fronds. I sucked in air. Mentally, I ordered the palm fronds to silence and stillness. They obeyed. Only the whisper of a breeze caused a slight motion of the fronds.

Safe! At least or a moment. But the respite lasted only a few scant seconds. Pablo rounded the corner of the mansion and headed my way. Forcing myself to hold my breath, my lungs felt close to exploding as I played statue and didn't move an eyelash.

Pablo passed my hiding place and kept jogging toward the front veranda. I couldn't see him, and thinking he must have reached the porch, I slunk from behind the palm thicket. This time I stepped into the grass beside the path and padded toward the front lane, knowing he would hear my footsteps if I broke into a run. Walking gave me time to catch my breath. The stabbing pain in my side eased.

Maybe I could make it down that long lane to the street. Maybe I could flag down a car once I reached the pavement. At this time of night? Forget that! I started running. It was my only chance.

No! Not my only chance. Use your brain, woman! Call Kane on your cell. No. I'd left my phone upstairs in the house. Dumb. Dumb. Dumb. Again, my lungs felt on fire.

I couldn't get my breath. I felt as if someone had tied a rope just above my waist. I gasped for air and then sharp pain hit low in my left groin. Surely someone must be jabbing a knife above my crotch. Jabbing and twisting.

I'd almost reached the street when I heard Pablo behind me. I hated giving in to him, but I saw no other choice. He threw himself at me, knocking me to the ground. Blood began to trickle down my leg again.

"Stand up, Rafa! Stand!"

"I can't. I can't."

"Stand. On your feet right now! Don't scream!"

I screamed.

"I guess a few screams won't make any difference. There's nobody around to hear you."

Pablo linked his left arm through my right arm and yanked me close to his side. Turning us around, he forced me to walk with him back toward the car.

THIRTY-SEVEN

"Where are you taking me?"

"You'll find out soon enough."

"Threnody. What have you done to her?"

"You gone blind? I think you saw what I did to her."

"She's dead." I didn't expect an argument. Pablo offered none. Had he gone mad? Was he bringing to life a scene predicted in the tarot cards?

"You're not going to get by with this, Pablo. First Diego. Now Threnody."

"And next, you. And of course I'll get by with it. I've made careful plans."

I had to keep him talking. "So you admit you killed Diego?"

"Had to. Learned that he and two of his buddy commissioners planned to vote against building a hotel at the marina, and in this case they formed a majority."

"The Gang of Three?"

Pablo gave a bitter laugh. "Gang of Three!

That's nothing but a political cliché. On any committee there's usually a majority. Could be a gang of five, seven, nine."

"You were sure that's how they planned to vote?"

"At the time I was sure of it. I wanted to see that hotel built."

"Wanted it enough to murder your own father?"

"We had our differences — money differences."

"What difference would the hotel have meant to you, with your dad dead?"

"I planned to let Brick build the hotel and insist that he appoint me as manager."

"Fat chance of that happening. Jessie's the one who'll get that job." Pablo was out of his mind, but I had to keep our conversation going.

"Who's to say? It's too late now for Dad's vote to count. The other two commissioners will vote in any way that's politically convenient for them at the moment. Without Dad's leadership and influence, I doubt they can pull enough strings to get the hotel vote to go his way when the matter comes up before the commissioners again."

"So what's the point in these needless murders?" I yanked on my arm to see if he'd tighten his grip. He did.

"The point is that I plan to run for Dad's place on the board of commissioners. I think people will vote for me. Son of the victim. I'll work on a tear-jerker act. Many people will feel it their duty to show their respect for Dad by voting for his son. And once I'm on the commission, I'll have influence on the ROGO."

"That's really looking into a cloudy future."

"I can countermand everything anyone else says, Rafa. Believe me. It's true. Right now Key West voters are in a building mood. They want to see Key West grow because they know that's the only way their incomes will grow. They want more cruise ships to visit our harbor. They want more t-shirt shops on Duval. They want more hotel rooms for an influx of tourists. I might have been a beach bum in the past, but I'm proud now to be able to be a part of the New Key West."

"I can't believe Key West's that full of Bubba politics."

"Sometimes Bubba politics are the best kind for everyone concerned. You scratch my back, I'll scratch your back."

"The thought of you scratching my back makes me want to puke." I choked on the bitterness at the base of my tongue and tried to swallow the tightness in my throat.

"Go ahead and puke — if you want that to be one of the few things you'll get to do before you join Dad and Threnody."

"You can't get away with this, Pablo. Everyone at the Frangi knows I planned to spend the night with Threnody. When they come here looking for me, they can see for themselves what has happened."

We had reached the back porch and my chances of escaping diminished. I had decided to make a run for it — a run for escape. I'd rather be a dead fugitive than Pablo's dead captive. In a sudden move, I yanked my arm free from Pablo's grip and turned to give him a shove. I hoped to throw him off balance. I knew he could outrun me in a foot race unless I had a head start.

In that instant a shot rang out and Pablo dropped to the ground. I thought for an instant that I'd been hit. But no.

Who? What? Maybe Kane had sensed my need for help and come to investigate.

I ran. If Kane hadn't shot Pablo, I had some other enemy. Or had Pablo been my deadline caller? Had I tripped over his foot last night at the Frangi? I couldn't remember where Pablo had been at the time I fell.

I could only concentrate on escaping. That bit of concentration wasn't enough. All hope dropped to my toes when I heard Brick's voice and felt him grab the arm I'd just freed from Pablo's grip.

"We meet again, Rafa."

Seeing my fishing rod leaning against the porch railing, I decided to make one last try for freedom before Brick had time to make a full assessment of our positions. I jerked my arm from his, at the same time placing one foot behind his ankles and giving him a strong shove backward. He lost his balance and I heard him fall and flounder on the ground behind me.

In those moments, I grabbed my fishing rod and ran, putting as much distance between us as I could. The moment Brick regained his balance and came rushing toward me, I took aim and, with the weighted lure hanging from the tip of my rod, I cast it, aiming for his head. I heard the thud of lead connecting with flesh and bone, but he didn't go down. Panicked, I ran again. Again, he caught me, pulled me close, and twisted my arm. The smell of rum on his breath turned my stomach.

"You make me sick, Brick Vexton. Sick. Sick. Sick." I tried to loosen his grip. No way.

"Oh come now, Rafa." He laughed. "You've forgotten the times I made you

375

happy. Very, very happy."

I couldn't be sure if his eyes looked glazed or if the moonlight glinted on them in a way that gave them a glazed appearance.

"You're a fool, Brick. Kane's right about you. You have an eye for the ladies. But I've never been one of your ladies. You may have noticed I've made it a point to keep plenty of distance between us."

Brick laughed. My voice snagged in my throat. I could think of no more insults. Some guys don't know an insult when they hear one. Once more I jerked my arm free and began to run toward the street again. In two strides Brick caught up with me, yanking me to his side and bending my thumb back until I thought he'd break it. With his other hand, he pulled a pistol from the slash pocket of his jumpsuit. I felt doomed when he locked his arm more tightly through mine and dragged me toward my car.

"Keep moving forward." Brick punctuated his words with a nudge of the gun.

I moved forward.

THIRTY-EIGHT

If fear and excitement gives one an empowering adrenalin rush, I failed to feel it. I hardly possessed the strength to put one foot ahead of the other. Moving forward or backward wouldn't have made any difference.

"Where are we going?" I asked, hardly expecting an answer.

"Thought we'd take a little drive, Rafa. You're so fond of the Prius, I thought I'd give you the pleasure of one final ride in it. So prepare yourself to enjoy."

His speech sounded slurred as he nudged me toward my car. Again I smelled rum on his breath. How many daiquiris had he downed tonight? I wondered how he would manage taking me for a ride I didn't want to go on. It turned out to be easy enough. He had it all planned. He opened the front passenger door and nudged me onto the seat.

"Hold out your hands, Rafa."

The temptation to refuse and to look over the seat at Threnody's body flashed through my mind. What if someone had discovered her while Pablo and I were playing chase-around-the-house for those few minutes? No such luck. Brick must have been the one who found her body.

One last hope. No. No Kane. No tell-tale noise from a cop hiding behind us. I stopped hoping for a miracle. I didn't look over the car seat. I did hold out my hands. Surely he planned to detain me with handcuffs.

Brick hesitated a bit when I thrust my wrists toward him, and I tried to plan how I could escape when he laid his gun aside in order to fasten the cuffs. But he didn't lay the gun aside. While taking careful aim at me with the gun in his right hand, he reached into another pocket of his dock master uniform with his left hand. I heard the clink of steel against steel when he pulled out the handcuffs.

"Where did you get those?" I asked, hoping the cuffs were toys. No. They were for real.

"Found them in my bag of magic tricks, doll." He clicked one bracelet around my right wrist. "Okay now. Arms behind your back. Don't try any tricks. Lean toward the dashboard and do as I say."

I leaned forward and felt cold steel scrape my skin moments before I heard the other bracelet snap around my left wrist. I refused to give him the satisfaction of begging for mercy. I knew by now neither he nor Pablo knew the meaning of the word mercy. I said nothing. Maybe I could kick him while he drove us to his secret destination. But he squelched those plans in the next moment.

"Okay, Rafa. Feet together. Ankles touching, please."

I followed instructions. It didn't surprise me when he pulled a coil of blue line from the same pocket that moments ago held handcuffs. He bound my ankles together. Then he smashed me back against the car seat and fastened my seat belt. Was he kidding! Why the sudden interest in my safety?

"Mustn't give the cops reason to pull us over, Rafa. Little traffic moving at this hour of the night. Bored policemen stop any car that looks the least bit suspicious to them. I've heard they get a bonus for any arrests they make between midnight and sunrise, so I'm making sure this car won't catch any cop's eye." He straightened himself behind the steering wheel, pausing a moment to wipe sweat from his forehead with his left arm before he fastened his own seat belt.

Breathing deeply for a few seconds, he wiped his forehead again before he hit the accelerator and we shot forward. Had my fishing lure hurt him, or had he enjoyed too many daiquiris?

"Where we going?" I tried to get back into my keep-him-talking mode, but having my hands and feet immobilized slowed my thought processes. So did having two captors in the same evening. I decided to say no more and wait to see what happened next. Maybe my silence would unnerve him, make him wonder what I was thinking — and planning.

He scooped the loop around Duval Street and Whitehead. We passed Southernmost Point. The presidential gate. Sloppy Joe's. Margaritaville. When a street light shone directly on his face, I thought again that his eyes looked glazed and glassy.

"Got a headache? That fishing lure gave you quite a whack."

"Hardly felt it, Rafa. Hardly f-felt it."

It pleased me to know I had hurt him — at least a little. Wish it had been a little more. Closed signs hung in the windows of the bars we passed. Sloppy's. Margaritaville. Schooner Reef. Hog's Breath. I guessed it might be about time for the early-morning garbage and trash trucks to take to the streets. Maybe I could signal someone. Those commercial truck seats rose above the seats of most cars. Maybe some truck driver would happen to look down into the Prius and see Threnody sprawled on the back seat or notice me mouthing the word "help."

I saw nobody out and about. Soon Brick chose a route that made our destination clear — Daiquiri Dock.

"I gave my dock masters the morning off for today, Rafa. Need a little t-time and working s-space to get a few chores done. The police will arrive soon after that, and I want to practice my surprised look as I lead them to Threnody's body. Surprised and horrified, of course."

"The husband's always the first suspect. You should know that."

"Of course. I've prepared for that. This time you're going to be the chief suspect."

"Don't know how you'll manage that." I hoped that comment would make him want to explain. Once I knew his plans, maybe I could figure out a way to escape and thwart them.

Brick made no explanations. He pulled his cell phone from the shirt pocket of his jumpsuit as if he might make a call. Then he dropped it back into his pocket. Too early

to talk to anyone? I wondered who he
wanted to call.

THIRTY-NINE

I'd never patronized any marina in the wee hours of the morning, but I expected to see a few security lights here and there. In fact, I expected to see several lights illuminating each catwalk, lights that kept the moored boats visible at all times. Tonight only the moon brightened the night, and as we approached the chandlery, clouds threaded across the sky and the moon. Dark. Light. Dark. Light. The frequent changes in visibility left me dizzy and off balance even though I sat securely fastened under the seat belt.

My car was the only one approaching the parking lot. At first I took that as a hopeful sign. Maybe some cop patrolling his beat would notice the Prius and stop to investigate. It surprised me when Brick drove around the chandlery building and headed into a mangrove thicket. I heard branches in the dense grove of trees scrape against the sides of the car. I could hardly breathe, but I gasped for air and tried to distract him.

"Brick! Stop! I'll need to have my car repainted."

"Someone will, but I doubt if it'll be you. In a few minutes you won't be worrying about paint or the Prius — or anything else. When the police find this car, they'll wonder how it got here. But finding it won't happen anytime soon. I doubt the cops know this thicket behind the chandlery exists. I'm guessing they've never investigated it or, if they're aware of it, even wondered about what it might hide."

"Of course they'll find my car. They're not stupid."

When Brick laughed, a flash of moonglow coming through the sunroof revealed a thread of drool seeping from his mouth and running onto his chin. He continued talking as if he didn't feel the wetness. "This is the area where people will see a new hotel in the near future."

"You can't build anything back here."

"Why do you say that? Wishful thinking?"

Keep him talking. Keep him talking. "You can't build a hotel or anything else here because it's against the law to destroy indigenous plants — like all of these mangrove trees. Mangroves are native to the Keys. They've been here forever. Mother's chairperson of the Preserve the Trees committee. That's a group of locals, men and women, who work on behalf of Key West's native palms and mangroves. Anyone abusing a tree faces a heavy fine and lots of negative publicity in the media. You might as well forget about building your fancy hotel at this location."

My mouth and throat felt so dry I didn't think I could say another word. I swallowed three times, trying to bring moisture to my mouth, my tongue.

"Laws can be changed." Brick spoke in a taunting tone. "Laws can be circumvented. I'll find loopholes in the building code that'll allow me to build here. What good is a bunch of ugly mangrove trees? No good at all. They'll come down. New hotel will go up. And Key West and the Vextons will be richer for the addition."

Brick gunned the car forward then back a few times, forcing the steering wheel to the right and then to the left, trying to create enough space to open the car doors. Branches scraped and scratched against the car every time he moved it. I closed my eyes and cringed. I gritted my teeth and said nothing. I hoped we were trapped here.

Maybe he couldn't force a space big enough to allow the doors to open.

Forward. Back. Forward. Back. He continued jogging the car inch by inch until he managed to force the driver's door open a crack wide enough for him to slip through it. Then he poked his head and shoulders back inside.

"Lean forward, Rafa."

"I can't lean forward. The seat belt — it's too tight."

He fumbled with the catch on the seat belt until it loosened and dropped to the car seat.

"Lean forward. Do it now. Lean!"

I leaned forward and he released the handcuffs. At first I thought I'd be able to whack him, but the pressure from the cuffs and the seat belt left my hands numb. They throbbed when the blood began to circulate through my wrists to my hands again. I clenched and unclenched my fingers, trying to make fists. Before the pain left, he jerked my left arm toward him. Was he going to break my elbow? I squinted and gritted my teeth in anticipation of more pain. Surprise. He replaced and locked one handcuff around my wrist and locked the other cuff to the steering wheel.

"You'll have to stay here a few minutes,

but don't get your hopes up. Nobody will see you, and I'll return quickly."

"The police will get you."

"The police will never find me back here."

He squeezed through the door opening again, faced the back seat, and began tugging on the rear door. At the same time he stamped his feet, breaking mangrove saplings until he could open that door. I couldn't bear to watch him. I kept looking forward.

"You won't get away with this."

No response.

When I heard him tugging Threnody's body from the back seat, I couldn't bear to turn to watch. After a few moments he stopped tugging. I hoped the mangroves would thwart his plan, whatever his plan might be. He closed the back door, forced himself alongside it to the car trunk, opened it. I turned to look. Moonlight gleamed on a blanket he must have planted there. He grabbed it then forced his way to the rear door again.

"The police will find you. You'll pay for this."

No response.

In the light from the ceiling dome, I watched him wrap Threnody's body in the blanket, pull her from the car, and heave her onto his shoulder.

I couldn't bear to look.

I couldn't bear to look away.

Brick was not a large person or a tall person, but he worked out every day. With Threnody balanced on his shoulder, he forced his way through the mangroves and out of my sight.

Tears burned behind my eyelids, but I refused to let Brick see me crying. I blinked them back. Several minutes passed before I heard him crashing through the thicket. Then he stood beside the driver's door again.

"Your turn, Rafa."

He released the cuff binding me to the steering wheel. I seized the chance to struggle, although my wrist felt like a piece of fish chum.

"No point in fighting the inevitable, Rafa. In a few moments it'll all be over. You'll join Diego and Threnody in eternity." He released the binding around my ankles, and pain shot up both legs. I could hardly stand to bear my weight on my feet. No chance I could ignore that pain and kick him. Blood trickled from the cuts on my leg. Good. Maybe the police would notice a bloody trail and find me — or my body.

"Want to see what I did with Threnody?"

"No."

"Want to hear more of my plans?"

"No."

Once we struggled from the mangrove thicket, Brick prodded me with his gun. He forced me to walk a step ahead of him down the catwalk toward *The Bail Bond.* Didn't he see the bloody trail I left? I refused to look at my feet until he reached up and forced my head down, made me look.

There on the slippery boards of the swaying catwalk, I saw Threnody's body. Her open eyes stared at nothingness. Her mouth gaped. Beside her lay a concrete block, a roll of gray duct tape, and a coil of blue line.

"Now it's your turn, Rafa."

I said nothing.

"Don't play dumb. Get to work. Stoop. Tape her ankles together. Now."

FORTY

He shoved me to my knees. Kneeling beside Threnody's body, I touched the cold skin of her ankles. Withdrawing my hand, I sobbed in spite of myself. Brick prodded me with his gun. Somehow in this awkward position I forced myself to peel duct tape from the roll and bind her ankles together.

"Now tie her ankles to the concrete block. I want your fingerprints on stuff, not mine."

Although my fingers felt cold and stiff as icicles, I forced myself to carry out Brick's orders.

"Good work. You're playing your part well. Now I'll help you. Together we'll dump her into the sea, close to the place where I dumped Diego a few days ago. The water's shallow at this tide, and it's clear. The police will see her body."

Together we performed this black deed. In moments I saw Threnody's head bobbing in the sea. Would my fingerprints wash off of the things I'd touched? Would Brick get away with this second murder? Third murder? How could this be happening! I'd be number four.

I vomited. Again.

Brick didn't jump out of the way soon enough. The vomit landed on his shoes and splashed onto his jumpsuit.

"You won't get away with this," I gasped.

"Of course I will." Brick fumbled in his pocket, bringing out the handcuffs again. He cuffed one ring around my wrist and the other around his wrist. "You've left a bloody trail to the body. The cops will think you murdered both Diego and Threnody. Similar location. Similar modus operandi. They'll come after you. You'll be convicted of murder — double murder. Maybe a triple murder if they count Diego."

"But when the police find me, I'll tell them exactly what happened."

"Dreamer! You'll be too dead to tell them anything. You're next, you know. They'll find your body next to Threnody's. Once you're dead — on second thought I may not wait long enough for you to die in the sea. Instead, I'll hack your body to bits and feed you piece by piece to the sharks that prowl here at night. Yes. That's my new plan. Feeding you to the sharks."

"Kane will come looking for me. Kane knows I didn't murder Diego. He'll know I didn't kill Threnody. Believe me, he'll raise a storm. He'll go straight to the police."

Brick laughed. "Be real, Rafa. It's almost impossible to prove a murder took place if there's no body left behind. Sharks do a good cleanup job when it comes to chunks of flesh in the water. They may find Threnody, but not you — after I finish with you."

"Well, my body isn't dead yet." Wind blew the clouds away. Brick stood laughing at me in the moonlight. "Why have you done this, Brick? Three murders. Why have you risked prison or death? So you thought Diego stood in your way, manipulated other council members until they agreed to hold your name back on the ROGO list. I can barely understand that as your motive for killing Diego. Then Pablo? Why? And Threnody. And now me. Why? Why? Why?"

"Think about Snipe Gross, Rafa. You and Threnody signed your death certificates when you went to see Snipe, pried info from him."

"You mean information about the bell?"

"Right. The bell."

"The bell told us nothing. Nothing at all. We were trying to trace the ownership of the blue line — the line you used to tie

Diego's feet and now Threnody's feet. We thought once we found the owner of that old line, we'd be closer to finding Diego's killer. Guess we were right."

"And this is what you get for being s-so n-nosey. You were getting too close to learning . . ." Brick wiped his forehead with the back of his arm. His voice faded away for a moment. What was wrong with him? My heart pounded. Had my fishing lure hurt him more than he admitted? I tried to take a step away from him, but the handcuffs jerked me to a stop. His reflexes hadn't slowed any. He yanked me toward him and finished the sentence he'd started.

". . . you were getting too close to learning the truth of Diego's death. Too close to suit me. You outsmarted yourselves. I dislike people who try to be smarter than I am."

Keep him talking. Keep him talking. I kept that mantra playing in my mind. But what good would it do at this point? How I regretted leaving my cell phone in that third-floor bedroom! Yet, maybe if I played to his ego I could win a few more minutes of life. I looked toward the chandlery. Surely someone would arrive before long. Even though he gave his staff the day off, some boat owner might arrive wanting to go fishing. I might be able to call for help.

Brick's gaze followed mine. "Don't be expecting help anytime soon. I've given all the dock masters the day off."

"Yes, you told me that and I believe you, but someone, maybe more than one, some boat owners may appear to use their boats. The owners can get their boats without the aid of a dock master if they want to. All they need is their key to the console."

"Wishful thinking, Rafa. Nobody will come around this early."

Brick's voice didn't hold the conviction it held earlier. My hold on life weakened. Dawn was turning the eastern sky from black to gray. The moon had changed from a golden globe to a pale circle of whiteness. It cast little light. I must keep talking. In my mind I willed some unexpected boat captain to appear. I tried to remember last night's weather advisory. Calm seas? Or small craft warnings? In spite of what Brick said, he must know he faced discovery from an early-rising boater, no matter what the weather. I forced myself to keep talking.

"Oh, we learned that the bell Snipe Gross told us about had been on Kane's boat. Also on Bucky Varnum's boat when he used it as a water taxi . . . Mariel Boatlift. Now the bell hangs at your front door. Right?" I paused for breath. "Is that bell for sale, Brick?"

"For sale?" Brick acted as if he'd never heard of a bell being for sale.

"Yes. Is the bell for sale? I'd like to buy it as a gift for Kane." I paused before I forced more words. "Kane's a history buff. Being able to display the boat's original bell would please him. At the same time, having that bell in its original place on *The Buccaneer* would give Kane brownie points with the officials who are allowing him to moor his boat at the historic harbor as an educational museum." I heard my voice trail off. Had Brick heard my words?

"These are the last moments of your life, Rafa Blue. You're not going to be alive long enough to be worrying about gifts for Kane. Don't think I don't realize you're trying to distract me."

"That's beside the point. I'll admit the bell didn't lead us to a murderer. It only led us to you, who we knew liked to collect artifacts from the past. Think about it. Will you sell me the bell? Will you let me share it with Kane and all the people who pay to step aboard and tour a former water taxi?"

"Why would Kane be interested in it?"

"You know why. I just told you why. Think about it."

Brick paused as if thinking. "You're stalling, Rafa. It's die time for you."

"You've had too much to drink, Brick. Remember, you'll have another body to hide. Bet you hadn't thought of that detail, had you?"

"Told you about the sharks. Don't you recall what happened to your father? Surely you haven't forgotten that. Like father, like daughter. You should consider it a fitting demise."

"The police may not find my body, but they'll find my car. Sooner or later they'll search all around the marina and the chandlery. How are you going to explain my car being stuck in the mangroves?"

"Easy, Rafa, easy. I'll tell them you must have hidden it there and then later found you couldn't get it out."

"Nobody's going to believe that. Everyone knows my pride in that car, knows I wouldn't intentionally damage it by driving it into a mangrove thicket."

"Too bad you won't be around to tell your reasoning to the police. Before the cops arrive, I'll get back in that car, clean up any signs of foul play. So they find your blood? They'll remember you cut your leg at the Frangi. Even DNA tests aren't going to incriminate me. I'm too smart for that."

I felt defeated. Exhausted. Why force myself into senseless conversation with a killer? My arm dropped to my side, pulling Brick's along with it. My body slumped toward Brick, but at that moment we both saw the flash of headlights. A vehicle turned into the entryway of the marina. A truck. It took me only moments to recognize it. Kane's work truck!

"Kane!" I shouted,

Brick clamped his hand over my mouth and pulled me closer to him. With my wrist cuffed to his, I couldn't regain my balance, but my feet were free. Somewhere, sometime during this wild night I lost my slippers, but now I kicked at Brick's shin with my bare heel and made contact.

"Damn you, bitch!" He cursed at me and dropped to the catwalk, pulling me down beside him. I thought my kick had hurt him. But no. He had forced us down to ensure a low profile for the truck driver. Kane didn't see us in the early morning gloom. His truck's motor along with the lapping of the sea covered my shout and Brick's curses.

The truck circled the parking lot and left the marina.

FORTY-ONE

"So much for Kane finding you!" Brick gloated. "He's long gone from here."

I kicked at Brick again, but my heel missed its target. "I hate you, Brick Vexton. Hate you! Hate you! Hate you!"

Brick laughed and jerked his arm to one side, pulling me even closer to him. "Easy, woman, easy. We both can remember a time when you loved me very much. Very much indeed."

My heart leaped. Now I was sure the fishing lure slamming into Brick's head had hurt him more than he'd admit. I studied his forehead as much as I could in the dim light of dawn, but I could only see a slight bruise near his left temple. Hope of some magic reprieve dropped to my toes again. But anger fueled my voice.

"I don't believe what you're saying, nor can I guess what you're trying to prove, Brick. You know I've never loved you. You must have embarrassed Threnody with your flirting, but I ignored you. I might have been one of the ladies you had an eye for, but I showed no interest in you. None. Not ever."

"How easily you've forgotten."

"Forgotten what? Ha! Refresh my memory."

"I didn't think you'd ever forget the Pla-Mor Hotel in Miami. Never thought you'd forget the handsome Mike Wilson."

I couldn't speak. My whole body froze. How did this man know about that sordid segment of my past!

"What do you think of that, Ms. Rafa Blue, *Citizen* columnist? Your parents did a super job of hushing up your passion for me. Even your grandmother helped try to quash the Blue family scandal. But your long-ago love for me — it's still there in your innermost memories, isn't it?"

"You don't know what you're talking about. I don't believe a word you're saying. You're out of your mind."

"Mike Wilson, sexy dancer. Mike Wilson, even sexier bed partner."

"You're making this up, Brick Vexton! You have no way of knowing such horrible things."

"Although many years have passed since that fun-and-games time we shared, I'm guessing you still lie in your cold bed in your posh hotel suite and dream of Mike Wilson. How cool is that? I've asked myself that question many times during the past years. What do you feel when you dream of Mike Wilson? Does your body tingle in places you'd almost forgotten?"

The cuff around my wrist cut into my flesh, sending pain up my arm. I didn't try to pull free. I let Brick rattle on and on until I could bear his words no longer.

"How did you know about Mike Wilson?"

"Oh! So you do remember me? We had some great times, didn't we? You were so young. It was my good fortune to be able to introduce a virgin to one of life's greatest pleasures. And you responded in such a mature way for a child your age. No, not a child. You were a child when I picked you up drinking a margarita at the hotel bar. But you were a woman when I finished bedding you. You should thank me for sharing my expertise with you."

I could only stare at him. I'd never seen this man when I was a child. How could he know about the secrets I'd revealed to no one? Not even my parents or my grandmother knew the details of the moments I'd spent with Mike Wilson. And certainly not the doctor who placed my feet in cold steel stirrups, spread my knees, and asked a million questions as he prodded and probed at my private parts. I'd kept the intimate details of my moments with Mike Wilson a secret. My secret.

"I'd never seen you before in all my life, Brick Vexton. I met you casually at a friend of my parents just before I left home to go abroad to college." Maybe the blow on his head had addled him. But here was something he wanted to talk about — a subject that inflated his ego. I'd keep him talking as long as I could, no matter how painful the subject.

"But you do remember Mike Wilson, don't you, Rafa? I won't release you into sweet death until you tell me you do remember Mike Wilson. Remember those brown eyes? Remember his sable-colored hair? Back then, many women told me my hair felt more like a silky pelt than real hair. Did you feel that way about it?"

"Why do you think you can convince me you're someone named Mike Wilson? Okay. So I'll admit I once knew a guy named Mike Wilson."

"Now we're getting somewhere." He jerked on his arm, making the cuff on my wrist cut into flesh, bringing tears to my eyes. "Of course you knew Mike Wilson."

"But you look nothing like the Mike Wilson I knew. Nothing at all. And your name? You're trying to tell me that the guy I knew as Mike Wilson of Miami is now Brick Vexton of Key West? You expect me to believe that?"

"It's simple for anyone to change his name. A person can do it upon request. Sometimes divorcees prefer to delete their married name from their lives and their memories and return to using their maiden names. No problem. Sometimes people hate their given names — and for good reason. What if Scarlet O'Hara had been named Pansy? Names make a difference."

"Scarlet and Pansy were potential characters in a novel. Easy enough for the author to click a few computer keys and change their names. But how did you go about changing your name?" I hoped that question would keep him talking a few more minutes. Bisque coloring now crept into the eastern sky. Maybe I could keep Brick talking until sunrise.

"Changing my name took a little money for fees here and there. But I had lots of money — the Mariel Boatlift, you know. The name change took some trips to a lawyer's office, then more trips to the courthouse and to a judge's chambers. But

at last my birth certificate read Brick Vexton."

"You went to all that trouble to keep me
from finding you again. You thought I'd
come searching for you?"

"I thought it a strong possibility, not that
I wanted to hide from you. You were very
good in bed. That's a good thing in a
woman — any woman."

"So you could and did change your name,
but what about your looks? The blue eyes,
for instance? Mike Wilson's eyes were
brown."

"Contacts. I dislike wearing them, but
someday I may remove them and tell anyone
inquiring that I'm wearing blue contacts.
Don't know why that might not work.
Should have tried it long ago. What do you
think?"

"The sable pelt? Tell me about that."

"At first I shaved my head and grew the
moustache and beard. Then age took care
of the hair problem. I'm probably the first
male in the world who welcomed baldness.
The beard, however, is natural. I think it
lends me a lot of dignity."

Now and then I heard a car passing on
the street below the marina. I willed some
driver to come to the chandlery. Clouds
began to cover the sliver of sun peeking

above the horizon, but they would soon burn off. Now I remembered that yesterday's weather forecast mentioned sunshine and temperatures in the eighties.

"Brick Vexton." I tried to ease away from him, but he jerked me back to his side. "How did you choose a new name? Did you have to find a name the courts and the judge approved, or could you pick any name you wanted?"

"I could choose and I chose Brick Vexton."

"Why?"

"Several reasons, Rafa. Brick has a strong sound. Don't you agree? The word *brick* leaves a strong picture in a person's mind."

"And you wanted to appear strong. Right?"

"Right."

"Vexton? Where did that name come from? Ancestors?"

Brick laughed. "People are strange, Rafa. Certain words call up taboo subjects. Any name with an *x* in it calls up the word *sex*. Vex, sex. You get the connection. I consider Vexton an attractive name, sexy, steamy."

I felt myself running out of questions, but I took a deep breath and kept talking. "So returning to Key West disguised as Brick Vexton made you a new person. But why was that change so important to you? Did you think I'd fall for you again in your new disguise? Guess you've learned by now you failed."

"Don't flatter yourself. I grew up in Key West and I wanted to live here again."

"So you are living here. I see no problem with that."

"I had a deep fear that one day you might recognize me, perhaps by my voice. But that proved to be no real problem. Maybe voices change over the years, too. But I had no real problem with my disguise until you and Threnody started poking around at Marathon, looking up and questioning Snipe Gross."

We were talking in circles. We'd been over this before, but I had everything to gain by talking and nothing to lose — except my life.

"What could Snipe Gross have told us that would send so much fear into you? That would make you so uneasy you had to murder Threnody?"

Brick hesitated so long before answering that I thought he might refuse to talk any longer. I prodded him with another question. "What did you think Snipe Gross might reveal to us?"

Brick remained silent.

"Did you think Captain Gross might reveal that you murdered Diego?"

Brick's laugh sounded more hollow than before. "No, Snipe had no way of knowing that."

"So what did he know that threatened you?"

"He knew my real name."

"Mike Wilson? That knowledge could endanger you?"

"He knew my original name."

I heard a siren wailing somewhere in the distance. How I wished I had a way of signaling that cop car to drive by the marina.

"Wishing you could call that cop up here, aren't you?" Brick asked, reading my mind.

"I won't lie to you. Yes. I wish the police would come, would find you here, would find Threnody's body, would find you threatening me."

"Well, that's unlikely to happen. In a few short moments you will join Threnody and Diego in eternity."

"Eternity. Nothing I can do to hurt you from there. So what will it matter now if you tell me your birth certificate name? You're a clever person, Brick Vexton, Mike Wilson, or whoever or whatever else your original birth certificate says."

Again, he hesitated. He wiped his forehead

with the sleeve of his jumpsuit and when he looked at me, his eyes glazed. He sat down on the catwalk, pulling me down with him. I squelched a scream as the handcuff cut more deeply into my wrist.

FORTY-TWO

"Brick, you'd feel more comfortable if you'd unlock the cuff. There's no reason to keep us bound together in this painful way."

"You mean *you'd* feel more comfortable without the cuff. Forget that. I'm not about to release it and let you make a bolt for freedom. Not that I couldn't bring you down with one shot. Think die, Rafa Blue. Your time is up."

"Be real. Please unlock the handcuff. How could I run away with you holding me at gunpoint?" I squirmed in my cramped position. With my leg hurting and bleeding, I doubted I could muster the strength to rise and run. Pain shot through my arm when I pulled on the handcuff, but pain must be coursing through Brick's arm, too. I gritted my teeth.

"Your birth certificate name, Brick. Who are you? Are you sure you really know who you are?"

"It's a secret I've kept for over two decades."

"So tell me now your real name so I'll know how smart you've been — how brilliant. I can understand why you're so proud of yourself. Not many people could have kept a secret that long."

"Reach into my shirt pocket and pull out the key to the cuffs. You may be right about our being more comfortable without them."

Hope soared. I found the key and held it where he could see it.

"Unlock the cuffs." He held the gun aimed at my heart. He lifted his wrist and mine so I could find the lock, insert the key, turn it. He pulled his wrist free first and I let my hand fall to my side before I struggled to free myself from the steely grip.

Pain stabbed my arm from my fingertips and wrist to my shoulder when the cuffs came loose and clanked to the catwalk. We both heaved sighs of relief. I wanted to shove the cuffs into the sea so he would have no chance to use them again, but that might arouse his anger. I left them where they fell. I struggled to stand, hoping he might rise, too, and help me to my feet. He remained seated and prodded me with the gun.

"Stay where you are and I'll let you live a few more minutes. How cool will that be?"

I remained seated beside him.

"Bucky Varnum."

At first I didn't realize he meant Bucky Varnum was his real name. But then I remembered Kane telling me about Bucky Varnum — the Mariel water taxi captain.

"Bucky Varnum." I repeated the name, giving myself a few moments to think, to plan what to do next.

"Clever, don't you think? Bucky Varnum. B.V. I kept my original initials. Thought I might need them someday when I returned to Key West."

"If you liked this rock so much, why did you leave?" I tried to ease away from him. He didn't prod me with the gun, but he lifted its barrel as if to take a better aim. I sat still.

"Didn't want to leave. Didn't want to leave at all."

"So why'd you go? You were rich, rich, rich. Kane told me you made millions running a water taxi between Key West and Cuba."

In dawn's growing light, I saw Brick smile. "Right. Few shrimpers controlled as much money as I did. I deposited my take in many banks throughout the Keys. Wanted nobody to know the extent of my wealth."

"Okay, so you had it made. You were set

for life. Smart guy. So what happened to all that money?"

"Wealth's a hard thing to keep secret. Truth leaked out. Gossip and rumor made my wealth expand with each telling."

"So that made you Mr. Important. At least Mr. Important to those who knew you on the shrimp docks."

Brick gave a short, derisive laugh. "Not just the shrimp docks. Throughout the island, people called me a big shot. Called me that behind my back. Called me that to my face."

"And how cool was that!" I repeated his favorite phrase, hoping he heard my touch of sarcasm.

"Not many shrimpers could afford to live high on the hog. Or should I say high on the shrimp shell. Most of them worked hard to eke out a living."

"So you were king. What happened?"

"Jealousy. Jealousy rides the tail of gossip. Island folk began to resent not only my wealth, but the way that I'd made it — no, not made it, earned it. Island loudmouths said I'd earned my wealth on the backs of helpless Cubans — refugees."

"Refugees like Diego?"

"There were thousands of them — all wanting to escape from under Castro's thumb."

"And you gave up your successful shrimp-ing business to help those poor people to a better life."

"Right. I did those people a big favor. And they did me a favor, too. A big, big favor."

"What favor did those poor people do for you?" *Keep him talking.*

"One day when we were waiting for the tide to change, they took me to Daiquiri."

Good. I had him rattled. "Took you to Daiquiri. Tell me about it."

"Yeah, they took me to Daiquiri, Cuba. A tiny village. Villagers were known for their daiquiris. At least that's the story they told me. Rum. Lime juice. Sugar. My favorite drink. Later, I named my dock after that drink to thank the thousands I took to Key West. Very lucky for them. They might have been trapped in Cuba with no freedom at all."

"Did you think that some of them might be criminals? Did you ask yourself if any of them might be mentally deranged?"

"Watch your mouth, woman! You hinting that I might have brought bad people here?"

"That's what President Carter realized — too late to do much about it."

"The Cubans I hauled felt nothing but grateful. I only charged two thousand a person. Could have squeezed them for three, if I'd put a little pressure on."

"I'm not surprised that the locals here on the island wanted you off the rock. But what did it matter to you. You created your own realm in Miami, right? For a while Mike Wilson was king."

"Right. He was — until you caused a problem that ruined that name and my marriage. But later, I was a little wiser in my name choice. When I returned to Key West, everyone had forgotten about Bucky Varnum and the Mariel Boatlift."

"So you changed your name again, married Threnody, opened a marina, and the rest is history."

"And I'm proud of it, very proud."

"Is that old ship's bell for sale, Brick? I told you before I'd love to buy it for Kane. It really belongs in its rightful place on *The Buccaneer.* In fact, now that Kane's opened his boat as a floating monument, a historical monument honoring Key West's former shrimping business, he may want to change the boat's name back to its original name."

"No. The bell isn't for sale. At least not to Kane Riley." Brick surprised me by standing. "Up, woman. Up. Need to see that Threnody's still in place before I take you to a more secret spot and help you join her

413

in death. Get up! Now!"

When I tried to stand, my head whirled. Maybe I'd lost too much blood. Bracing my uninjured hand on a dew-damp catwalk board, I pushed myself up until I stood beside Brick. He prodded me with the gun and we both stood looking down at Thren-ody's head bobbing under the surface of the water.

I wanted to vomit again, but nothing remained in my stomach. I gagged and shuddered while dry heaves wracked my body. It took me a few moments to realize I no longer felt the pressure of Brick's gun on my side. I hadn't heard him fall, but when I turned to look at him, he lay sprawled on the catwalk by my feet.

Run! Run! I tried to run, but I had no strength left. At first, I thought Brick had fainted. Closer inspection told me he was no longer breathing. Was he dead? Had the fishing lure's blow to his head felled him at last? Elation made me want to jump at this chance to escape. But I couldn't move. Instead, I dropped down beside him. I grabbed the gun from his hand, clutching it so he couldn't take it from me if he rose up in anger.

Dead? At least he lay there immobile. When I'd pulled the handcuff key from his shirt pocket, I'd felt his cell phone. Laying the gun on the catwalk as far from Brick's body as I could reach, I forced myself to fumble into that pocket again and grab the cell.

I punched in 911. When the dispatcher's voice answered and began asking questions, I said, "Daiquiri Dock Marina," and closed the cell before I keyed Kane's number.

"Rafa! What's up? Where are you?"

"I'm at Daiquiri Dock, and I may have killed a man."

FORTY-THREE

"Rafa!" Kane shouted into my ear. "What makes you think you've killed someone?"

"Brick's lying here beside me on the catwalk. I'm not sure, but I don't think he's breathing."

"You call the police?"

"Right, I did."

"When they get there, don't tell them a thing. Don't say a word. Don't answer any of their questions. I'm coming. I'll bring a lawyer. Don't say a word until you have a lawyer at your side to advise you. Learned that on *Law and Order.*"

Kane hung up, and I sat holding Brick's phone, unable to bear the thought of touching him, of slipping it back into his pocket. Instead, I picked up his gun, still afraid he might rise and spring into action. Maybe I'd won only a short reprieve.

The police arrived first with lights flashing, sirens wailing. Then an ambulance.

Then a fire truck. I didn't call out, and it took the officers a few moments to find me — and Brick — on the middle of the catwalk. From a distance I recognized Chief Ramsey and Detective Lyon. Lyon ran down the catwalk toward me. Ramsey held the safety line and plodded toward me at a slower pace.

"Rafa Blue!" Lyon exclaimed. "Are you all right? What's happened here?"

Pulling my knees to my chin, I remained seated, turned my face away from him, and rested my head on my knees. I followed Kane's advice and said nothing.

"Miss Blue." Ramsey spoke in monosyllables without raising his voice. "Miss Blue, please tell us what has happened here?"

I didn't reply.

Lyon hunkered down on the catwalk beside me. "Rafa, please. This is an official call that you instigated. Answer our questions."

When I refused to reply, Lyon rose to his full height. He and Ramsey began talking to each other. They didn't look into the water and see Threnody. What if they looked in a few seconds and thought I killed both Brick and Threnody? And Diego.

Lyon pulled a ballpoint from his pocket, eased it into the gun barrel, and lifted the weapon, dropping it into a plastic bag he pulled from his other pocket. Both men studied the gun and then looked down at me. Lyon sniffed at the gun but made no comment.

"Don't touch anything else until the M.E. arrives," Ramsey ordered.

The medical examiner arrived, stopping in front of the chandlery at the same time Kane pulled up, stopping his truck beside the M.E. By craning my neck, I could see a man dressed in pajamas and a robe step from the truck. The lawyer? Why did I want to laugh?

"Is he dead?" the chief asked the medical examiner.

"Yes," the M.E. replied.

"Cause of death?" Ramsey asked.

"Can't determine that at this point, sir. Need an autopsy."

"Okay. Okay," Ramsey said. "See any bullet wounds?"

The M.E. didn't reply. And they still hadn't seen Threnody's body in the sea behind them. In the next few minutes photographers arrived, and cops with crime scene tape tried to cordon off the area of the unexplained death.

"May I take Rafa to my truck?" Kane asked the chief.

"Yes. But don't leave the scene."

"Yes, sir."

With Kane leading the way, he and I and the lawyer, who'd he introduced as Attorney Albury, walked to the truck. I felt the catwalk swaying from the weight and movement of so many people on it. Gripping the security line, I struggled to keep my balance.

When we reached Kane's truck, he reached into the truck bed and pulled out a yellow slicker that reeked of shrimp and mildew. Without protest, I let him help me into it. I snapped it on over my sleep shirt before we climbed onto the truck seat and he again introduced me to Attorney Albury.

"Miss Blue," Attorney Albury said. "Can you tell us what happened here tonight?"

I looked at Kane for his go-ahead, and after he nodded, I related the whole story. They listened without interrupting

"Then, you didn't shoot him?" Albury asked. "I need to be quite clear about that and I need to know you're telling me the truth."

"I'm telling the truth. Every word of it."

We sat in the truck a long time. More cops arrived, spinning their patrol car wheels in the graveled driveway as they hurried to turn onlookers away from the marina. At last, the M.E. approached us, looking directly at me.

"In my opinion, a blow to the temple downed Mr. Vexton. But only an autopsy will tell us for sure."

Chief Ramsey, who had been following at the medical examiner's heels, stepped forward. "Miss Blue, did you observe Mr. Vexton receive a blow to his head?"

"My client prefers not to answer that question at this time," Attorney Albury said. "She's taking the Fifth Amendment."

I wanted to protest. I felt that taking the Fifth Amendment equated admitting guilt. But the chief allowed nobody to question me further at that time. Admitting guilt? Me? A murderess?

FORTY-FOUR

Both my father and Kane had put their trust in ALBURY ATTORNEYS AT LAW in Key West, and I don't know why I doubted Attorney Albury's order to take the Fifth Amendment. I soon learned it was the right thing to do. By ordering me to say nothing upon first questioning, and later to answer no questions from reporters, he steered me in the right direction. Although my name later made headlines in connection with the murders of Threnody and Brick Vexton, I tried to tolerate them with good grace.

Of course, nobody could, or would want to, squelch the news media entirely. People have a right to know what's going on in their world. Many human interest stories about the Vexton deaths appeared in the *Citizen,* the *Keynoter,* and even the *Miami Herald.* Due to Albury's adept legal counsel on my behalf, the courts accepted the fact that I acted in self-defense when I cast my fishing lure at Brick Vexton — the blow to his temple that took his life, but spared mine.

Someday I'd learn to live with the knowledge that I'd killed another human being. Later. Not today. Nor tomorrow. Someday. Maybe.

We closed the Frangi for a few days out of respect for Threnody, Pablo, and Diego — and even Brick, regardless of his misguided actions.

During one of our nights off, Kane took me to a special dinner at Pier House. I asked him to go for a drive with me afterward.

"Where to?"

"That's my secret — at least for a while. Are you willing or will I be forced to kidnap you?"

"No force needed."

So on this moonlit night, I drove up the Keys to Big Pine. I turned left onto Ship's Way and we passed several avenues, each one named for a famous American battleship. We turned left again when I reached the avenue where my grandmother lived — Independence. After easing to the end of her street that stopped a few yards short of the huge boulders that prevented drivers from dropping off into the Gulf of Mexico, I braked the car.

"Why are you stopping in Pine Channel Estates?" Kane asked. "I remember headlines a few years ago. Headlines about a serial killer who lived in this area. Creepy stuff."

"That guy's dead now. Shot himself."

"Good riddance. But something like that could happen again. County needs to put up some pole lights on these streets. They're dark as pits."

"Except for the moonlight. I love the moonlight." I turned into a private drive and cut the headlights.

"Taking up trespassing, Rafa?"

"No trespassing. This is where I spent two years of my life, Kane. Not in this ground-level cottage, however, but here on Big Pine. Gram's moved here from the other side of the island — the woods, as she called the location of her old stilt home. She's up north visiting friends for a week, but she's given me all-time permission to use her cottage whenever I care to. I'd like you to see it tonight. Will you come in with me?"

"Of course. Lead the way."

When we left the car, I took Kane's hand and led him toward the cottage door. Moonlight lit our way across the pea-graveled lawn, past a grapefruit tree, an orange tree, and lengths of croton hedge on either side of the entry.

"Where does she go during hurricanes? All the other houses are built on high pilings."

"This is an older home, built before the eight-foot height level became a law, but the house is a CBS structure — concrete block and stucco. Gram takes her chances — doesn't even carry insurance." I fitted the key in the lock, turned it, and opened the front door. Once we stepped inside, a tiny nightlight illumined a large oil painting of two pelicans perched on a group of four dock pilings. On the wall to our right, a smaller painting of two parrots almost seemed to call out a greeting to us. By the light of the moon shining through a wide sliding glass door, we walked through Gram's office where a white wicker screen set her computer desk and files off from the tiny living room. There, casual furniture covered in Florida floral prints invited guests to linger.

"How about some lights?" Kane asked. "Don't want to stumble and damage something."

"Just follow me." I took his hand and pulled him along behind me through a small dining room and onto a screened porch. "Here is the reason Gram bought this house

— this wonderful porch. She sits here reading, writing, or playing bridge with friends while they watch boats navigate their way up and down the canal. Have a chair."

Kane sat in the chair I offered. "No light but moonlight needed out here."

"Right. I love the silvery glow on the canal waters. Gram swims here almost every day — winter or summer. It's one of the many things about her new home that she heartily approves of."

"No scary things in the water?"

"I've never seen any — except once. We both saw a large barracuda. The neighbors said it was harmless, a pet. No sharks roam here during daylight hours. They feed at night."

"Iguanas?"

"We see them in the water now and then. They swim, you know. Harmless. When I've asked Gram to move into our hotel, she begs for reasons as to why she should leave this paradise for the noise and commotion of Key West. I have no reasons to offer. This is her personal Garden of Eden, and I come to visit now and then."

"Why tonight? Why when she's away from home?"

"There's something I want to ask you."

"Okay. Have it your way. Be a lady of

mystery. What's your question?"

I pulled Kane into the bright moonlight and looked into his eyes. Standing on tiptoe, I kissed him lightly on the cheek.

"Kane, will you marry me?"

Startled for only a moment, Kane regained his composure when he turned my light caress into a more probing kiss. When we broke to breathe, he nuzzled his lips along my neck.

"Rafa! I've asked you dozens of time to marry me only to hear you say no. I never thought of you asking me."

"I couldn't ask you until you knew the worst about me and my past, my past that haunted me right into my future — until a few days ago. Can you accept me as your wife?"

"Yes. With all my heart, yes! When can we tell all our friends at the Frangi?"

"Tomorrow night, on one condition."

"Okay. What condition?'

"That I ask Dolly to write a poem to commemorate the event, and that I ask her to become a published poet by filling my column space with her poetry for one week this month."

Kane hid his groan behind a smile. "Your wish is my command."

We stayed until dawn, enjoying the moonlight, the breeze, the water, and I knew this special night was another thing Gram would have approved of.

ABOUT THE AUTHOR

Dorothy Francis, an award-winning author, works from her home studios in Iowa and Florida. She is a member of Mystery Writers of America, Sisters in Crime, Short Mystery Fiction Society, Society of Children's Writers and Illustrators, and Key West Writer's Guild. Her first four novels for adults — *Conch Shell Murder, Pier Pressure, Cold Case Killer,* and *Eden Palms Murder* — received critical acclaim from *Publishers Weekly, Booklist,* and *Crime Scene Magazine.* She lives with her husband Richard, a Jazz Hall of Fame musician and avid fisherman.

For more information, visit her Web site at www.dorothyfrancis.com.